THE SEVEN MEN AT MIMBRES SPRINGS

The best secret agent the South had was L. L. Henderson. She was also a beautiful woman and a counterspy for the Union army. Her men were dangerous hard cases: hired guns, drunks, drifters, a murderous freed slave and the sweet-talker who was her lover. They set out to win the Civil War by sealing off California and her gold. But they hadn't reckoned with Mangas Coloradas, 'Red Sleeves', the Apache chieftain. When his warriors sprung their ambush trap, the race for death was on. Then they knew they must reach Mimbres Springs—or never see sunrise.

THE SEVEN MEN AT MIMBRES SPRINGS

Will Henry

GUNSMOKE

First published in the UK by Corgi Books

This hardback edition 2005
by BBC Audiobooks Ltd
by arrangement with
Golden West Literary Agency

ISBN 1 4056 8035 0

British Library Cataloguing in Publication Data available.

to
AUGUST
LENNIGER

Printed and bound in Great Britain by
Antony Rowe Ltd., Chippenham, Wiltshire

Some years ago, on an Indian reservation outside a bustling atomic-age town in New Mexico, there died at the reported age of 108 years a tall, gaunt, green-eyed squaw entered upon the Agency records under the Mimbreño Apache name, Waska-na-chay, but known locally and for lack of definite legal identification, simply as "Apache Annie."

The attending physician, noting among her effects an age-yellowed diary written in English, with hand-lettered map, and certain other interesting objects—which no modern Apache could explain—pressed her only son, himself a wrinkled oldster close to ninety, for permission to borrow and transcribe the strange document.

The old man politely refused.

The doctor could not take the little book away with him, nor could he have any copies of it made. He would be allowed, on the other hand, to read it if he cared to, while the old man watched him. Would he want to do that?

Indeed, said the physician, he would.

When the doctor had finished, the old man took the faded diary from him and put it calmly into the wickiup fire.

"It belongs to another time," was all he said.

1

The lone woman passenger on the El Paso stage was very young, pretty, plainly frightened. It was not a good feeling to be riding the ancient Concord toward El Paso that April 11th of 1861. The accommodations did not help. The interior of the decaying coach had the classic severity of a Victorian hearse, the passenger comfort of an artillery caisson. The young lady's mood fitted perfectly this aura of funereal gloom and military meanness of appointment.

Adding to her depression was the constant surveillance of the four men with whom she shared the journey. They were patently Southerners. She was, as clearly, from the North. Their attitude of sullen suspicion was but harmless personal projection of a public resentment which had begun to grow uncomfortably from the moment the stage route had veered south out of Arkansas and the Indian Territory. Yet the very immediacy of their regard seemed to increase the tensions of the coming conflict tenfold, and to focus upon her, with each passing mile, the dangers of the assignment she had undertaken.

To begin with, the war was no longer a matter of conjecture or Congressional debate. It was a shooting certainty. It could start any minute. It might be on even now, as she thought of it, touched off by some ambitious garrison commander or nervous outpost gunner since the stage rolled past the last telegraph station.

Secondly, she was working, under cover, for the American Mail Company, old John Waterfield's pioneering stage line to the Pacific Coast. Only the month previous, an emergency act of Congress had uprooted the Waterfield line from its threatened Texas route, transferring it to the mid-continent safety of the old California Central trail. Subsequently, the company had succeeded in getting out of the Southwest all of its main traffic units with the exception of the Western

Division staff in El Paso. This seven-man crew had been kept in the field to mask the withdrawal of the line's Texas stations eastward, but its members were never apprised officially of this fact. Now, suddenly, it had grown too late to get them out openly.

A new factor of intelligence had reached the home office in St. Louis within the fortnight: it was not American Mail's line equipment which was the primary target of the Rebel planners in west Texas; it was the complete set of operational records kept in the El Paso office.

Texas was full of horses and mules and of men who could break and train horses and mules. For rolling stock enough to set up and maintain the skeleton line necessary to keep open the vital Confederate link with California and her wealth of gold, there was the old Jim Birch Line equipment, such as the El Paso travelers' present conveyance, now being put into service along the deserted Texas sections of the Waterfield route.

The operational records were something else again. They had cost doughty old John Waterfield over one-half of his original joint stock company capitalization of $2,000,000 to pioneer and put into active being. They composed, in effect, the written-out directions for running a relay stage line successfully through the desolate wastes of Texas, New Mexico and Arizona, to the Bear State treasure with which the Confederacy hoped to finance a major part of her war effort.

The young woman's assignment, then, was to get those operational records out of El Paso and out of Texas, and to get out with them, if possible, the seven faithful employees who guarded them.

The time was dangerously late, the Southern temper already exceedingly ugly. Small wonder the young woman was worried.

Yet there were even further odds against her gamble than those apparent ones of time and place. The nature of those odds contributed grimly to the upset she was suffering as the stage topped the last dusty rise in the dreary mesaland east of the Rio Grande and the forgetful old driver bawled lustily, "El Paso, five minutes! Hung onto your seats and hold onto your water!" The latter's hastily called down, "Oh, excuse me, ma'am—plumb forgot you was along," did little to improve matters or uplift depressed emotions. Over the bone-jarring course of the following reckless gallop across the mesa, the Northern girl could think of her mission only in its personal terms. These were three in number. And they

4

marched repeatedly, in the ascending order of their importance, through her weary mind.

She was not a "Northerner" at all, but by blood and birth a Southerner.

Her real name was not N. S. Benedict, as listed on the passenger manifest, but Lucille Louise Henderson.

She was a professional Union spy, posing as a Confederate secret agent.

To the Texas stage traveler, El Paso came as something of a shock. After the 458 miles of merciless landscape from Fort Chadbourne, the town was well nigh unbelievable.

It appeared, in the sparkling high-plains air, to be no more than a mile or two away. The drive proved, nonetheless, to be a brakeshoe-burning, four-mile plunge from the mesa's rim to the lush outskirts of the desert jewel which was the centuries-old Ciudad del Paso.

The place was an irrigated paradise within a purgatory of prickly pear. It was as welcome to the parched stage passenger of 1861 as must have been the sweet wells of ancient Canaan to the wandering Israelite of twenty centuries gone. Yet despite this surprise benison of desert beauty, Lucy Henderson's premonition of waiting danger became only the more intense as she drew nearer to it.

With the harness-lathered, bit-tossing horses slowing to enter the town limits, her formless apprehension mounted unbearably. It required every effort of her trained will to force her thoughts to follow her eyes in their preliminary study of the strange little foreign city on American soil.

She recorded the visible facts in her first guarded glance. Down the dusty street, directly ahead, loomed the squat adobe structure which housed the Western Division offices of the American Mail Company. Hovering sociably off its sun-faded flanks were several dozen smaller adobes, each the faithful copy of its neighbor. These would be the residences of the native townfolk, the colorful Spanish-Americans about whose proper racial nomenclature no newcomer was left long in doubt. Lucy Henderson received her education when she now chanced a remark to one of her fellow passengers.

The latter, a big, florid man of virile good looks, had seemed to be showing too much interest in her study of the passing sights. His undue regard led her to test him with some ingenuous comment along the lines of "the perfectly

5

precious quaintness of these outlandish Spanish-Americans." As an offhand cast, it was close. Her companion rose at once to the lure.

Smiling unexpectedly, he observed that the inhabitants were indeed a quaint lot but scarcely precious or anything approaching perfect. "They are, in fact, ma'am," he emphasized in the twangy Southwestern drawl which stamped him a Texan, "*Mexicans.*"

As this was the first friendly address any of the four Southerners had made her since boarding the stage at Horsehead Crossing of the Pecos, the Union girl determined to exploit it. She threw the big Texan a side glance heavily salted with smiling innocence. Again, he came nobly to the bait.

Sweeping off his flat-crowned black hat, he bowed as low as his lanky height and the confines of the coach would permit.

"Cullross, ma'am. Price Cullross. At your service . . ."

The girl let her smile become a low laugh.

Knowing that since the recent, and continuing, withdrawals of the Federal garrisons in the Southwest had been begun, no stages operated beyond El Paso, she understood that the destination of Cullross and his friends must be the same as hers. Accordingly, she felt the moment right for a return name-dropping.

"Benedict," she nodded back gaily, mimicking his own succinct introduction. "Nancy Sue Benedict. At my own service, sirs; exploring Texas and loving every minute of it!"

Her entire thanks for this gambit was a stiffening grin from Cullross and a ripple of curt hat-brim touchings from his three companions. Returning the abbreviated gestures with a forced smile, she quickly went back to her detailing of the settlement's geography.

In and about the clustered adobes, giving the place its hushed air and antiquity so remindful of a Biblical watering-spot, towered a grove of cottonwood and pear trees. The great size and careful spacing of these patriarchs spoke of Spanish hand-planting dim centuries gone. Beyond their airy shade began the open land, the rich complex of vineyards, corn, melon, bean and red chili fields, which, with the silver mountings of the ancient *acequias*, or irrigation ditches, composed the setting for the desert emerald that was El Paso in the twilight hours of the dissolving Union.

In the gentle channels of plashing green water drawn from the sandy breast of the Rio Grande, the sloe-eyed Mexican youngsters laughed and swam with the abandon of natural children unspoiled by higher civilization. With them swam their parents, perhaps not so innocent of worldly care but certainly of covering, as their naked offspring.

Embarrassed by the unexpected display, Lucy Henderson averted her eyes until the coach was past the last of the outer fields and bearing down on the stage station.

How those last yards were traversed without killing any of the sleeping dogs, foraging pigs, dusting chickens, dozing old men, crawling fat brown babies or wandering burros which peopled the main thoroughfare, the tense girl never knew. But by some miracle of providence, the human and animal inhabitants were spared a crushing death beneath the wheels of the ancient Concord, and the driver brought the careening vehicle to a safe stop in front of the Waterfield office. With vast relief, and to the accompaniment of the old rascal's happy bawl, "All out, end of the line!" Lucy allowed herself to be handed down by a no longer gracious Price Cullross.

The latter, after a hasty bow, excused himself. She stood, rather put out, and watched him hurry across the street after his companions in the direction of the town cantina. When the unpainted slats of the double-hung doors, familiar from the Potomac to the Pecos, had swung shut behind the last of them, she came about to survey the remainder of her surroundings; this, before going on to inquire for lodgings of the American Mail Company's beleaguered staff.

It was a task which took little time. Including the solitary saloon just noted (B. Dowell, Prop.), there were apparently but three business enterprises functioning in that far southwest corner of Texas. The other two were a dilapidated flour mill (Simeon Hart, Res. Owner and Op.) and a customerless general merchandise store labeled Coonts & Magoffin.

Suppressing a shudder, the tired girl turned away. Seconds later she was standing in the blind inner gloom of the stage line office. And seconds after that, she was listening to a timbrey, deep Southern voice whose greeting completely unnerved her.

"Evenin', ma'am," was all it said. "I knew one day you'd come through that door."

But those eleven slow-spoken words reached out and enfolded Lucy Henderson like the arms of a lover. There was implied in them something far more meaningful than she was prepared to acknowledge. She was, moreover, lonely, hungry, hot, stage-sick and afraid. She did what would come naturally to any woman in like circumstances; lost her temper and struck out at the nearest thing to her.

In this case it happened to be an Alabama boy named Linn Sparhawk, general stablehand and hostler for the El Paso station and presently standing in for the regular front-office man, who was up the street having his supper.

Sparhawk was a man of monumental patience. He understood not only horses but women; a not uncommon combination of skills in a Southerner. He waited.

Presently the young lady in front of the ticket counter had got rid of the required number of hard words. Her femininity defended, her eyesight adjusted to the cool shade of the old adobe, she was ready for her first good look at the deep-voiced clerk whose peculiar greeting had so disconcerted her.

Sparhawk stood obediently for examination. In no way did he measure up to his voice. He was a pale, sickly-looking young man who could not have reached six feet with the help of his three-inch boot heels. His weight would not exceed 140 pounds with his disreputable pockets full of creek sand. His eyes, large and heavily lashed, were an odd shade of cobalt blue. His sensitive mouth was delicately drawn and red as lip rouge. His hair, long, soft and curly brown, was unkempt and pendent as the ear-feathers of a mongrel water spaniel. The only thing the worn-out Union girl liked about him was that he made her feel so superior that she was sure, should she snap her fingers, he would roll over on his back, all fours waving, in the spaniel attitude of craven surrender.

She broke off her belligerent regard of him, satisfied she was once more in control of herself, and the situation.

"I wonder if I might trouble you to direct me to the nearest public lodging?" she inquired civilly.

"Ma'am?"

He had that disorganizing Southern habit of looking at a person without letting him catch him at it, and of appearing to listen politely, while actually paying no attention at all. The girl brought him up short.

"I need a place to spend the night. Is that too difficult to comprehend?"

"No, ma'am."

"Good. Then I trust you can see I am in want of a little rest."

"Yes, ma'am, and a little repair too."

8

Lucy Henderson lifted her chin.

"*I beg your pardon!*"

"No offense, miss. Nine days in a stagecoach isn't very kind to any woman."

"Indeed it is not!" she snapped. "Now if you will just kindly tell me . . ." She started to ask about the lodgings again, but he cut her off with his shy smile.

"Shucks, I'll do better than tell you, ma'am. I'll take you." He moved around the counter to pick up her straw suitcase but she would not surrender it to him. Seizing it firmly, she faced him down.

"Young man, please be good enough . . ."

"I want to do it for you, lady."

His hand had found the handle of the suitcase and, in consequence, her hand. The touch of his thin fingers was as unsettling as the tone of his voice. It sent a shiver through Lucy Henderson that she did not like. Yet she found herself giving up the suitcase and following him out into the street.

Trudging through the ankle-deep dust up the main street, she had just composed a sharp speech to put him in his stableboy's place, when once more his soft voice surprised her completely.

"Ma'am, I think a lot about Mr. Lincoln and the Union. A man can see you're from back there. I was wondering if there wasn't something you could tell me about the war. Is it actually coming so soon? Is everybody so sure about it? It just doesn't seem possible to a man who truly loves the old flag and all it stands for."

His opening words had alerted her, his closing ones only confirmed the warning.

This shabbily clad, shaggy-haired youth was a Southerner. His accent was deep South. His every look and gesture bespoke a Rebel background. Yet he talked invitingly of the Union. Could it be she had walked squarely into her Confederate contact in El Paso?

If so, it was a rare piece of luck. And espionage agents who take to depending on luck do not last long. Despite the cleverly forged papers in her reticule, identifying her as a Southern operative, Lucy Henderson played it carefully. "Oh, come now, Mr. . . ." She suspended it deliberately, meanwhile arching an eyebrow to bring him along with the desired information.

He looked at her obliquely, wondering if she thought to deceive him with her naïveté, or whether it was genuine. He

9

had already decided this girl needed a lesson in good manners. Now he made up his mind that her acting ability could also do with some brushing up.

"Sparhawk," ma'am," he said humbly. "But not 'mister,' please. Just make it Linn. Spelled L-i-n-n. Mama's name was Willie Jean Linn, you see, and that's where it comes from. All right?"

"Of course," she sparred. "How do you spell Sparhawk, Linn? I may as well have the full course while we're about it."

"Sure. Just like it sounds," he grinned happily. "Spar and hawk. Down home, Sparhawks and Linns are thicker than Jacksons and Calhouns up in the Carolinas. I reckon we're commoner than blue-heeled niggers in Mississippi. Especially down around Montgomery, where I come from."

He said "Mungumrih," and from that she knew he was from Alabama—more, that he was no doubt as desperate a slaver as any secessionist up or down the river. Her own mother had come from Lowndes County just south of Montgomery. She did not have to assume; she knew what the Alabama political temper was apt to be.

What she did not know was that her gentle, blue-eyed guide was quite aware of her suspicions.

He kept watching her covertly, still wondering what her game was and what she hoped to gain by playing it with him.

These were bad times. A man of his convictions could not be too careful. Yet . . .

"You were about to tell me, ma'am," he ventured, "something about the war. Particularly how strong and safe the Union feeling is up North. Remember?" He waited for her, the picture of complete honesty and seriousness, and her suspicions could not help but falter under his wide-eyed regard. Besides, she was very, very tired.

"What I started to tell you"—she forced the white-lipped smile—"was something along the lines of 'Oh, come now, Mr. Sparhawk, let's not talk politics!'" She shrugged appealingly, went on quickly. "I'm really quite weary and beginning to wonder where you're taking me. Just how much farther is it to this Mrs. Sanchez's you told me about? I thought you said it was just up the street?"

He looked at her, didn't believe her but didn't bat an eye to tell her so.

"Oh, it is, ma'am," he assured her. "But you've got to re-

member this street runs from here to Horsehead Crossing."
Lucy Henderson was not amused.

By now the furnace heat of late afternoon was bearing down insufferably. Of a sudden the Union girl was no longer in the mood for her work, nor of a mind to carry the charade with Linn Sparhawk another syllable further. She simply let the conversation lapse. Stumbling through the dust kicked up by her clumsy-booted escort, she was entirely miserable. There was no doubt whatever that she looked as grim as an awful pair of orange-colored high-button shoes, hideous yellow-straw suitcase and molting purple bird-of-paradise hat could manage to make a pretty girl look. As she looked, so she felt; like a cheap, tawdry, bedraggled streetwalker reporting for work in a new house.

Given any choice in the matter at that moment, Miss Henderson would gladly have traded all her Union loyalties for a good bath, a soft bed and a set of clean, fresh linen sheets.

2

The house of Lucia Sanchez was not quite the image of its neighbors. It was built on the square about an inner patio, like the others, and flush to the street. But beyond that there was a certain hushed richness about the place, an air of size and solid respectability, almost of subdued elegance, which bespoke well of the good widow's business acumen.

Lucy Henderson was impressed. As for Sparhawk, he had told his Yanqui turista only that Mrs. Sanchez was a hardworking lady who kept the most popular place in El Paso.

Now, as he waited with her outside the widow's high front wall, he was enjoying the sweet fruits of his taciturnity.

La turista was still examining the widow Sanchez's patio garden through the little grilled opening in the heavily planked street door, when they heard the warning slap-slap of the señora's bare feet moving toward them over the polished tiles of the inner paving. Sparhawk stepped back, just as the scarred panels swung open to reveal Lucia Sanchez. It was quite a revelation.

From what Sparhawk had said, or perhaps from what he

11

had not said, the American girl had drawn a picture of her hostess as a motherly old dueña with iron-gray hair, spider-web skin and a proper black rebozo. Ay de mí! as the Spaniards say. No woman is so blind as the one who will not remember that man is born to deceive. Lucia Sanchez was beautiful. The most beautiful woman, in a savagely feline way, Lucy Henderson had ever seen. The girl was still staring at the thinly clad wickedness of Señora Sanchez's body when Sparhawk broke out a suggestive grin and a string of border Spanish.

The Sanchez woman returned both the smile and the Spanish with a sidelong look and low laugh that made the white girl blush without understanding a word that had been said.

She wheeled accusingly on her guide, but he was already retreating. He paused only long enough to set down her suit-case, wink broadly at the beautiful Mexican, tip his disreputable hat to both ladies. After that, he eased about and strolled off into the purpling sunset whistling as sweetly on key and unmindful of worldly cares as a river-bed bobolink.

"Qué hombre curioso!" sighed Lucia Sanchez happily. "That Sparhawk! The thoughts he has. The things he tells a woman. The tricks he plays. Tch! tch! Even such as I, por Dios, am made to blush a little!"

Lucy Henderson's eyes narrowed.

"Un momento, señora"—she made deliberate use of her guidebook Spanish—"I have a small question. What was it Sparhawk said that made 'even such as you blush a little'? What is your little joke on a friendless stranger in your land who has trusted you both? Por favor, señora."

Here was a calculated gamble based upon the Mexican people's inherent regard for good manners, and it worked. La Sanchez stared hard, threw up her lovely hands, surrendered. "I cannot go through with it, señorita. It is not a respectable thing. Sparhawk will never forgive me, but I cannot do it. . . ."

Her white guest waited in demanding silence. Lucia Sanchez dropped her eyes. "He thought you needed to be humbled, señorita; broke to rein a little more smoothly, as the caballeros say. It was in his mind that you were too nice a girl to be so haughty and bad-tempered. And so, since he liked you a great deal, he decided he would bring you here as a lesson."

"And where," said the American girl, "is here?"

Lucia Sanchez looked at her as though she truly doubted

12

any sister of the sex could be so blind. Finally, with typical Latin reluctance to use the declarative in a situation of delicacy, she replied with a question of her own.

"You are sure you do not know, that you cannot guess, señorita?"

"Guess what, for heaven's sake?"

"To what kind of a place it is that your friend Sparhawk has brought you to spend the night?"

That at last brought the light—that and the chorus of stifled, girlish giggling which suddenly penetrated the silence from the direction of the cross-patio "sleeping" rooms. All at once Lucy Henderson knew exactly to what kind of a place she had been brought to spend the night. The oldest kind in the world. And the least likely to enhance any decent girl's standing in a new community.

"Her friend Sparhawk" had a sense of humor. He had referred her to the one and only "*Madam Lucy's*," the best known and highest class house of ill repute west of the Pecos River. It was time to take a second look at the Alabaman—and at herself.

For a girl who imagined her superior intellect and passing good looks fitted her for playing with grown men in a game where one's first called-bluff was apt to be her last, the badly embarrassed Miss Henderson thought she was off to a famous start.

How long had she been in El Paso now? Twenty minutes? Half an hour? Whichever, it had been time enough. In its brief span she had managed to let herself be made an utter fool of by a stage line swamper who looked as though the effort of his next breath would kill him, and acted as if he agreed the world would be the winner if it did.

Well, in this business you met all kinds. And, besides, it wasn't far from being a fairly good joke at that. When she laughed, Lucia Sanchez, previously watching her reaction anxiously, laughed with her.

By the time they had crossed the patio to the main *sala*, they were arm-in-arm and on the way to becoming the best of friends. By the further time the lithe madam had shown her where to put her things and given her a generous glass of the tawny local Malaga, the American girl was calling her new landlady "Luz," the latter was calling her "Lucy," and they were happily bound for the back-garden irrigation reservoir to take a cooling sunset swim in the gently swirling, sleepy green waters of the old Rio Grande.

That brief immersion in Lucia Sanchez's pool was mem-

13

orable for more than one reason. To begin with, it was an unbelievably beautiful evening.

As was the early spring habit of the atmosphere in the high country of the Southwest, it had showered late in the afternoon. Immediately overhead, the tumbled clouds, black with lateness now, still hovered, their undersides filigreed with the glimmering heat lightning. Off to the east, the horizon sky was pale and pure green as the heart of a Karachi emerald. To the west, it was deep-fired as the inner prism of a pigeon-blood ruby. And everywhere, all about everything, lay the exciting raindust smell and misty yellow light of the thirsty earth expressing her gratitude for the reviving shower just past.

The ceramic-tiled Sanchez reservoir served alike as a source of irrigation for the lush inner garden and as a swimming plunge, *muy elegante*, for Lucia and her house guests. Its site had been most carefully planted to screen its users from views, on the one hand, of the Mexican field workers and, on the other, of the El Paso road travelers, the latter route passing directly along the rear wall.

Lucia now dropped away her Shuntung dressing gown and slid into the sparkling pool. Her American guest quickly followed her hostess's breath-taking example (the Mexican woman's body was even more superb than her filmy negligee had promised), slipping out of her own borrowed gown and diving after her into the clear green water.

After a few lazy turns she surfaced, to float upon her back in the slight current of mid-pool, letting the gently moving water caress and cleanse her tired limbs.

She was still in this posture when she chanced to glance up and see Price Cullross staring down at her from atop the garden wall.

The moment their eyes met, the big man laughed hoarsely. Waving his black hat, he swung the second of his straddling legs across the wall and dropped himself down on the inside. When he hit the ground and started for the pool, he was no longer smiling. His face was flushed and dark, his nostrils pinched with the heaviness of his breathing. He had already removed his coat and vest, was slipping down his galluses and kicking off his congress gaiters as he came to the water.

To this point frozen with mortification, the shocked girl now reacted with desperate speed. Churning to the house-side of the pool, she flashed out upon its tiled edge, swept up her dressing gown and ran frantically across the garden. Cull-

14

ross did not follow her and perhaps he never intended to. The one frightened look the fleeing American girl stole over her bare shoulder, as she reached the main sala's casement doors, showed her that she was no longer in danger, if she had been at first. The amorous Texan had seen Lucia Sanchez.

In view of that fact, no pale Northerner was of further interest. The man who looked for the first time upon Lucia Sanchez as the generous Lord had made her was spoiled for all other and more ordinary women.

As the madam's youthful guest dashed on across the sala to her room, she heard behind her her hostess's teasing laugh and the eager splash of Cullross's heavy body striking the water in response to its age-old invitation. She could still hear them laughing and calling back and forth to one another while she dressed and repacked her suitcase. By the time she passed again through the sala on her way to the street door there were no more sounds of gay voices or pursuitful splashings coming from the garden pool.

It was very quiet out there. No woman had to ask why.

Sparhawk came out of the Cockroach Cafe, his stomach full but his mind unsatisfied. It wasn't that the food at La Cucaracha was any worse than usual; it was that angular-built green-eyed Southern girl, who for some reason was masquerading as a Yankee tourist. She wasn't doing a bad job of it, either. A man had to admire her ability. She would fool most of the locals, likely. But a fellow Southerner . . .

The Waterfield stablehand paused in mid-thought, his glance narrowing as it turned up Main and came to rest on the very figure in question. Angular? Yes, he decided, but interesting, very interesting. The angles just made the curves that much more impressive. Continuing upward, his appraisal came to rest on Lucy Henderson's face, and again his thoughts were interrupted. Mister, she was mad.

Sparhawk eased behind a two-foot square adobe column, wanting to watch but not be seen. By golly, maybe she had a bad temper, but there sure wasn't anything bad about what went with it. Well, it was the same in horses. Any man knew that—you scratched a good-looker, you found a bad actor. Now you take her gait, for instance. She went loose and easy with plenty of reach and swing. Her fetlocks were trim, her cannons slim, her hips . . .

For the third time the Alabaman's thoughts broke in mid-stride. The girl had come to a doubtful pause under the

15

lights from Ben Dowell's saloon directly across the way, clearly disturbed and trying to make up her mind about something. The halt gave Sparhawk his best look yet. With it, he felt better.

He had begun to suffer some remorse about steering her out to Sanchez's, the same guilty feeling compounded by just now seeing her come walking back into town, so plainly angry and discouraged.

Well, mad she might be, and unrested and rumpled up and out looking for Linn Sparhawk with Southern blood in her eye. But one thing she was not, any longer, and that was dirty. She was, in fact, so clean and dewy-fresh from the bath, a man imagined he could smell the lovely fragrance of her clear across the street.

And that—being clean—was a signal achievement, all by itself, under the circumstances of contemporary stage travel in southwest Texas. Certainly Linn Sparhawk appreciated that.

The interim coaches trying to take over the old Waterfield routes did not travel straight through with stationed changes of horses but instead followed the previous Jim Birch and San Antonio & San Diego Mail-Line custom of using the same six horses or mules from one end of a given run to the other.

To manage this meant stopping the coach and spanning out the teams every night. The passengers under this arrangement made shift the best they could, shivering through the raw prairie darkness till their prayers for daylight were at last rewarded. As often as not they spent the night sitting bolt upright in the coach itself, rather than risk the verminous mud hovels or airy, snake-infested ramadas provided as rest shelters by the amateur Texas stagers.

These ramadas were the generic sagebrush arbors of the Southwest. They consisted of four cottonwood poles set like fence posts in the naked earth and roofed over with whatever weeds were in season. You could never tell when a packrat or lizard was going to fall out of this overhead brush pile, or a horned toad or Texas sidewinder slither in out of the open desert to join you if the rats and lizards didn't.

Food, of course, was furnished by the passenger and if he failed to bring along enough for the nine days from Fort Chadbourne to El Paso—exactly twice the old Waterfield time—he was like as not to starve somewhere between Horsehead Crossing and the Guadalupe Salt Flats.

Water was even more of a problem, as it could not be car-

16

ried in quantity on anyone's person. Frequently the unlucky ticket holders were without so much as a drop to drink between wells, along the way; and never was enough provided for the brave lady travelers to de-calcimine a dust-painted face or dampen a dehydrated spit curl. It was an unmentionably dirty way to travel, an utterly demoralizing way to run a stage line. And if the Rebels did not quickly figure out some way to get onto old John Waterfield's secrets of round-the-clock schedules, with perfectly rehearsed team changes and ten-mile-an-hour minimum speeds maintained, they were going to find themselves in the same spot they had put old man Waterfield—owning a lot of stage line with no place to run it to.

Well, that was another matter and only showed how a worried man's mind could get off the track. What happened to the American Mail Company's property in El Paso was no concern of Linn Sparhawk's. They were paying him to pitch manure, not pontificate on the organizational woes of their makeshift successors in the Texas stage line business.

Moreover, at the moment, he had his own fences to mend. The main one concerned a growing sense of guilt about his call-house trick on Miss Lucy Henderson, yonder. Dogged if it hadn't been a shabby stunt and damned if he wasn't going to cross over and tell her so, right now. Ennobled by his resolve, Sparhawks stepped out of the shadows and started across the street.

Lucy Henderson stood in the pool of light from Ben Dowell's Longhorn Saloon, measuring her next move. It was not that she was suffering any waverings of her original agreement, nor doubts of its importance. The efforts of the Confederates to reactivate the Waterfield Line centered on their need to secure California's gold. The Union strategy to frustrate them was bedded in the same placer deposits. The yellow ore was that vital to both causes. There was only one disquieting complication—the one responsible for Lucy Henderson's presence in El Paso.

Shortly before her departure from Washington, the Confederates had the idea of seizing the stage line's operational records and actually sent through an order for the Texas Rebels to strike for them on April 15, barring prior declaration of war. However, a Federal secret service man in Richmond intercepted the order and reported it. On consideration, the Union authorities resealed the order and let it go through to the unsuspecting Confederates. Then Washington sent Lucy Henderson by fastest route to get those records out of El Paso before the Rebels could do so. It was this Southern order which was turning in the Union girl's mind, together with some purely personal plans for taking eventual care of Mr. Linn Sparhawk.

She drew limpingly abreast of the Longhorn. Now she had had her moment to think, and must move on, or in. Her instructions clearly gave the proprietor of the Longhorn as the man to see for local information. Caution was urged in the introductory phase but it was understood and accepted that Dowell was a free thinker, although certainly no Unionist. So there was really no choice. She hesitated to go into a saloon. Ladies just didn't do that. Still, her moral standing in El Paso had already suffered one blow that evening. What harm could come from a second?

On the point of deciding this question she received some help from an unexpected quarter. It came in the form of a soft Southern voice and what it said was, "Excuse me, Miss Nancy Sue. I got something I want to tell you."

Coming around, she saw Sparhawk had her cut off from her other considered move—going into La Cucaracha Café to eat before interviewing Ben Dowell—and she snapped at him that he had absolutely nothing to say to her, ever, and turned and marched into the Longhorn as though she meant to take an ax to it.

Mr. Ben Dowell was impressed. Lucy's dossier indicated that Dowell was inclined to promotional speeches on behalf of El Paso; all the curious traveler need do was inquire. Dowell stood unflinchingly to his reputation.

"Well, young lady," he began, in considered rebuttal to her opening resolution that war conditions across the country were bad and due to get a lot worse before they got any better, "out here along the Big Bend we see things a bit different. You see, we don't have any cotton to chop out here. It follows we don't need any darkies to chop it. So the South's main grief is no sorrow to us. On the other hand, old King Abraham didn't get any plurality in El Paso, you can bet. Matter of fact, miss, we aim to go our own gait out here. We don't think much about today or tomorrow. but mostly of the day after. Come along over here to the door, I'll show you what I mean."

They left the bar and, peering out over the tops of the slatted street panels, Ben Dowell flung his arm across the dramatic view of open rangeland beyond the town's edge, and went on.

18

"Standing here, I can look at history all four ways of the compass. North and south, this street runs into the oldest freight line in the United States. She goes 2,000 miles from the City of Mexico clean out to Santa Fe. Looking the other way, I can see the youngest trail in these dis-United States of ours. That's the one old John Waterfield's men laid out from the settlements back east to California. It's like Baron von Humboldt said in his book. He predicted that one day a tremendous big city, the metropolis of all *Nueva Méjico* and *America del Norte*, would be built where the Rio Grande makes her big bend to cut through these mountains. The minute I read that, I knew he had to mean El Paso. So here I came and here I stay until the tourists start coming and I retire rich.

"That's about it, miss," he trailed off. "As for the war, we don't rightly favor either side, except that naturally most of us feel our kinship to the South." He held up a long moment and she thought he was looking out across the rain-washed plains he loved so well, into that misty land of the day after, which is visible only to the world's Ben Dowells. She was wrong. Of a sudden he put his big, gentle hand on her shoulder.

"Miss," he said, "was I a pretty young 'Northern' girl looking for somebody with Confederate delusions, I reckon I'd try me them four slick-ears from San Antone that showed up on this afternoon's stage. But, miss"—the gnarled fingers tightened and the wise, friendly eyes found hers with the warning—"I allow I'd try them big-city strays almighty careful and cautious. Especially the one that handed me down out of that old Jim Birch Concord not two hours gone."

He patted her on the shoulder, nodded good luck and was gone back to his bar-polishing before she could think even to thank him. She stood looking after him an undecided moment.

Then it dawned on her that the game was over and that Ben Dowell had played it exactly as predicted. Except that his information had not been accidental. With the grateful thought, Lucy Henderson laughed softly from pure good feeling. At the sound Dowell looked up from his labors. She blew him an impulsive kiss and moved on out through the swinging doors of his Longhorn Saloon.

It began to look like her night, after all. She had got what she wanted from Mr. Ben Dowell. All that remained was to get as much from Mr. Price Cullross.

19

3

Price Cullross gave up his information in a rather more difficult way than Ben Dowell. Still, he gave it up.

It was nearing eight o'clock when Lucy Henderson came out of the hole-in-the-abode-wall restaurant next door to the stage station. The early spring darkness was well down and she did not see the big Texan until he lounged out from under the Waterfield building's sidewalk roof and spoke to her.

In the same instant she recognized him, she thought she recognized the man to whom he had been talking when her appearance broke off their guarded conference. Unless she did not remember his pale face and poor physique, Cullross's companion had been the bright young employee of the American Mail Company who had left her in charge of Lucia Sanchez that same afternoon. Her instant suspicion, of course, was that Sparhawk and Cullross were in collusion to seize the company records. But she was given no time to react to the idea. The latter was up to her, doffing his wide black hat and bowing sardonically. The other man, whoever it was, remained in the background.

She was sufficiently glad, then, that it was dark.

"Good evening, Miss Nancy," he said, eyeing her boldly. "I trust we're still speaking."

He was smooth as country butter but the implication was clear.

"I would like to warn you, sir," she told the Texan stiffly, "that you will make a grievous error should you draw any improper conclusions from this afternoon's unfortunate affair."

Price Cullross was immediately the picture of gentlemanly contrition.

"I have indeed misjudged you, ma'am." He bowed. "I can only hope you will show your forgiveness by joining me in a stroll about the town." He widened the polite smile, deepened the bow, gallantly offered his arm. Lucy grew watchful. Here was a time for careful treading.

"I accept your apology, sir, but I have no time for strolls.

20

I am faced with finding some manner of decent lodging for the night."

Cullross came to the lead beautifully.

"Ah, then! Perhaps you will allow me to introduce you to Mrs. Brown, with whom my friends and I are staying. A most delightful lady, and entirely circumspect."

His companion knew all about the respectable Mrs. Brown, having made inquiry in the Cockroach Café, but she let the Texan think he had rushed forward just in time.

"Oh, would you!" she cried. "That would be ever so kind of you."

"Nonsense, ma'am." The black hat was off again, the ready arm once more put forward. "I've wronged you and I mean to make it up to you."

Lucy Henderson was quite proud of herself. At least, considering it was her first important job. She really had her Confederate hawk coming nicely to hand. Giving the latter her warmest smile, she took his proffered arm and started away up the street with him.

Shortly they were both chatting as aimlessly as though they had been brought up in the same small town. But they had progressed no more than a few hundred leisurely feet, reaching the north end of Main, a desolate spot marked by the crumbling ruin of an old adobe courtyard, when the lightness evaporated out of their conversation and the moonlight stopped sparkling on Price Cullross's fine white teeth.

The Texan seized her high up on both arms, whirled her off the road into the musty court. There he slammed her rudely against the inner wall. It was done so swiftly, so expertly, she had no time to struggle or cry out.

"Now then," snarled her assailant, "we'll just dispense with all this damned play-acting, miss. You're in a real deep hole, I'd advise you not to pull any more topdirt down on you."

Lucy Henderson was in trouble. She didn't have to consult her dossier to realize that.

"Why, Mr. Cullross," she gasped, not knowing which way to go with him now and stalling for the time to find out. "Whatever do you mean?"

Her scowling captor was not to be stalled.

"I mean you had better talk, damn you. Low and clear and to the point. Do you understand?"

She understood. Between the dropping of the polite "ma'ams" and the addition of the blunt profanity, Lucy Henderson understood several things. She was in pressing

21

danger. She had stepped squarely into the middle of the conspiracy she had been sent west to frustrate. It was time to stop fencing with the big Confederate and commit herself.

"I am quite ready to talk, Mr. Cullross," she told him quietly. "But I'll not say a word until you release me. You are trying the idea sorely, but I would still like to think of you as a Southern gentleman."

She felt his muscles go loose, as his hands fell away from her. "Yes, ma'am," he said through his teeth, "and I would still like to think of you as a Northern lady, except that you are entirely too damned nosey to suit my loyalty to the South."

It took her like a piece of bare ice at the base of the neck, but she held steady, staying with her pose.

"Surely you're not serious," she smiled.

"Try me," said Cullross.

It wasn't going right. The frightened girl backed off, came in from another direction.

"You're not making sense, sir. Surely you realize that you and I are in El Paso on the same business?"

"And what business might that be, ma'am?"

"Confederate business, of course."

The succeeding pause was not long but it was very painful.

"I'm sorry you said that, miss," said Price Cullross at last. "It was the wrong answer."

She saw the dull glint of the moonlight bounce off the double-barreled derringer, as it appeared in his hand.

"I knew all along you were a Yankee agent but I surely didn't want to believe it," he apologized.

"You're a fool, Mr. Cullross," she said with desperate calm. "And I shall so report you when I get back to Richmond."

"You never left Richmond, ma'am, and you're never going to get back there. Surely you know that."

"I know no such thing!"

This was the time. Lucy Henderson made or broke her case for Confederate acceptance right here.

"You will kindly put that pistol away, sir," she ordered him. "We haven't much time. I am with the Richmond office and have the necessary papers to prove it."

"It won't wash, miss," said Price Cullross regretfully. "You're the fool, you see. We found out about your regular agent in Richmond. We know he intercepted our orders for taking the Waterfield papers here in El Paso. You've been

22

followed all the way from St. Louis. My friends and I simply took over the job at Fort Chadbourne. I'm sorry."

She heard the twin clicks of the derringer's hammers being put on cock, but would not accept the sound at face value. It was impossible he meant to discharge the piece. She had to assume this was a continuing part of a try at breaking her Confederate agent story. It was rather too much to imagine he actually meant to murder her.

Fortunately for Lucy Henderson, she did not have to call Cullross's hand.

It was called for her by a section of 2 x 4 scantling in the possession of Linn Sparhawk, who had slid around the far end of the wall and come up behind the Southern agent as the latter raised the derringer.

The wood came into the back of Cullross's head with a bone-hard bounce. The big Texan gave a soft grunt and pitched forward into a rank weedpatch at the old wall's base. Stepping over him, Sparhawk removed his ragged hat and gestured with it toward the break in the wall through which the wide-eyed Union girl had been dragged.

"After you, ma'am," he said. "I don't like to rush you but I've a notion we'd best get a move on." To his listener's amazement he stooped down and successfully shouldered Price Cullross's heavy body. "I've met Mr. Cullross's three friends, you see, and under the circumstances I don't care to renew the acquaintance. You follow me, ma'am?"

His slender companion was already moving.

"Better than that," she assured him fervently, "I'll accept your original invitation and precede you."

Taking action to suit the statement, she went ahead of him through the hole in the weathered courtyard wall, and out upon El Paso's deserted main street. Little time was taken loitering there. Ten minutes later, under guttering lamplight and behind closed front shutters, Linn Sparhawk and Lucy Henderson were once more staring at each other across the worn oak ticket counter of the American Mail Company's Western Division office.

The situation was apparent enough; only the solution seemed obscure. Neither of them could know what to do about trusting the other.

Sparhawk could not be sure the girl wasn't what she appeared to be; a Southern sympathizer masquerading as a Northerner. Lucy Henderson dared not discount the possibility of the Alabaman being in league with Cullross, despite her rescue. The slight stablehand might kill her as certainly as his possible compatriot on the floor. Yet she had to move, and so did Sparhawk.

Price Cullross was beginning to stir. Above the counter, the old office clock ticked rustily. Sparhawk waited. Lucy Henderson suffered. She looked up at the clock again, then back at Cullross, now struggling to sit up and beginning to mumble incoherently. Finally she had to look back at the Alabaman and when she did she said impulsively, "For God's sake, do something! Can't you see he's coming to?"

Sparhawk nodded. He went over to the office woodbox and selected a good piece of split cedar from the Davis Mountains. Recrossing the room, he put it to the back of the big Texan's head, stepped back and struck him sharply behind the ear with it.

"Now then, miss," he suggested quietly, "I'd say it was time you left off fretting yourself about my Southern bloodlines and got on with telling me the rest of what Mr. Cullross didn't quite scare out of you, yonder in the old courtyard. If you're a Union spy, like he said, you had better let your friends know it quick." He trapped her uncertain glance, finished low-voiced and urgent. "You could do a lot worse than starting off with me, ma'am."

The frightening fact of the truth in what the skinny Waterfield hostler said, unnerved Lucy Henderson. She had been without any real sleep, or decent food, or anyone to talk to for the past nine days. She was not an experienced agent and had been poorly picked for the job that needed doing in El Paso. She had courage and wanted adventure and would have made a good operative in time. But there was no time and she was tired, badly shaken up and only a few days past nineteen years old. The soft voice of Linn Sparhawk unlocked her last reserve and out spilled her complete story, including her real name.

When she was done Linn didn't let on that he saw she was crying, but only said, "Well, come on, Miss Lucy, ma'am, I reckon we'd better start a'bailing."

"We'd better what?" she asked, grateful to him for his tact but bitter with herself for breaking down.

"Start dipping with the old bait can, ma'am," he grinned. "We're sure as sin both in the same leaky boat."

Before she could answer, he bent quickly, tipped the lamp's chimney, blew out its smoking wick. He handed Lucy the cedar chunk and nodded to Cullross on the floor.

"You watch him till I get back," he said.

"Hold on!" she whispered apprehensively. "Where do you think you're going?"

"To round up the office crew for sure and sudden," he replied. "We got to get out of here."

"Now?" she gulped.

"You know a better time, Miss Lucy?" he asked.

"You mean run for it? With the company records and all? Right now?"

"This minute, yes."

"But I don't see it. We've got Cullross. That makes it their move. Why not just wait them out?"

"Hmmmmm," said Linn Sparhawk.

"Hmmmmm what?" she demanded.

"Just like a woman," he said. "Fast, loose and far from sweet reason. You're forgetting the facts, ma'am."

"Which are?"

"Firstly, the total white population of El Paso."

"Fifteen, Mr. Dowell told me."

"Fifteen B.C., before Cullross, ma'am."

"Oh, very well. With his bunch it makes nineteen."

"Wrong again. It makes twenty-nine."

"Sparhawk."

"Yes, ma'am?"

"You're crazy."

"It's been mentioned. But I can still count to ten. And I can still tell a Confederate when I see one sitting a dusty saddle in the south-of-town sagebrush of an early April evening."

"What in heaven's name are you talking about?"

Sparhawk stopped smiling. "Those ten Texas night-riders waiting out yonder where Cullross met with them while you were out to Lucia Sanchez's," he said.

"What!"

"Yes, ma'am. Cullross and his three friends on the stage were only the advance patrol. The main rebel bunch is hid out in the brush south of town." He paused, nodding softly. "Our main gamble has come right down to this, ma'am: what will that bunch out there do when their boss doesn't show up to lead them into town on the agreed schedule for taking over the Waterfield office?"

Lucy Henderson suddenly felt very inadequate, very young, and far from home.

But the question was waiting to be asked. Failing to ask it would not make the answer go away.

25

"That schedule," she said huskily. "What's your guess as to the exact time they've picked?"

"No guess to it, Miss Lucy. Cullross told me."

The Union girl could hear the rusted innards of the old wall clock wheezing away again. The loud seconds splashed into the stillness like drops of cold black cave water. Her mouth got dry and the word came out with considerable difficulty. "Tonight?" she said.

"Tonight," echoed Linn Sparhawk, and glided on out the creaking door and down the shadowed dust of the moonlit main street.

4

By the smoking light of a hooded stable lantern, Sparhawk guided Lucy Henderson down the long rows of deserted stalls to the feed room of the horse barn behind the Waterfield station in El Paso. Shuttering the single window with a horse blanket, he unhooded the lantern.

"Pick a bale of hay and sit down," he told her. "The men will be along directly. Meanwhile, I'll warn you a little about these 'seven loyal Northerners' you've been given to understand work in this office."

Pausing, Sparhawk winced. It was a hell of a thing to have to hit her with at a time like this. As if she didn't already have enough troubles without adding to them the truth about the El Paso staff. Well, there was no help for it. A man had to do what needed doing.

"First off," he said, "there's me. Alabaman by birth, drifter by choice, loyal Unionist by suspected declaration, head stock tender for Waterfield in El Paso by temporary chance.

"Then you've got Red Mike O'Hanlon, a back east bullyboy from Boston. Mike's a fighting man from a fighting clan and wants to make sure everybody within range of his ten-mile tenor hears about it. He is also chief baggage smasher for the Tucson run of the Western Division, and a very tiresome sort to be around.

"Third man is Doc Harnaday. Doc's a sometime practicing veterinarian and prodigal drunk, presently driving the

26

twice-monthly San Antonio stage for lack of steadier work.

"Fourth, I give you Alvah C. Barton, relief driver. The boys call him 'Preacher' and you'll shortly hear why. He's an unfrocked minister that we understand left his home town two jumps ahead of the folks of a seventeen-year-old parishioner who had come to him for spiritual guidance and settled for physical demonstration.

"Fifth of your 'youthful Unionists' is Jake Bergerman. Jake's company clerk. He's sixty if he's a day. He's a German Jew and a humble, devout man. His quietness is mistaken around here for a lack of spirit. I think he's most likely lonely for the left-behind life of the big city he came from in Europe. But his homesickness is locally put down to 'Dutch pigheadedness' and he's scarcely more popular than 'Preacher' Barton. Myself, I rate him high and would trust him anywhere.

"Now in number six you've got a man. Frank L. Swango. Frank's a thin-lipped, far-eyed one, who has been much used by life. He says little, sees much, thinks what he wants to think, with no man the wiser. He's never been really tested in his job of Tucson run conductor—that's the company way of spelling 'shotgun rider,' ma'am—but it's my opinion he's a retired gunman; that is to say, ma'am, retired on a fast horse with a high price on his head.

"Seventh man is not a man at all, but a boy. Far from being a Northerner, he's the width of the river south of being even a Southerner, being born in Ciudad Juarez across the Rio in Mexico. His name is Ceferino Sanchez and he's the sixteen-year-old brother of Luz. They're half-breeds, you know, and Cipher Reno—that's what I call him, ma'am— he's dead set on being considered an *americano*. It's his whole life and all he ever talks about. He works as a stable flunky for me and thinks I'm about the grestest gringo since *Jorge Washington*. That's because I keep telling him all he's got to do to be an *americano*, is to live like one. You see, that makes him think he can do it and sort of keeps him happy."

Finishing the list, Sparhawk explained that Cipher Reno wouldn't be along right away, as he had posted him out on the main street with orders to report immediately the arrival of any "out of town" horsemen.

Yet the closing of the official list of employees did not account for the full membership of the coming meeting, which fact the Alabaman now quickly pointed out to his white-faced listener.

27

"We've got to figure on three more passengers out of El Paso tonight, like it or not," he noded. "There's Cullross and you and Simon Peter."

"Simon who?" asked the surprised girl.

"Peter," said Sparhawk. "I call him 'Sim,' but the locals call him 'Simple Simon.'"

"Well, who is he?" asked Lucy Henderson.

Sparhawk shook his head. "He's an ex-plantation slave, ma'am, bought-free by me in Shreveport and carried along to Texas with me when I came out, three years ago. He's a six and a half foot giant with the body of a black Hercules and the apparent mind of a retarded child. Yet, ma'am, he has a strange habit of 'looking over' the white man's head, and this has earned him the bad reputation of an 'uppity nigger,' and made him scarcely more popular here than it would down South. However, he's faithful as the family dog to me. I've tried repeatedly to turn him loose and he won't go. Says that when the time comes for him to go free, he will know it and will go. Until then, he says he will 'walk humble,' as he calls it, calling all men mister and no man master. He's a strange creature, and I think I love him as surely as I know he loves me."

Outside the feed room there was a sound of footsteps, interrupting the Alabaman. "Douse it, Linn," they heard a hard voice say. "We're coming in."

Sparhawk hooded the lantern, the door squeaked open, the muted shadows of men blocked its black square.

The hinges complained again and the hard voice said, "All right, turn her up."

Sparkhawk flicked back the sooty hood. The yellow light spilled around on the motley array of humanity Lucy Henderson had just mentioned. The warning had been far short of the wares displayed. Sparhawk could see that as he watched the girl's eyes go wide.

Well, he thought, you couldn't blame her; it was a hell of a looking cast of characters. Truly, a man had to admit, it looked like a bad opening night for traveling Union actresses in Ciudad del Paso.

All they needed now was for Cipher Reno to leave his guard post and come legging it down the alley yelling that the Rebels were inside the city, had taken the Longhorn Saloon and run up the thirteen-starred battle flag over Ben Dowell's private piece of west Texas.

When Sparhawk had made his speech introducing her

28

and her mission to the Waterfield men, it seemed to Lucy Henderson as though one could have sliced the ensuing silence and served it in sandwiches. Then everybody, with the narrow-eyed exception of Frank Swango, started to talk at once. Talk, that was, not say anything.

Disappointingly, Sparhawk stood back and let them take the meeting away from him. Lucy had hoped, from the way he had been acting since downing Cullross, that he was going to be the man they needed to handle things from there on. But she had apparently figured him right in the first place. He was a real weakling. By himself he did not look too bad; here in the company of men, his humility was disgusting.

Fortunately, he was not the model for his fellows. Among the latter were several adult males, "hombres with whiskers on their briskets," as old Doc Harnaday called them. And their actions now showed the Union girl that not only was Sparhawk's courage limited to sneaking up behind better men in the dark, but also that his judgment of his co-workers was atrocious. Barton and O'Hanlon, the only two he had singled out for deprecatory comment, were the first to speak out and make sense. Barton led off.

"Now, men, calm yourselves. We have a problem but the dear Lord will furnish the answer. If we come unto Him seeking, He will provide." The general manager raised his hands in blessing, cleared his throat in good preacher style, and concluded graciously. "To start the discussion, I side with Miss Henderson and the Union."

Bergerman held up his hand. "You will excuse me, please," he began hesitantly, "but maybe I ain't heard something." He gestured helplessly. "Exactly what does it mean, you 'side' with the young lady?"

Lucy Henderson bit her lip. How could Sparhawk think as well as he did of this pathetic, frightened little man? How could he be so wrong? Fortunately for them all, Red Mike proved a better judge of the poor bookkeeper.

"Sure now, Jake, and it means that Mr. Barton is for giving the bloody Confederates a run for their thieving money!"

"And what does *that* mean?" said Frank Swango quietly. Red Mike spun around on him, small eyes snapping.

"Sure now, Swango lad," he nodded carefully, "you can understand the king's English."

"I can," said Swango. "It's yours that throws me."

Red Mike's eyes blazed again, but Bergerman broke in on his rage. "But please, Mike, Frank and me we only want to know what Mr. Barton was recommending, and you ain't said it yet."

"Ah well, now," offered the Irishman, "if you'll quit waving your paws, I'll try again. The question is whether we surrender to the sneaking Rebs, or grab the company records and make a run for it. Now, Mr. Barton says he's for making the run and so, by heaven, am I!"

Warmed by his own oratory, he put a freckled hand on the little Jew's thin shoulder. "In other words, Jake my lad, here's our two votes for fighting our way past Cullross's boys, and we're passing the franchise your way for number three. What do you say now? Will you lay down and quit, or stand up and fight?"

Bergerman shrugged patiently. "What can I say? What do you want I should say? I will do whatever the others think right."

"Spoken like a true son of Father Jacob," sighed Red Mike resignedly. "Swango, lad?"

"I'm with Jake. I pass."

It was a bad surprise. Clearly, the big Irishman was not ready for it. He looked at the gray-haired shotgun rider as though he were going to qualify his vote, as he had Bergerman's, by moral suasion. Directly, he thought better of it; wisely went on to easier fields.

"Doc, my fine bucko!"—he grinned at the grizzled driver —"for certain 'tis a yes you'll be having for me. Am I right now?"

"As a Democrat in Dallas," grumped the old man. "I wouldn't give them San Antonio Rebs the sweat off the back of my whiphand. They ain't real Texicans, by God!"

"Aye! That's the spirit! Three to one for taking off with the company papers!" crowed Red Mike. "Sparrowhawk, my Southern friend, which will she be for you?"

Sparhawk grinned sheepishly.

"Shucks, I don't rightly know, Mike. But it does seem that so long as the company's paying us, we'd ought to do what's proper by them."

"Sure and that's the idea, Sparrowhawk. Now the Mex kid ain't here and ain't old enough to vote anyways, so I'm exercising his proxy for him. Five to two in favor of a fight and the polls just closed for keeps." He glared about him, daring his listeners to deny him. None did. "All right, Mr. Barton," he nodded triumphantly, "your motion is carried and the floor's open for the best ways and means of getting

30

them operational records out of town. Who's got what to say on the subject . . .?"

Again the discussion became general. But this time, their thoughts channeled by Alvah Barton's ministerial calm and Red Mike O'Hanlon's infectious courage, the men talked in sober turn. Inside of ten minutes the whole risky plan took shape.

It was now becoming very exciting to the young girl who had brought it, indirectly, into being. She seemed to sense at work here something much deeper than the safety of the Waterfield papers. No set of statistics on how to run a stage line could possibly mean this much to the men who merely sold the tickets, polished the coaches, skinned the mules, watered the horses, kept the books, pitched the manure or rode the shotgun guard. The entire abstract area of Union loyalty, what it meant to men who were obviously ready to die in its name, was in ferment here. In the end, Lucy Henderson could only come down to her own case, to what she was doing here, and then apply the same indistinct motive to the ill-assorted El Paso seven: they were simply "for the Union," the same as she.

There was no time for further thought on the root stems of patriotism. The plan, largely Barton's idea, was now complete. The core of it was that Preacher and Red Mike would take the light spring wagon, which was Mr. Waterfield's personal route-inspection rig, and start south for the border as though making for Mexico. Since they had the speed rig and the fast horses—Mr. Waterfield's prize pair of matched Kentucky bays—the Confederates would naturally assume they were carrying the company records.

While they were thus drawing off the pursuit, the rest would take the one Celerity coach in the El Paso barns, hook it to the six fresh mules which were all ready to go on the return run to San Antonio, and make their break due north up the Santa Fe branch line. The records, of course, would ride with them.

The simple remainder of the plan was that Barton and O'Hanlon would abandon the spring wagon short of the river, swing up on the bays, circle to the north and join their comrades at Coyote Wells along about daylight.

Quickly the various members of the escape party were detailed to their particular jobs of preparation and the meeting was over. It was just 9:30 P.M. when Barton blew out the lantern and said, "Well, my friends, let us go and may the dear Lord bless our venture."

It was exactly five seconds later, freezing every one of the departing shadows in its track, that the sounds of bare feet running in deep dust were heard thudding down the alley. The next sounds were a string of strident Spanish words raised in the high-pitched voice of Sparhawk's small Mexican lookout.

"*Señores! Amigos!* Watch out! Here come those strangers!"

There was no need for translation, not even for Lucy Henderson. Cullross's men were on the town.

No one moved; no one made a sound. The noisome darkness was a smothering hand, repressing breath itself. Hearts pounded, throats ached, imaginations stampeded. Then it was Frank Swango who pulled aside the horse blanket at the window and asked calmly, "Where are the riders, *amigo?*"

"Across the street in the cantina," whispered the half-breed boy. "Where is Señor Linn?"

"Here," answered Sparhawk for himself. "What goes on, *hermano?*"

The boy spoke rapidly in Spanish and they could all see the accepting nod of the Alabaman's shaggy head. When he had finished, Sparhawk issued him a return flow of Spanish orders, to which the youth replied with a quickly grinned Latin shrug of understanding.

"Sure, of course, señor. *Adiós.*"

Lucia Sanchez's little brother was gone as swiftly as he had appeared. Before Sparhawk could turn from the window to explain the exchange, Red Mike's belligerent challenge rasped out. "Now and what in the name of hell was that all about? Speak up, damn it. You know I don't savvy that tamale talk!"

The Alabaman did not get to answer. "It was all about us," Frank Swango informed the beefy freight handler. "Sparhawk's sent the kid back to keep an eye on the Rebs. They've gone in Ben Dowell's bar. When they come out to go for their horses, the kid's to let us know. Meanwhile, we're going to hump our tails toward getting out of town, as planned."

The lean-headed shotgun rider laid a deliberate emphasis on the last two words. His twangy Arizona drawl was dry as the buzz of a rattlesnake. His sage-gray eyes watched Barton and O'Hanlon like a crouched cat's.

Both the latter were showing clear signs of nervousness.

"Well, now, wait a minute, Frank," began the office manager. "I think this development alters everything. With the Confederates already in town we haven't a . . ."

32

"You're right, Preacher," said Swango, cutting him off. "We haven't a minute to lose."

"That's not what he meant!" edged in Red Mike. "He meant, with them already atop of us we ain't got a chance to get out of here. There's only one thing to do; lay low till they're gone, *then* set out."

"I say we go now," said Frank Swango, not raising his voice a flat syllable.

"And me," said Linn Sparhawk softly.

"The same," growled Doc Harnaday.

"Well," shrugged Bergerman resignedly, an undoubted gleam of small triumph in his bright old eyes, "so many have already said *ja*, Bergerman says *ja*."

Red Mike ignored them all, save Swango. Flexing his huge fists, he moved in on the slender shotgun rider.

"All right now, Swango, I'm giving you one last chance. I want to know who's running this show—you or Mr. Barton?" He loomed over the dry-framed Tucson conductor, dwarfing him pitifully. The latter didn't move a muscle.

Eyeing the loud-talking Irishman, Frank Swango dropped his right hand toward his dusty thigh, letting its curving fingers brush the scarred walnut butt of the big cap-and-ball Colt which rode so easily there.

"That answer your question?" he said, in a voice as quiet and cool and soothing as moving spring water.

It did, and more. It answered Preacher Barton's whole objection.

"Frank's right, of course," the latter interjected quickly, catching O'Hanlon's eye with the surrender and giving the big Irishman the nod. "We mustn't stampede. Now, let's see, we'll start by . . ."

"We'll start by you and your tame Irish ape hooking up them bays of the old man's by the time I count ten," said Frank Swango. "One . . ."

"Frank, wait now." Barton held up his hand. "We've got this Cullross to dispose of."

"Two."

"And Miss Henderson, the dear young lady from Washington. Good heavens, man, you can't mean to take an innocent woman out into that Indian country."

"Three."

"The Apaches, Frank. Think, man, think!"

"Four."

"We'll never get past Mesilla. I heard today that the troops pulled out of Fort Fillmore up there last week."

"Five."

"Sparhawk, I appeal to you!"

"You'll find the bays in the two end stalls, Mr. Barton. That make it six, Frank?" replied the Alabaman.

"And one makes seven," said the shotgun rider.

"Swango!"

"Eight."

"All right, all right, for God's sake, we'll go. But . . ."

"Nine," said Frank Swango, and dropped his hand.

There was no need for the last count. Barton, followed by the cursing O'Hanlon, broke away down the center aisle of the barn, toward the stalls of the Waterfield bays, "a'stumbling and a'mumbling," as old Doc put it later.

"Now then, kid," Swango turned his easy voice on Sparhawk, "let's get that Celerity loaded. You, Doc, span in them mules. If I hear a loose chain rattle, I'll throw down on you." Doc growled something profane and was gone into the darkness after Linn. A third and startling figure loomed at the shotgun rider's side. "How about me, Mr. Frank?" purred the lion-deep voice of Simon Peter.

Lucy Henderson, seemingly forgotten in the subdued hum of activity, studied the giant ex-slave through the stable gloom. His magnificent physique, of course, demanded attention, and even a kind of awed respect. But far beyond that, one felt a sense of some great simple dignity here, a kingliness that would not be denied by any claims of childlike mentality or handicaps of dark skin color.

"You go along with Mr. Linn same as usual," Swango directed him. "He can use you, likely."

"Thank you, Mr. Frank," muttered Sim, and padded noiselessly away.

"Jake," ordered the shotgun rider, "drift on out front and check with the Mex kid. Send him on home when you have."

The quiet-spoken little bookkeeper was gone with as little argument as the huge black Sim, and it was Lucy Henderson's turn.

She made the mistake of taking it with put-on flippancy.

"And how about me, 'Mr. Frank'? Doesn't a pretty girl rate any attention at all around here? Surely there's something I can do to help."

"There is, miss," said Frank Swango. "Get in that coach and start praying. Barton wasn't fooling about them Indians."

"That bad?" she asked uncertainly.

"I wouldn't put off on you, miss. There hasn't been a

34

stage, or a freight wagon, or a flatbed farmer's outfit to go west or north out of El Paso since the soldiers started pulling out of Arizona and Cochise closed the roads behind them."

"These Indians—they're Apaches, aren't they?"

"Yes'm."

"Mescaleros, did Barton say?"

"Providing we're lucky, yes'm."

"Lucky?"

"Yes'm, it could be the Mimbreños we run into," said Frank Swango, and drifted off into the darkness and away from her.

She stood there a moment, thinking about the Indians. Then she thought, in turn, about the gray-eyed shotgun rider, and the musty darkness of the Waterfield feed room lightened appreciably. And why not? Any of the troubles ahead of them, from rebel Confederate guerrillas to marauding Apache warriors, could be handled by the right man in the right place at the right time.

This was surely the place. This was certainly the time. And Lucy Henderson was satisfied they had just found the right man.

The excited girl was not left alone long in the feed room. Shortly, the door scraped open and Linn Sparhawk was there. "Sit tight, miss," he said. "I'm going to make a light."

The wooden sulphur match scratched and spurted, the smoky lantern flared again.

In the Alabaman's hand was a rusty pair of foot-long scissors, a bit of broken mirror, a currycomb. Under his arm he carried a bundle of well-used work clothes: a pair of patched rider pants, a faded cotton shirt, an old beaver hat, a pair of cracked Texas boots, a set of red flannel winter drawers, complete with buttoned front and drop seat.

Lucy Henderson stared. What, she asked Sparhawk, did he intend to do with those rags? Dress a scarecrow to put in the Waterfield office window to make the Confederates think American Mail was still in business?

The Alabaman said, yes, he guessed you could say he was going to dress a scarecrow. But he wasn't going to put it in the office window. He was going to take it along on the Santa Fe run. Maybe they might use it to scare off the Mescaleros or to hang out the coach window to spook the mules into full effort.

While he talked, he laid out the clothes on a handy bale

35

of hay, hung the shard of mirror on the wall, knocked the dried horse sweat out of the currycomb, spat on the dirty shear blades to break their seal of caked grease. Then, with a testing snap or two, he turned around.

It came to Lucy Henderson, incredulously, what he meant to do.

She drew back, throwing up her elbows.

"Don't you touch me with those things!" she cried, falling backward over her bale of hay. "I'll call Swango . . .!"

"You do and you'll spend the rest of the war picking Dixie cotton." He waved the shears disapprovingly. "Besides, get up off the floor and make yourself decent. You're showing more underside than a bull calf at a branding fire."

Lucy stopped waving her legs, pulled her dress down, got to her feet.

"Thank you," said Sparhawk soberly. "Now sit still. These here are sheep shears, ma'am, and you're going to get shorn by them."

"I'll die first."

"You dying is what I'm thinking of. So you get a change of clothes and a man's haircut."

"Never!"

"Right now."

He moved in on her and she struck at him angrily. He caught her arm, twisting it with surprising strength.

"Make up your mind, miss. Would you rather I scalped you with these sheep shears or some Mescalero buck did the job with a wooden-handled butcher knife?"

She glared at him, trying to hide her fear.

"Are you trying to be funny, Sparhawk?"

"Depends on your sense of humor, ma'am."

"I don't understand," she faltered.

"Look at it this way, then. The Indians in these parts, Mescalero, Mimbreño or whatever, will do anything to get their hands on a white woman. Having a pretty young girl along when they're raising hell is like having a side of fresh meat hanging in camp in bad wolf country. Except that I'd rather be a dead side of meat than a live white woman in Apache country. You understand *that?*"

Lucy Henderson understood it. Twenty minutes later, short-cropped, roughly clad and very badly scared, she was following him meekly down the dark center aisle of the Waterfield horse barn.

The Celerity coach was a special Concord built by Abbott

36

& Downing to John Waterfield's personal design, for use on the rocky Western two-thirds of his stage route to California. Slung almost two feet lower than the standard Concord, it was well nigh impossible to tip over. And next to a good hitch of gun-sound horses or long-gaited mules and a top grade shotgun rider, nothing so guaranteed a safe passage through Apacheland as a coach that would not tip or leave the road when the warbows were bending and the Springfields blasting back at them. With their lightweight canvas tops and let-down seats they were the darlings of the Western drivers and the despair of the frustrated Apaches who chased them.

It was this type of stage into which the last of the office records, carried out by Sim, were now being loaded. Sparhawk, coming up to the scene with Lucy, left her to help Doc Harnaday with the mules.

Down at the far end of the barn Barton and O'Hanlon were ready to go. They were easing wide the big rear doors which opened into the sagebrush back of town. Nearer at hand stood the Celerity, with Sim now beginning to load into it a variety of guns and boxed ammunition from the front office. Bergerman, Cullross and the Mexican lad were nowhere to be seen.

At this point Alvah Barton came up through the gloom to inform Swango he and O'Hanlon were leaving. While Lucy listened to the shotgun rider tell him how best to drive the first miles of the decoy run, Sparhawk appeared again. "Come along with me," he said. "Swango says we're to give the office a last look-see."

"Swango says?" she repeated, holding back.

"It saves time doesn't it, miss?" he asked her with a sharpness she could not fail to note.

"What does?"

"To say 'Swango says.' That's the way you'd rather have it, isn't it?"

She got his point and was surprised he'd had the spunk to make it. So her favoring of Frank was showing through? Well, let it. She certainly didn't care.

They went into the office. One quick look proved enough. The job in there had been done right. The place was as clean as the inside of a butchered shoat. She nodded "all right" to Sparhawk and they went out and across the stock corral to the horse barn. When they got there, Barton and O'Hanlon were gone.

Somehow that frightened Lucy Henderson.

"All right, little lady." She jumped as Swango touched her arm. "Up you go. Watch the step, it's a high one."

Another unseen hand, softer and more hesitant, reached down to take her from the shotgun rider. "Careful now, lady," directed the gentle voice of Jake Bergerman. "Don't step on the passenger."

"It's Cullross, miss," amplified Swango. "He's on the floor, bound and gagged. Don't ask me why. Sparhawk's idea. It's hardly the way I'd have gotten shut of him."

Lucy could believe that last without enlargement. She had a very good notion of the way Frank Swango would have eliminated the problem of Price Cullross. As she thought of it, she heard the shotgun rider's arid voice beginning to check their running gear with Linn Sparhawk, and her spine stiffened.

"Water?"

"Two side barrels, twenty gallons each."

"Grub?"

"Sack of flour, half sack of beans, side and a half of salt meat, coffee, sugar, salt, soda."

"Guns?"

"The six from the office rack. Four Springfields, two Sharps."

"Shells?"

"Enough for a Confederate regiment. Mostly the new brass-case stuff."

"All right. Everybody got his personal things aboard? We're going to close the boot."

The boot was the drop-style leather trunk on the rear of the coach designed to carry 600 pounds of U.S. mail or anything else that could be crammed into it. In reply to Swango's question concerning it, each of the crew answered up in the affirmative and the shotgun rider went on.

"Doc, your mules ready?"

"As they ever will be, the miserable sons of b—"

"Save it. We got a lady present. Sparhawk?"

"All set."

"How about Sim?"

"Up front, holding the leaders."

"Good, here we go. Sim, take 'em out easy. Doc, up you go. You too, Linn."

There was clear surprise in the order, and Sparhawk's reply echoed it instantly. "Me on top?"

"I said it, kid."

"How come, Frank?"

38

"Get up. You're riding my shotgun seat to the Wells."

"The hell! What about you?"

"Me, I got something else to do. Head out. See you at the Wells."

With the brusque dismissal and farewell, Swango legged up on his gingery roan and leaned in at Lucy Henderson's window. "Don't you worry now, miss. Linn's a good boy. Hell of a sight better than he looks. He'll get you through."

It was mighty small comfort to the upset girl. To say she was disorganized by the shotgun rider's apparent desertion would be the least of the truth. But she could think of nothing to say to him, and he swung the roan and was gone before she could even begin to try to reply.

She sank down in her seat. There was nothing else she could do, except maybe to take Frank Swango's earlier advice and start praying. The Waterfield records were safely loaded into the Celerity's boot. The rest was up to God and good luck.

As the mules eased into their collars and the low-slung coach started to move down the deep dust of the barn aisle, she heard behind her the wheezy striking of the old wall clock in the abandoned office.

The discordant chimes had time to announce the full hour before the mules had cleared the barn and the Celerity was in the sagebrush.

It was ten P.M. In two hours it would be April 12, 1861. In two hours it would be the day the Civil War began.

5

The road north followed the river. It was level, smooth, firm-bedded. The big Celerity moved easily, making deceptive time. They had a three-quarter moon with drifting broken clouds running high and bright.

The wind, light and steady from the west, came to them across the water. It laid their slight dust and put into the night air the bracing fragrance of sage and juniper. The mules liked the going. They lay into their collars, ate eagerly into the forty-six miles stretching toward Mesilla, the Union fugitives' first goal. To the latter it did not seem as though a tug or trace chain slackened, or a singletree dropped below hock level, until shortly after one A.M., when, at deserted Cottonwood Station, twenty-two miles north of El Paso, Doc Harnaday pulled up his six-mule hitch for a half-hour rest halt.

While the tough little brutes stood stomping and blowing, the travelers got down to stretch cramped limbs and see to other natural reliefs.

Lucy Henderson walked stiffly over to, and out upon, a rocky promontory commanding a sweeping view southward of the river. Here she tried to put her mind to the quickly changing circumstances of the El Paso adventure. As she did, her eyes insisted on straying off into the soft beauties of the night.

Nothing, of course, looks real in the magic of white moonlight. Yet that Mesilla road desertscape went beyond the merely unreal. It was fantastic, the city-bred girl thought. Fantastically beautiful, fantastically big, fantastically frightening.

As the feeling took hold of her, Linn Sparhawk came up and in his soft, quiet way began to talk to her, unbidden, on the very subject.

"There is no land, ma'am," he led off, "like this high Southwestern grassland. To attempt to describe it is hopeless. Worse, it's downright profane. Nobody who hasn't seen it will believe you. Anybody who has will resent you trying to tell him about it. It's just best to see it as sort of a sacred thing, or anyway past easy describing, like motherhood, or young love, or being a kid, or growing old with dignity. It's just too big for the eye to get around, or the mind to capture. You can quote all the words ever put down on paper about it and not begin to tell the truth about New Mexico in the moonlight."

He paused and they both were quiet until he startled his strangely humbled listener with a second touch of his deep voice. "What you thinking, ma'am . . .?"

She could sense in the appeal that he was vastly lonely and wanting to talk. Of a sudden, so was she.

"Linn," she said, "sit down and say something sweet to me. I'm so scared and lonesome I could cry."

"I know that feeling, miss. I know it like you can only know something you've lived with all your life. Lonesomeness is like a woman; you've never really known her till you've slept with her."

He hadn't meant to be bold with it, but she took him that

40

way. "Lonesomeness is a woman, Linn. This woman . . ."

She deliberately teased his hand, as she took it in both of hers, and he came to her with the invitation.

She let him kiss her and he was not at all awkward or unskilled about it as she had expected him to be. It turned into a long, hungry kiss and was going beyond that when old Doc Harnaday's bawling voice blaspheming his offside wheeler for backing over its singletree and in the same breath ordering his passengers to "load up and be goddamn lively about it!" broke their lips apart. They went at once toward the stage, and without talking. Each knew their relationship would not be the same now.

When she had touched the Alabaman he had taken it hard. When their lips closed, it had shaken him like the swamp fever. It was her fault and she was ashamed again. She was ashamed as she had been when she had kissed her first boy, and he had put his hands on her where they shouldn't be. Yet, right or wrong, there would be no undoing the damage of that willful kiss. It was Lucy Henderson's poor little joke and she was stuck with it. Linn Sparhawk was in love.

Four A.M. came and was galloped under. El Paso lay forty miles south. In the ghost light they rolled past historic Fort Fillmore, with its lone adobe stationhouse, corral and the great barracks quadrangle flanking it off in the shadows to the east.

Report had reached El Paso that the large Union garrison at Fillmore had been pulled out the past week. From the lonely stillness of the moonlit post, the report appeared reliable. Not even a dog barked as the Celerity rattled past the Waterfield station, on around the irrigation system of the post gardens between the stage road and the river, and then north again along the Rio Grande toward Coyote Wells.

It was a bad break, those soldier boys pulling out like that. If they had still been there, the Waterfield papers could have been safe in the hands of their commanding officer in another ten minutes, and Lucy Henderson and her seven men would never have gone on to Mimbres Springs. But the troops were plainly gone. Old Doc growled, laid the leather to his mules, and the shadowy walls of Fort Fillmore fell behind and were forgotten.

Fate, they say, plays no favorites. She certainly showed no mercy to the fleeing employees of the American Mail Company the early dawn on April 12, 1861.

41

The irony of it was that Major Gilbert René Paul and 380 Federal regulars were asleep behind the brick and adobe ramparts past which, within 400 feet, Doc Harnaday whipped and cursed his lathered mules on toward Mesilla.

No pursuit by Cullross's men developed. The party rolled on through the false dawn, nothing chasing them but their shadows. Full day came on. They made Coyote Wells, south of Mesilla.

The wells were pothole water tanks, rock *tinajas*, like those at famed Hueco Tanks west of Guadalupe Peak. The Celerity reached a higher altitude during the night and there was now more cover, particularly the pungent ten- and fifteen-foot junipers.

The approach to the water had to be made on the qui vive, for again, as at Hueco Tanks, Coyote Wells was a favorite haunt of the nomad Apache.

The tension mounted as Doc started in through the heavy brush. He inched his mules along at checkreined walk. Linn Sparhawk stood up back of the dashboard, his Springfield carbine poked out front, quartering the morning breeze. Suddenly they broke clear of the screening juniper and could see the rocky pools.

They were the most beautiful sight any of them had seen in a long spell. Best of all was the angular silhouette of Frank Swango watering his sweat-streaked roan at the nearest one of their red-rock depressions. His crisp black outline slouched lean against the pale sun was glad sight enough to make a person want to let down and shout—especially Lucy Henderson.

There is in every young girl's life that one remembered older man who is the exciting superior of all the more callow, youthful swains put together. For Lucy that man was Frank Swango. Nor did she care that he was nearing fifty.

He was some inches over six feet, lean, dark-skinned, graceful. His face had about it the sculptured spareness of a Plains Indian's, but this romantic notion of war-bonneted forebears was belied by his light gray eyes and deep curling, silver hair. His habitual expression was a sort of cautious, quizzical squint, "the look," Doc once complained, "of a man who's spent the best years of his life looking where he's been instead of where he's going."

But the Union girl admired everything about him, including the hunted look and the half-century of harsh experience. The emotional stir proved hers alone. Frank Swango had other things on his mind, including something hidden behind a nearby juniper clump.

He disappeared around that brush clump, as Doc set the Celerity's brakes and clambered down to unhook the mules for watering. Sparhawk scrambled up the sand hill dominating the Wells to mount Apache-guard for the stop. He had just reached the top and raised his field glasses to begin his scanning arc, when Swango came back from behind the junipers. He was leading John Waterfield's two prize bay buggy horses. The nervous geldings were caked gray with alkali dust but their saddles had not been sat in recently and stood empty as the eye sockets of a drying steer skull.

"Tie 'em to the boot," said the shotgun rider, handing the bays to big Sim who, with Jake Bergerman, had just crawled out of the coach. The giant Negro nodded and took the horses. When he had gone behind the stage with them, Lucy Henderson crowded forward to welcome the returned Tucson conductor.

"Well . . ." she began, and got no further.

"Be quiet," said Swango, and put two fingers in his mouth and whistled up at Sparhawk.

The latter waved back quickly, came sliding down off the hill on the double. Clearly, the situation was tightening up. The Alabaman trotted up to Swango, hooked a thumb at the Waterfield bays and grinned swiftly.

"What happened, Frank?"

"Just ran out a hunch, kid."

"Whereabouts?"

"Just past Luz Sanchez's."

"Mike and the Preacher, eh?" asked Sparhawk, looking again at the riderless bays.

"For sure," answered Swango. "The double-crossing sons ditched the wagon and saddled up the team for a getaway on their own not a mile out of town. Down at the Big Bend, it was. They never figured to stick with us in the first place."

"Apparently not. Anybody get bad hurt, Frank?"

"The loud-mouth Mick felt his. I had to use two on him; he stood tough. Barton went easy. He never knew what hit him."

"You must have gotten up hand-close to them," muttered Sparhawk, eying him half accusingly. "Two-for-three is pretty good for a night shoot."

"Dark or daylight," said Swango, "it's all the same in this business. You get up as close as you can."

Sparhawk felt the chill of the look and nodded awkwardly.

43

"Yeah. Well anyways, we can use the horses, I reckon."

"I reckon," agreed Swango in terse return. Then, sharply: "You see anything of Cullross's bunch last night, kid?"

"Nope, did you?"

"No. Let's get out of here. Doc . . .!"

"Yo, Frank?" queried the old man, calling up from the tanks.

"Get your teams hooked up again, *pronto.*"

"All right. Linn, gimme a hand down here. This bank's steeper'n the price of panther juice in Prescott."

As the Alabaman started sliding down the incline to help the old man with the mules, the other travelers were spun about by a coughing grunt of surprise that sounded like it had come out of a lion. There, grinning the first grin any of them had seen on his dark face, they saw big Sim standing by the Celerity's opened boot. In one huge hand dangled Cipher Reno Sanchez, caught up and carried like a guilty puppy by the scruff of the neck.

"He said he came to fight the Indians, Mr. Frank," Sim rumbled. "He says he wants to help me take care of the little boss."

He pointed to Sparhawk down by the water and Swango answered, straight-faced, "Set the kid down and sign him on, full pay."

The released half-breed youngster was thankful for many things beyond his liberation from the cramped and airless mail boot. Not the least of these was his pride in being accepted by the widely feared Señor Frank. "Gracias, *Patrón!*" he shouted, dancing about. "*Mil gracias, mil gracias!*"

"*De nada, hombre.*" Swango would not smile but his gray eyes squinted an extra crow's-foot for the occasion. "Go help with the mules." The happy boy dashed down the embankment and the shotgun rider turned on Bergerman.

"Jake . . ."

"No, no, Frank, I swear it! I done exactly what you told me!" The little Jew spread his hands in eloquent testimony to his innocence. "*Himmel!* Look at me and say I would lie to you!"

"I'm looking and you would. You told that kid I said he was to go home, didn't you? And then you turned right around and snuck him into the barn behind my back and stowed him in the boot, anyways."

"Frank, I swear to you . . ."

"*Jake.*"

"Well, all right. So I did it. So shoot me."

"I've a good mind to."

Swango said it as though he meant it but Bergerman knew better. "He wants only to be one of us, Frank. A man among men, no questions asked about color or religion. The way it is supposed to be in this land of ours; for me, for Sim, maybe even for you too, eh, Frank? You know what it's like to be alone, to be one who cannot come in and be welcome. I know you, Frank. You are as soft with the boy as old Jake. Only with you there is the . . ."

"Only with me there is 'the nothing,'" broke in Swango roughly. "Shut up and climb back in that coach. I wish to God Indians could be talked to death and we had along a dozen 'Dutchmen' as gabby as you, Jake. There wouldn't be an Apache left alive in New Mexico by the time we got to Mesilla."

"Linn!" bellowed Doc Harnaday from the front of the coach. "Get up here with them goddamn leaders! Christ A'mighty, boy, you're slower'n the eighth scab on the seven year itch. Get a move on!"

"Sticks and stones may break my bones," Sparhawk panted up the slope, "but flattery will get you nowhere."

"In fact," put in Swango, "any more flattery like that, Doc, and I'm going to wash your mouth out with soapweed. You forget once more we got a lady aboard, I'm going to come down on you like a ton of hot steer guts. You hear me?"

"You and what special deatchment of Rip Ford's Texas Rangers?" demanded the old man angrily, elevating his bony fists as though he actually meant to square off about it.

"Lead team's in," called Sparhawk. "Let's go."

"We're gone," nodded Swango, and swung open the door for Lucy Henderson.

"Up you go, miss. We're running late."

"I only wanted to ask . . ."

"It'll keep. Get aboard."

He reached for her, clamping her arm hard. It hurt her and she pulled away from him. "I only wanted to ask you what happened to Barton and O'Hanlon!" she finished defiantly.

"You heard me telling Linn, miss."

"Listening to you and Sparhawk," she spat back at him, "is about as understandable as eavesdropping on a couple of cigar-store Indians."

The shotgun rider only nodded.

45

"You know what happened to Barton and O'Hanlon, miss, and why, and when, and how it happened to them. I'm not going to make you no detailed diagrams of it."

Lucy Henderson swallowed hard. She looked up at him and said it much more quietly. "*Both* of them?"

His lean head bobbed again.

"Are they . . .?" she had to know, still smaller voiced.

"They are," said Frank Swango softly. "Bellies up and toes abobbing. In the backwater at Big Bend."

6

It was just six o'clock when they made the westward turning in the river road south of Mesilla. A mile and a half away, across the scrubby bottoms, lay the town. The river lay directly ahead.

Fortunately the stream was low and they had no trouble with their crossing. This was a real blessing with a watercourse which could be either an inches-deep, sandy-clear trickle or a muddy flood 400 feet wide and twelve feet deep, depending on the weather upcountry.

As Doc Harnaday brought the Celerity out on the far side and shook up the tired mules with a slap of the lines, the purple shadows were retreating swiftly toward the eastern scarps of the Organ Mountains. The sun, well above the ragged peaks now, was diffusing the grassy bottomlands with pink warmth. The cactus wrens sang in the sage. The redwings sawed rustily in the river reeds. The western larks belled sweetly in the blue-gray grama grass. It was, indeed, a surpassingly fresh and lovely morning—until they cleared the last brush-screened bend in the winding road.

Then all the beauty drained out of the new day. Old Doc threw on the brakes. He stood up on the box, spread his legs, lay back on all six lines at once.

The lead steam sat back on their singletrees. Behind them the wheel and swing teams braced their forelegs, showering back red dirt and rock sparks. The big Celerity skidded, teetered, turned broadside-to, stopped safely upright. All the Waterfield party, from Frank Swango, frozen on his ear-pricked roan, to Cipher Reno Sanchez, hiding with Lucy

46

Henderson behind the Celerity's leather side curtains, sat and stared in shocked dismay.

A half mile away across the open flat lay the several score adobe houses of Mesilla, quiet in the morning sun. On the near, or southeast, flank of the settlement stood the lone landmark cottonwood tree which shaded the abandoned Waterfield stationhouse, hay barn and stock corral. Somewhere a forlorn rooster crowded unchallenged in the dusty streets. On the mesa beyond the last house a skulking cur, early afoot to run down his breakfast in the sagebrush, put up his gaunt head to howl a doleful warning of strangers upon the land. Mesilla slumbered on. Very clearly its predominantly Spanish-American population did not practice the gringo habit of early-to-rise.

But it was not the town's sleepy stillness which riveted the travelers' attention. They were looking 300 yards to their left.

Over there, at about the same distance from Mesilla as themselves, and having popped out of the bottomland brush in the same moment as they, were thirteen mounted men.

For a long half-minute no member of either party moved. Both sides sat quietly, remaking history. Beauregard's bombardment and young Union Major Robert Anderson's subsequent gallant surrender of Fort Sumter at noon of April 13 was not the first Confederate action of the war. It was the second. The first, by some thirty-six hours, was the abortive strike at Mesilla, New Mexico, sometime before seven A.M. of April 12, by the thirteen Texas irregulars of Price Cullross's San Antonio command.

Those were "Cullross's Rangers" staring at the Waterfield fugitives across that silent, grassy flat.

Clearly, the Southern guerrillas, missing them in El Paso and correctly guessing their Santa Fe destination, had raced to cut them off at Mesilla. That they had failed by five minutes of getting into the town in time to set up a classic ambush meant little. They had won the race, no matter. Or had they?

When the Rebel horsemen held their mounts disdainfully, Frank Swango glanced up at Linn Sparhawk.

"You game for a little run to the company corral, kid?" he asked quietly.

"Game but a little gut-shrunk," grinned the Alabaman. "Doc?"

"Me, too. Shaking like a bobcat passing buckshot."

Across the morning stillness they could hear the Confed-

47

erate horses grunting and blowing to ease their wind. In the motionless air the flank steam arose from their sweated quarters in pungent, curling fingers. They could see the lips of their riders moving in subdued, watchful conversation.

"All right," said Swango softly, "I allow we'll take a set at it."

With the nod, he put his spurs into his sidling roan and went, as Doc later described it, "away from there like a tail-burnt bat looking for a bucket of sitting grease."

Across the flat the Confederates milled a moment in surprise. Then, raising a ragged guerrilla yell, they streamed off after Swango. At the same time Doc kicked off the brake, laid the leather and the language to his six-mule hitch, and the run was on.

After the starting yells on both sides, the race was made in dead silence by all concerned. Frank called his gelding Blue Bolt. The little horse, squat, muscular and ugly as a sourmug bulldog, rated the name. He could run like a turpentined cat. The stage road curved like a drawn bow between the river brush and the company corral. The Southerners, being to the left, were running against the long outer curve, while Frank cut across the short inner side. The difference, with his sprint horse's speed, made it possible for Blue Bolt and him to get the guerrillas headed. With half the original course covered and but a scant quarter-mile remaining, the Confederates saw that Frank would go under the wire a long pistol-shot in the lead. At once they veered and came for the Celerity.

Doc saw them make the swing. With a warning yell to Linn, who was riding the top of the coach, he wrapped his lines and jumped down off the seat box to land between the wildly galloping wheelers. He hit the wagon tongue and stayed on it. Crouched atop the whipping timber, he yowled four-letter endearments to his straining mules, while blasting away across their churning withers with his ancient Walker Colt.

The old gun was the best part of a foot long and weighed four pounds. It bucked and roared and belched flame like a piece of wheeled artillery; and created nearly as much consternation among the startled foe. Flat on his stomach on the canvas roof of the crazily pitching stage, Linn Sparhawk offered no more target than old Doc down between his shielding mules. Too, his heavy Springfield carbine was snapping out its big .50 caliber slugs as valiantly as the rusted Walker revolver.

Cullross's Rangers were, in a word, getting a bit more than they had come prepared to handle.

Left with nothing but the coach itself to shoot at, they did a thorough job of ventilating the Celerity's vulnerable canvas. Yet, miraculously, none of its occupants was struck. Jake Bergerman's skullcap and Cipher Reno Sanchez's straw sombrero got knocked off, but that was from cracking their heads together while diving for the floor. Lucy Henderson followed them when a whistling rifle bullet went through the crown of her borrowed man's hat. The only ones remaining upright in the coach were Sim and Price Cullross, and of the two only the big Negro was so by choice. The captive guerrilla leader was there solely because his pinioned arms and legs, plus the point of Sim's Bowie knife in his nearest ribs, would not permit him gracefully to be elsewhere.

The passengers on the floor of the coach had to interpret the short remainder of the race by translation of its outside sounds, augmented by what small views they could get through the rocking, dust-clouded oblongs of the Celerity's narrow window openings.

The image, nonetheless, was graphic. Doc's chainfire of unbelievable profanity provided a good picture all by itself. From the old man's curses and Linn Sparhawk's occasional puppy yips, they made out that Doc had winged one, and the slender Alabaman two, of the converging horsemen; and, better yet, that Frank Swango had opened up on them from the cover of the adobe-wall stock corral.

Caught thus between two lines of aimed fire, and themselves under the severe handicap of shooting from their mounts, the Rebel racers broke their strides badly.

They had meanwhile got between the Celerity coach and the town of Mesilla, but did not seem to know what to do with their tactical advantage. Halting in mid-road, they all began yelling orders at once. As they did, the passengers inside the Celerity heard their hoarse shouts nearly in their ears, and saw the blurred images of their big hats, their angry faces and the foam-flecked heads of their rearing horses flash past the coach windows.

Undaunted, Doc Harnaday had simply driven the big stage straight through their loosely bunched effort to block off the road in front of him.

The next thing his astonished passengers knew, he had rolled the proud Celerity to an unhurried, schedule-speed stop in front of the empty-windowed Waterfield stationhouse in Mesilla, New Mexico, and was hollering down his standard-run "All out, end of the line!"

In the same minute the routed Confederates swung their horses wide out around the reach of Swango's rifle, heading north to invest the town and flank the corral from the safer approach of the Santa Fe side.

While Doc worked carelessly in the open to unhook his panting mules, Sparhawk dropped cautiously off the stage roof by the protected rear way of the boot. Once down, he went to work gentling and untying old John Waterfield's two wild-eyed bays. Both he and Doc had got their livestock loose and were running it toward the corral gates before their companions inside the coach caught up with the hard facts of life under fire.

This was war. Nobody, as old Doc would probably have put it, was going to be opening any stage doors for nobody. The common thought struck Jake Bergerman and Cipher Reno Sanchez at the identical time it did Lucy Henderson. The three of them got stuck in the doorway on the exit end of the same shameless dive.

Then they all had the good sense and humor to laugh about it. They untangled themselves and got through the door in the time-honored social order—women and children first. But once out of the coach, just the same, they all broke and scuttled for the corral like nerveless rabbits. After them, dragging the half-dead Price Cullross behind him, stalked the unimpressed Sim.

Sixty seconds later they were all safely inside the corral, the ponderous plank gates closed and cross-bolted.

Shortly, they gathered close beneath the shelter of adobe bastions made eight feet high and two feet thick to repulse the raiding Apache. They each looked up to the sunbaked ramparts as if they were old friends. They snuggled up to their warm, smooth surfaces, patting them as they would good and faithful dogs. The same thought was in the mind of every one of them: surely, if these mud-brick walls had held off the wily Mimbreño and frustrated the savage Mescalero, certainly they could stem any straightaway assaults by civilized white guerrillas.

Well, perhaps they could, for a time. But time is a troublesome thing. It will not hold still for mice or men or badly frightened young women, or for mortally shot-up stage mules; or, indeed, for scant food supplies or short rations of barrel-stale water.

50

Frank Swango, the hard-eyed shotgun rider of the El Paso crew, was explaining this fact of frontier life to his strangely assorted companions even as the latter were blessing the stout adobe fortifications of Mesilla Station. He kept his illustrations short, his text professionally brief. No one argued. It was all new to them; Frank Swango had been there many times before.

It was quiet enough to hear a cricket sigh. They all sat perfectly still, their attention riveted. Swango's dusty Arizona accent continued. Cullross's men, said the shotgun rider, could win any starve-out that went past four days. The reason for that was the basic weakness of the Seven. They had only what water was in the two small barrels still tied to the coach. Of food, also still in the coach, they had only enough to get them decently to Santa Fe. The guerrillas, on the other hand, could quarter on the town. They would find real good pickings once they dug under the strange look of desertion which hung over the place. They would scare up plenty of Spanish-American supplies the minute they got around to pounding on a few doors with their rifle butts. As for the handful of white merchants in Mesilla, they had learned from their dusky customers how to survive hostile invasion—ignore it. They were no more likely to take sides in the argument at the Waterfield corral than the Mexicans.

That was the dry side of the slice. Turning it over, it looked a little fresher. They had, the way Frank saw it, the valuable advantage of the Confederates not knowing about them any of the bad things they knew about themselves. Doubt, said the pale-eyed shotgun rider, had won more stand-offs than Colt and Remington put together.

After all, the San Antonians were most likely out for nothing more than a little local notoriety; something which might aid the cause of the South only insofar as it advanced their own home-town interests. It didn't seem reasonable they would be ready to die in any great numbers just to come by the Waterfield papers—papers of which very likely they didn't begin to realize the true importance. They were in that final respect much like Miss Lucy, herself. They had been sent out to do a job without any real idea of what they were doing, or just how to do it, or how much it might matter to their side if they did or didn't get it done.

There was, in Frank's terminal opinion, a time to fight and a time to wait. They had made their best move; now let the Confederates make theirs. If it was to be a wait-out, it could

51

be bad, but they had no choice in the matter. Not with four of their six stage mules so shot up they wouldn't be standing by next daylight. No, their best chance was to hang tough, hoping the Rebels would get tired and go home in two or three days. For sure, it was a cold-deck bluff, and why not? If they all had a dollar for every pot that had been stolen in the history of cutthroat poker they wouldn't have to worry about *waiting* out the guerrillas; they could buy them out.

The end-guess was still no. The Confederates would not go for a showdown fight. For a long while after that, the quiet continued unbroken. Then, to everyone's surprise, Linn Sparhawk shook his homely head.

No, drawled the Alabaman, Swango was wrong—dead wrong. *Those men were Southerners; they would fight.*

The shotgun rider looked at him, a peculiar light growing in his narrowed eyes. "Kid," he said, "what you getting at underneath the mint juleps and magnolias?"

For once Sparhawk did not drop his glance.

"You've got to understand, Frank," he answered soberly, "that there is a real difference between the way a Southern man and a Northern man will take the same situation. It's not an easy thing to get across to a Northerner. It's all bound up with regional pride and pedigreed blood and a man's God-given right to walk where he wants, when he wants and with whoever he pleases, accepting no affront from any man, tolerating no insult to any woman. I guess you might call it a sort of line-bred passion for personal freedom and the rights of the individual to do as he wants with no interference from anybody."

"You mean," said Frank Swango slowly, "like you exercise on the poor damned niggers down there?"

Sparhawk flinched, but stood to it.

"No, that's different. That's a sickness that will surely kill the South one day. Still it doesn't take away from the white Southern sense of personal right and pride. Frank, they've been hurt, and a hurt Southerner is a man who will kill you no matter he may have started out sparring with you halfway in fun. You've got to believe me, you hear? You wing a Southerner, you've wounded a fighter. A bad, mean, knee-in-the-groin man who will kill you exactly like I said."

"Like you maybe?" said Frank Swango quietly.

Sparhawk recoiled under the question. His companions saw the pain of it twist his sensitive mouth, darken his odd-colored eyes. He looked the picture of that shame-sick misery known only to the physical coward. And while he sought

52

desperately for an answer to the gray-haired gunman's insult, a better man stepped in and supplied it for him.

"No, not like *him*." The reply, strangely subdued in level and language, came from Doc Harnaday. "Linn's no fighter, except in his heart. He can't be much else with the trouble he's got. You know that, Frank. What in the hell is the matter with you, you lost your damned mind?"

"Doc," said Sparhawk, "shut up. You're talking too much."

The old man nodded and stepped back, for some unaccountable reason not arguing it.

The Alabaman stood nervously licking his lips, apparently looking around for help that wasn't there. Finally he got on with it.

"You all know this is Frank's show," he said. "I'm not trying to tell him how to run it. It's only that I'm in the best position to know the enemy and thought I ought to speak my piece on him. Frank's still bossing the main drive, regardless."

"I sure don't want to boss it," said the other, plainly embarrassed and appealing to them all. "But somebody's got to take the reins. Doc's too old and full of wind. Cipher Reno ain't got his citizenship papers. Sim's too dumb and Linn don't weigh enough. Jake can't. So who's left?"

"You," said Sparhawk simply, and that was that.

They made themselves as comfortable as might be. There was nothing else they could do until night came on and gave them the cover of darkness to go out and unload the coach.

The day dragged along without sight or sound of the Confederates. The local citizens stayed put as predicted. The town dogs wandered the alleys, the chickens scratched and dusted in the main street, the burros switched flies and browsed the gutters in search of sustenance. High noon blazed and cooled. Sunset lit its red fires over west. Twilight doused them. Full dark came on.

Sim crept out with Sparhawk and brought in some of the food and the Waterfield records. The Alabaman also produced Lucy Henderson's old straw suitcase, which, for some reason not apparent to anyone, he had smuggled into the boot at El Paso. The big Negro, having been shown the route, made the second trip alone, toting back the first of the water barrels. He was starting on the third and last trip for the remaining barrel, when Swango hissed at him to lay low and stay quiet.

The silence grew like a fungus, stifling, choking.

They held their breaths, waiting. Out by the Celerity there

was a sound of muffled footsteps in the dust. Swango and Doc Harnaday both fired. The stillness again.

Presently the sodden "thunk!" of an ax blade caving in barrel staves echoed wetly. Then the heart-sinking sound and smell of fresh water puddling in deep dust filtered through the dark. Shortly, another familiar, but this time out-of-place, smell came seeping to them over the corral wall.

Puzzlement for an acrid minute. Then uneasy frowns. Coal oil? What the devil?

No time to wonder. In the empty well of darkness beyond the coach, the scrape and flicker of a sulphur match spurted. This was followed by the scuttle of running figures bent double and zigzagging. Then came the vicious crack and futile whining ricochets of Frank's incredibly fast shots. A pale flutter of growing light appeared within the coach; then, *ssshhhboom!* the belch and flare of the oil-drenched interior exploding in a ball of greasy yellow flame. They all knew then, the answer to that morning's argument. Sparhawk had been right. The Southerners would not play a waiting game. Nor would the Seven for very long.

7

Sim built the supper fire in the chimney corner of the stationhouse. Cipher Reno cooked the tasteless mess of wheatflour tortillas, which, with a rusted tin of coffee, was their first hot food in twenty-four hours.

The rest of the company waited by the front wall of the corral, not saying much, thinking a great deal.

When the "Chihuahua cornplasters"—Doc Harnaday's jaundiced description—were ready, they ate. Only when the last one of them was washed down and the coffee tin being passed for the third time, did the talk begin.

Linn Sparhawk led off with a sobering résumé of their position, as he saw it, debited and credited.

The debit side: Their Celerity coach and four of its six mules were gone. With them had gone all their spare clothing, toilet articles, half their water, over half their food, both long-range Sharps rifles, one case of the boxed ammunition for the Springfield carbines.

The credit side: They had twenty gallons of water, one sack of flour, one side of bacon, two pounds of coffee, a handful of salt, a half box of baking soda. They had two sound mules, two spooky bay geldings broke to ride or drive, but no wheeled rig of any kind to which they might hook them. They had four breech-loading carbines and 500 rounds of brass-cased ammunition for same. Other weapons included Lucy Henderson's Elliott Patent Remington pepperbox, Doc's old model Sharps bullgun, Swango's 1850 Ethan Allen shotgun and 1860 Army model Colt revolver. Past these, there was very little, as neither Sparhawk, Bergerman, Sim nor Cipher Reno normally went fire-armed. Linn packed a pocketknife, Jake a cigar clipper, Sim his "Texas toothpick," and young Sanchez a cottonwood slingshot and six or eight smooth stones suitable for anything up to bullfrogs or scarab beetles.

That was the inventory of their fighting stock in the opinion of the pale Alabaman. None of the others could add materially to it.

Soon enough the talk began to swing toward ways and means of making some kind of a deal with the guerrillas. The spirit of adventure seemed to have evaporated rather suddenly since sundown. Lucy Henderson heard no further mentions, her own or anyone else's, of company loyalty or Union dedication. The simple truth appeared to be that with the chips down none of them meant to get killed over the Waterfield operational records.

Nor was the questionable worth of old John Waterfield's paper the only embarrassment presently challenging the common sense of the El Paso Unionists. There was the little matter of the Apaches. This worry was very much in the mind of Linn Sparhawk as he listened to his friends fretting about doing business with Cullross's men.

Of course there had been some Indian risk understood from the beginning. All hands had either known or been told that. And it hadn't bothered any of them too much at the time. Men like old Doc Harnaday and Frank Swango could never have held any serious doubts about their ability to take a well-armed coach through to Santa Fe. Old-timers in the staging business seemed to develop a simply magnificent contempt for the red men in any kind of a Concord running fight. But that was only so long as they had a good coach and six sound mules to roll it. Now they had neither, and the Indians were out there waiting for them just the same, when, as and if they broke out of the Confederate surround.

That last part of the proposition brought a person squarely up against the most immediate stumbler in his summation —which would be those same silent guerrillas sneaking around somewhere out there in the dark streets of Mesilla, New Mexico. They were tonight's problem.

What to do about them composed the main content of company thought presently going on behind those high adobe walls. The scarcely veiled suggestions of the Alabaman's companions now began to admit as much, with definite overtones in favor of the aforementioned "deal."

Jake Bergerman announced that he was not mad at anybody, and that some of the finest men he had ever done business with had been Texans. Cipher Reno let it be known that he didn't care what "hoppened to heem," so long as he didn't get "hort." Sim had nothing to say other than to mutter, "I will go where you go," when Sparhawk asked him what he wanted to do. Even old Doc hedged a little, allowing that, "maybe it isn't rightly fitten to run no more risk of innocent people getting themselves killed." He didn't offer to identify which of the company he considered innocent, but did manage to leave the impression he felt himself to be considerably blameless.

Frank Swango, characteristically, said nothing. Linn, by the same token, spoke his full share. "Well," he volunteered, "it seems like now is the time for us to 'pluck up that which is planted.' "

"Come again?" said Swango.

"Cullross," shrugged the Alabaman. "It's why I figured to bring him along in the first place; to trade him off in case we got in a real tight."

"By God!" crowed Doc excitedly, "I'd clean forgot the slick-ear son of a bitch! Maybe we can swap him for a twenty-four hour pass through their damned lines!"

"Not without we tie them company papers to his Texas tail when we turn him loose," gritted Swango.

"No, wait," urged Sparhawk, "there's another way. I was thinking of Barton and O'Hanlon."

Frank's face was invisible in the darkness but none of them needed to see it. The change in his voice was clear enough. "Go right on thinking about them," he said, "but do it out loud."

Sparhawk nodded. "Well, you see," he went on quickly,

"I was thinking that Cullross heard you and me talking about what happened to Mike and the Preacher back yonder at Coyote Wells. Now, not knowing you like I do, how will Cullross be sure you won't give him a shot of the same lead strychnine you gave them? I mean if he bows his neck and gets balky on us."

"All right . . ."

"All right, I just thought maybe we could let him think you would. Then, most likely, he'd be more of a mind to try and swing a little deal in our favor with his friends, out there." The Alabaman gestured off into the street darkness and Swango nodded noncommittally. "So . . .?"

"So maybe his pals might toss in their cards to Cullross's call where they'd stay and see ours, figuring we were bluffing from a busted flush. But with Cullross himself doing the ante-ing, they just might buy our bet. What you say, Frank? You think maybe?"

"I dunno. It might work, kid." Swango was over his hard streak, thinking straight again. "Where'd Sim put him?"

"In the harness shed yonder." Sparhawk bent his head toward the small lean-to built against the hay barn at the rear of the corral. Swango turned to the big Negro.

"Sim," he said, "go fetch Mr. Cullross up here."

The ex-slave grunted something pleasurable in a language that certainly wasn't English, and disappeared on his errand. He was back in a minute, Price Cullross slung over his shoulder. He dumped him at Swango's feet and faded back to his watch on the front wall.

"We got you some supper here, Cullross," the shotgun rider told him, showing him the coffee tin and three cold tortillas, "but first you're going to have to sing for it."

Cullross, who hadn't uttered a word since regaining consciousness the night before, only bobbed his head now.

Swango went on, sketching the situation of the suggested barter. "You make the deal to get us out of here," he concluded, "you go free. Otherwise . . ."

"Never mind the threats," said Price Cullross quietly. "I understand very well the morals and mentalities of express messengers."

"The what?"

Frank Swango was not a bright man. He didn't have to be. He had obviously made his way in the world with other tools than a college vocabulary.

"No man," Cullross answered him evenly, "takes a job like yours except by clear choice."

57

"Which is to say?"

"You're a hired killer, Swango. You like the work, you earn the pay. Let's get on with it."

"Suits me," said Frank Swango.

He took Cullross by the bound arm, spun him around.

"Hop up on them old boxes by the front wall. Yonder where you see Sparkhawk's black man. Sim," he called over, "you see that Mr. Cullross makes a good speech. If he starts talking about anything but getting Mr. Linn and the rest of us turned free, you stand away from him in a hell of a hurry. Comprende?"

"Si, señor. Es muy comprensible, muy claro."

Lucy Henderson, hearing the fluent Spanish of Sim's reply, shook her head. How had the giant ex-slave ever earned the sobriquet of Simple Simon? If his was a child's mind, she decided, the world would be a better place with a lot more backward adults of his dark hue in it. And maybe a lot fewer of the so-called superior, light-skinned varieties. Furthermore . . .

The indignantly developing argument was cut off by the intrusion of a sterner sociology—that which surrounded them all in the inky darkness of the Waterfield corral.

Cullross stood in front of Swango as though he did not mean to obey his command to mount the wall.

Surprised, the shotgun rider said easily, "Maybe you didn't understand me, Cullross."

"I understood you."

"In that case I'll count to three."

Swango punctuated his laconic statement with the double period of his twelve gauge's twin hammers being put on cock. The hard-nerved Cullross laughed low and quick and said, "Now that's a language I understand. Why didn't you say so in the first place," and started for the wall.

There, Sim's lion growl muttered some guttural instructions to the Texan and the latter answered lightly, "Never you fear, you black rascal. There's two things I'll not argue with in any man's hand—a broken bottle or a Bowie knife. Give me room, I'm ready to orate."

With that, the swashbuckling prisoner was calling out clearly and carefully to his invisible henchmen.

"Boys, it's me, Price Cullross."

There was a significant pause.

Cullross raised his voice sharply. "Willis? Beaufort? Randall? Travis? You all hear me out there? Speak up!"

There was a second lengthening pause before a noncom-

58

mittal Southern drawl replied that he was, indeed, being heard out there.

"All right, then," he went on, beginning to push a little. "Now think straight on this. These people in here want to make a deal. They offer to release me unharmed if you will let them go along up to Santa Fe with the Waterfield papers.

"Let me repeat that.

"They mean to trade me for their own safe passage north out of Mesilla. If you don't do as they require, they say they will burn the papers and put a bullet through me. I might add they've got a hired gunhand in here who I believe might do it. Now do you understand the situation clearly?"

There was a third pause, longer even than the others. From out of the street darkness came the subdued mutter of several voices in urgent discussion. Swango stood waiting, loose and easy, his old Ethan Allen twelve idly wandering over the shoulders of Price Cullross's pin-striped coat. He was in no way tense. It was perfectly clear that Frank Swango was used to people doing precisely what he told them and doing it with no more backtalk than he was currently getting from Price Cullross.

Over on the other side of the street, the guerillas had finally made up their minds. "All right, Price," their spokesman called back. "We understand. So what do you want us to do about it?"

"Nothing!" yelled the Texan, to the Waterfield party's stunned amazement. "By God! Not a damned single Yankee thing, you hear! Give 'em hell, boys! Three cheers for the Stars and Bars!"

Frank Swango was a man lightning quick to shoot; what was called in the Southwest at the time "a very fast gun." But this time he came out second.

As he shifted his double twelve calmly upward, presumably to blow off Price Cullross's defiant head, Linn Sparhawk struck the weapon's barrels down and aside. The left bore's charge went into the wall alongside Cullross; that of the right, into the packing boxes upon which he stood. Before any of the others realized what had happened, Sim had dragged the Texan down to the ground and was asking Swango, "What do you want me to do with him, Mr. Frank?"

"I'd like to have you pin him to that wall by his dammed Rebel ears!" snapped the shotgun rider, showing more emotion than any of them thought he had in him.

They could all see the white flash of Sim's beautiful teeth

59

in the rare grin. He whirled Cullross around, seizing him by the coat collar. In an instant he had plastered him flat up against the wall and driven his heavy knife into what looked like the Texan's head.

Horrified, Lucy Henderson gasped and cried out. Doc cursed. Bergerman groaned. Cipher Reno said something in Spanish to God.

But Sim was still grinning. When he stepped back, away from his victim, they saw why. The huge Negro had driven his blade's steel through the doubled cloth of Cullross's coat collar six inches into the loose adobe of the wall behind the Texan. The guerilla leader was hung up as helplessly and humblingly as a hickory-smoked ham.

"Sorry, Mr. Frank," Sim mumbled expressionlessly. "His ears are quite small, I missed them in the dark."

"You see in the dark like a cat."

Linn Sparhawk's soft-voiced accusation cut in from the wall shadow before Swango could answer. He followed it with a flat order.

"Take Mr. Cullross down from that wall this minute, Sim, do you hear me?"

"Leave him hang," said Swango, stepping forward.

"Sim, you heard me," said Sparhawk.

Lucy Henderson crowded forward unconsciously. She had not heard that tone in the little Alabaman's voice. There was a great firmness in it and not a small inclusion of fear. It had some kinship to the controlled tone an animal trainer takes with a dangerous and uncertain brute with which he has had trouble before. Whatever it was, Sim heard it.

"Yes, Bwana."

It was the first time the big black had used the formal African address and the Union girl sensed in it the same nameless change in relationship which had been in Sparhawk's command. Then in a flash she had it. Here was the master speaking to the slave, and the slave responding to the master, with neither white man nor black conscious of the reversion. Here, at last, was that ugly Southern sickness of which Linn had spoken so feelingly before, showing up in the Alabaman himself.

"Take Mr. Cullross down off that wall," repeated Sparhawk, low-voiced. "Now."

"Don't touch him," countermanded Swango and dropped his right hand.

With that reference to the gun, Sparhawk began spanieling again, obsequious as ever. "Now, please, Frank . . ."

60

"Don't put off on me, kid." The interruption was brittle as breaking glass, and Sparhawk waved his hands.

"Sure not, Frank. I only want to ask you what you'd have done in Cullross's place. Would you have begged for your life up on that wall with a shotgun in your back?"

The listening Lucy Henderson shook her head in frank admiration. The little Southerner was nothing if not devious. All in a simple twist of words he had turned an ugly situation inside out. The entire angry atmosphere was at once made harmless, requiring only a straight answer to an innocuous question to dissipate the gunman's gathering wrath.

The latter was not quick enough of mind to understand how this had happened, yet he was not so slow that he didn't realize it had. In some puzzling way the thin-chested stablehand had put him in a corner he could not shoot his way out of. He didn't like that, but he was too much a man to lie about it. The Alabaman boy had him cold.

"Well, hell," he shrugged. "Since you put it that way, kid, I reckon I'd have done the same as him. Cut him down, Sim."

He brought his hand away from his holster in an unfamiliar gesture of surrender, at the same time easing back the quick step he had moved forward the moment before. Sim hesitated, then grunted his agreement. The others could see the relief sag Sparhawk's bony shoulders as the murderous-looking Negro moved to obey Swango and free Price Cullross.

The Alabaman walked away from the tableau at the wall, breathing heavily and mopping his pale face with his ragged shirtsleeve. He got out his bandanna and blew his nose. He sighed to himself, sank down unknowingly on the same pile of corral poles Lucy Henderson had sought out seconds before. He did not see her until she spoke.

"Well, Linn, that was close."

He was too tired even to look up. "Very," he granted her.

"For a minute there I thought it was going to be Cullross. Then Sim. Then you. It was hard to tell."

Sparhawk shook his head. "It was never going to be anybody but Frank," he said.

"Frank?" she frowned. "You're crazy, Linn."

"No, I'm not," he said. "But Sim is."

He paused, wiping his face again, still breathing with difficulty. "Sometimes I almost wish I believed in slavery. Or at least that I'd left him stay where I found him. It gets to be like having a pet tiger on a string."

"You mean Sim? Tell me about him, Linn. I know he's not what he looks or lets on to be."

Sparhawk took his time, thinking about what he was going to say. In the end it could not be much for he did not know much about his giant shadow, and so he made it brief.

"You're right, he's no ordinary colored man," he began. "He wasn't a field worker, but a house companion to a sickly white boy whose daddy owned one of the biggest plantations in Louisiana. That's where he got his good English and other learning; right along with his young master the way they do down South. Well, the boy died and his daddy put Sim out in the cotton but Sim wouldn't be put out in the cotton. He went surly and they sent him to market in Shreveport, where I found him.

"He took to me right off, mostly I suppose because I was puny like the boy he'd been taught to protect and grown to love back on the plantation; you know the way strong things will do with weak ones. Anyway, we got on fine. And we still do, saving for times like just now when his wild blood gets stirred up. Then he'll make you sweat for a minute, I'll allow."

He broke off, shaking his head again, and she prompted him softly. "What do you mean, Linn?"

"Firstly, that dumb act of his is only to keep the white folks from bothering him and in the process getting him riled. He's no more simple than any of us, and a good bit smarter than most. And he's proud, proud as hell; that's where the trouble comes in and the wild blood I was talking about."

She waited and he went on.

"Sim's not a native Negro. He's an African Massai caught and sold north through Arabia when he was already a man grown. That Massai is the highest blood there is. The other Negroes call them 'lion killers' and I wouldn't want to argue the idea any. They're a real handful and mostly the slavers won't fool with them.

"But once in a while one comes through, like Sim, and they either have to sell him or shoot him, and believe me they're not in the business of shooting the poor devils so long as they can stand up and look halfway alive in the slave ring at Shreveport, or wherever.

"So Sim got sold. By the time I bought him free, he was surface-broke and putting on that simple-minded act so nobody would buy him for field work. You see, he knew full well the overseers don't take to the idea of turning a 'crazy nigger' loose with a cane knife or a chopping hoe. But like I said back at the beginning, I'm half a mind to wish now I'd have bought him a steamboat ticket north, instead of bringing him along to Texas with me. I reckon we'd both find our nerves benefited by the change."

Lucy waited again and then, seeing he wasn't intending to go right on, nudged him back into his story. "What did you mean about Frank being in danger just now, and not you or Price Cullross? I'll admit I don't see that yet, though I see some other things about Sim, true enough."

"Miss Lucy," Sparhawk told her, dropping his voice dramatically, "if Frank had come one step closer to me, or moved his hand another inch to pull his gun, Sim would have killed him. He would have torn him apart with his bare hands. Him or any other man alive who might make a motion to harm me. Now do you see what I meant?"

Somehow it didn't sound theatrical the way he said it, and Lucy knew it was the unadorned truth. She just said yes very quietly, and sat there trying to think up some less uneasy subject. She had not yet found it when the flesh and form of their suspended talk materialized out of the dark at Sparhawk's elbow.

"You want me to put him back in the little shed now, Mr. Linn? He has eaten his food. He ate well, too. A little fast, perhaps, but well."

In one great hand Sim held a length of picket rope. At the end of the strand, collared like a stray and miserable dog, stood Price Cullross.

"Yes," said Sparhawk. "Trot him around a little bit first, though. He's been tied up too long to put him right back. And when you do bed him down, see he has fresh hay and a clean, decent place. Mr. Cullross," he added to the Texan. "I'm sorry, but it's the best we can do under the circumstances."

"Under the circumstances," shrugged the other, "you'd get no better from me."

Sim gave the rope a pull and started off. Cullross hung back and the big Negro stopped.

"Sparhawk," said the Texan, "I owe you one on that shotgun."

"Shucks, man, that was nothing."

"It was something."

"All right then," Sparhawk smiled, "just put it on the bill."

"No," said Cullross, "I'll pay cash."

Linn waited him out, seeing that he was having a tough time phrasing his gratitude for his having knocked aside Swango's murderous weapon. Presently, the guerrilla leader had made his mental settlement, nodded at the Alabaman.

"Back of that harmless shed yonder," he pointed, "shoved in between it and the corral wall, and covered over with old pack-mule tarps and moldy hay, is a sight I reckon you'd be mightily pleased to see. I made it out through a crack in the boards where your nigra dumped me before supper. Likely the Waterfield people had to store it there in a hurry when they pulled out."

"Don't tell me," laughed the little Southerner, "that there's a spare stagecoach squeezed in there!"

"No," said Price Cullross, after a deliberate wait, "but there is a perfectly damned good springbed wagon."

8

The discovery of the wagon wrought a singular change in Sparhawk. To the imaginative Alabaman it meant, provided they were free to do so, they might once more resume their journey. With it, plus their two strong mules and two fast horses, they could make even better time than they had with the Celerity and six mules. His companions, by no means as intrigued as he by Cullross's revelation, listened with indifference as he tried to show them the altered situation and its patent opportunities.

"Now please listen, you all," he pleaded with them. "We've got a real chance here if only you'll see it and take it." None of them nodded or looked up in response to this plainly earnest supplication, but he hurried on regardless of their apparent apathy.

"It stacks up this simple, folks, and we're as good as gone out of here, right now, I'll guarantee you."

"For God's sake, boy," complained Doc Harnaday. "Get on with it. You're wearing us out with how easy it is."

Sparhawk grinned and galloped on. "We know they expect us to go north," he pointed out. "You will recall Cullross made a point of stressing that when he spoke to his friends a bit ago. Of course, we don't know how many of them are on watch over yonder across the street, or where the rest of them are camped. But it's a good bet the main bunch is out on the north edge of town where they can watch both the stage road and the river-bed brush between us and Sante Fe. That's so they can jump us, either way, should we try to rush the ones on guard, straightaway, or pull an over-the-wall sneak-out on foot up the Rio. You agree so far?"

A half-attentive series of grunts from his listeners told him that they might or might not.

Again, he went on regardless. "All right then. Now all of us know the only other road out of Mesilla runs west. Doc, you and Frank can call that run in your sleep. Picacho, Rough and Ready, Goodsight, Mimbres Springs, Membrace Station and Fort Webster, Cow Springs, San Simon Creek, Apache Pass, Dragoon Wells, Tucson."

He rolled off the list of sunbaked mud huts and sagebrush ramadas as though they were real towns and up and coming centers of frontier activity, whereas, as a matter of converse, lonely fact, the whole of western New Mexico and eastern Arizona did not hold a hundred white people in that spring of 1861. El Paso, with a voting population of fifteen adult Anglo-Saxon males, was the biggest town, American count, between San Antonio and Tucson.

Lucy Henderson shivered a little. She had been well briefed by the Waterfield people at the St. Louis home office. Her memory mirrored a detailed map of the company route beyond Mesilla. Though the rangeland night was warm as August corn weather, the mere mental image of all those waterless, brassy miles west of their present position gave her a second ugly chill.

However, Sparhawk was not similarly affected. "Now then, don't you see," he continued happily, "if we can get that little old wagon out of this corral and onto the Tucson Road without we're caught doing it, we'll have seen the last of 'Cullross's Rangers'!"

It was he who had first given the name to the Texas saddle-toughs. Usually he got a smile out of it. This time he didn't.

"Yeah," said Frank Swango icily. "I reckon we will. And they'll have seen the last of us, too. Them and everybody else in Arizona and New Mexico."

"*Hein?*" asked Jake Bergerman anxiously. "What you mean, Frank?"

"He means the Apaches, Jake."

Sparhawk didn't duck it, back off from it, or try to swing wide around it. It was there like a jagged rock in the middle of the proposed Tucson road and he admitted it. But then just as quick as he did, he also pointed out they didn't necessarily have to bust their bedsprings driving over it. There was a way, he said, that they could get through to Tucson and safety without too much risk, or any real risk at all.

"Sure," nodded Swango pleasantly. "Fly."

"No," spat Doc Harnaday, just as searingly, "that's too easy. What we do is strip to our g-strings, paint ourselves red, start eating boiled dog and roast mule and cutting off our womenfolks' noses when we catch them blanketed with a strange buck and all the likes of that. Hell's tinkling hot brass bells! there ain't nothing to it. If you can't outthink 'em, by Christ, throw in with them."

He whirled on Linn, stained whiskers jutting.

"You're a forty-carrot genyus, boy! Now who the hell you want to be? Nachez, Geronimo or Nakay-do-klinny?"

"Unlock your wheels, Doc, you're burning brakeshoe leather. Ease up and I'll tell you all about it."

"You'll tell me nothing, you leppy little Alabama stray. I was talking Apache backward before you was old enough to pee without somebody pointing you. Now, by God, you listen to me!"

"No, Doc," insisted Sparhawk patiently, "you're going to listen to me. Don't you realize yet," he asked the old man, "that we're in real trouble here in Mesilla?"

"The kid's right," said Swango out of the dark. "Those Dixie roosters of Cullross's mean business now. They ain't just scratching dust no more. Linn was right about that when he said it to begin with. Now you shut up, Doc, or I'll come down on you, you hear?"

Doc heard. And Linn shot ahead. "I figure all we got to do is just steer clear of any daytime driving once we get west of Picacho," he explained.

"You know how those Indians are about night work; they don't take to it. They won't fight at night or even travel after dark if they can help it. They'd rather take a rawhiding than to get caught uncamped come sundown. So all we do is lay low during the day, drive like hell all night. We'll get through slick as hot grease down a gun barrel."

"That all there is to it?" asked Frank cryptically.

"Nope," replied the Alabaman confidently. "Besides that, we got a kicker out by Membrace Station."

"You mean Fort Webster?" said Frank interestedly.

"Sure. We can check with the Army before going on past Membrace Station. And, hell!" he added enthusiastically, "we can get that far tonight!"

"It's crazy!" snorted old Doc angrily.

"And it might work," said Frank Swango thoughtfully.

"Sure it'll work." The Alabaman shrugged it off as though they were already rubbing down their tired teams in Tucson. "You don't think I'd be recommending a run like this without that garrison was out there to guarantee us the choice of turning back, do you? You know me better than that, Frank."

"Yeah, I reckon. To tell you the truth, kid, I'd forgot all about that orphan bunch of soldier boys stuck out there."

"I hadn't, by Tophet. I've had them in mind from the minute we left El Paso. And especially from the minute we rolled past Fillmore in the dark and didn't get any dog barks. Finding Fillmore empty was bad, no bluffing that. I think we'd all halfway hoped the rumor was wrong, and that we'd find troops still there. But barring that, having those other Union boys out yonder at Webster will do till we get a better hand. Having them to count on is like being dealt four natural aces in a no-draw showdown game. We can't lose."

"We might," said Frank carefully. "What makes you so certain *that* command is still out there? You got connections we don't know about? That Major Mobry's a red-hot Rebel from the talk I've heard. What's to have kept him from pulling out to go home and help?"

"Nothing," admitted Linn. "But I know the garrison is still at Webster."

"How you know?" Frank asked.

"Well, we been a day here in Mesilla and we haven't seen them come through here, right? And before that we were all night on the road from El Paso and we didn't meet them alongway. Between here and there we went by Fillmore and saw she was deserted. Now if they had pulled out of Webster, where would they go? Tucson? Hell no, that's over 200 miles. Santa Fe? Across open country? Not this spring, mister. Mesilla, that's where they'd come. And where would they be going from Mesilla? Fillmore, where else? So if they didn't get to El Paso and they weren't at Fillmore and they aren't at Mesilla, where are they? Still out at Webster where they ought to be, Major Mobry or no Major Mobry, and that's how come I know that."

Frank spat into the corral dust and said, "Well, kid, you can go longer without taking a breath than I can. I throw in. But I still wish talk could kill Indians. Between you and Bergerman we could go to Tucson in broad daylight and never chamber a cartridge getting there."

He looked around for Doc Harnaday. "What you say, Doc? You think he's got it figured?"

The old Waterfield driver wagged his beard. "I dunno, Frank, I dunno. I wish we'd stopped at Fillmore now. All of a sudden I wish like hell we'd stopped there. God, I never thought of it, going by last night, but it's on me heavy and strong now that somebody was there. We should have stopped."

"What's that got to do with them troops being still out at Wedster?" Frank was short with it. Too much talk was piling up here, confusing the trial ahead.

"Nothing," grumped the old man. "Just that it might have been them that was there."

"There wasn't anybody there." Swango said it flat, and he had made his decision. "Kid," he agreed, "I'll ride your hunch a ways with you. What you got in mind for out past Mobry's post, happen we find the major to home?"

"Well, Frank, granting he's there and clears us past Membrace Station, the road from there is high and hard across good upland grass. Right? Any kind of a decent rig can make five miles an hour on that stretch. Correct? With our light wagon and the speed we stand to get from the Waterfield bays, we'll make seven, maybe eight miles an hour. Say, anyhow, fifty miles a night and more likely sixty. You go with that?"

"I might. Then what?"

"Then Tucson's only 250 miles from Membrace Station. We figure to roll it easy in five nights and not collect a single smoke signal doing it. Unless, naturally, we get careless."

"Or," qualified Swango acridly, "just plain unlucky."

"All right, you've said it many times yourself, Frank. Life's a lot like the Camptown Races. Somebody bets on the bobtailed nag, somebody bets on the bay. And damned if the black doesn't get up in the last furlong to win it going away. If we all had a dollar for all the long shots . . ."

"Yeah, yeah, kid, that's right. A man gambles every time he gets out of bed."

"He does," agreed Doc, giving in. "He might put his foot in the thundermug, fall and break his leg and have to be shot."

"Or anyways," finished Frank, "bow a tendon and get put out to pasture for six months."

"Well then?" asked Linn.

There was no immediate answer. But there was also no least doubt remaining that the Alabaman had done it again. There was a tangible change in the air. A person could taste it and it tasted good. Somehow, the skinny stock tender had sneaked the spirit of adventure back into the situation.

"Well then," said Frank Swango, at last, "let's get on with it. Faint heart never filled no inside straights. What you got in mind for getting us over the wall and on the way?"

Linn laughed that soft beautiful laugh of his and laid it out for them. The plan was innocently simple in conception. Nor was it entirely unreasonable of execution. Yet it had a certain original insanity about it which stamped it as vintage Sparhawk. None of his astounded auditors should have been surprised, yet they were. And with some cause. Whether or not they initially thought the Alabaman knew a hoot owl from a hay hook when the wind was off the wood lot, they had now to reconsider their opinions in light of his proposition.

The Confederate guerrillas, in circling the town after getting beat in the race to the corral, had certainly seen there was no rear way which would pass a horse and rider out of either that enclosure or the adjoining stationhouse. They must know, then, that the only exit they had to watch was the street gate to the corral. This much, at any rate, the cornered El Pasans had to assume.

Now then, of course, the Confederates knew nothing of the hidden springbed wagon. And even if they had, it would only have served to assure them further they had only to watch the front gate. Which was precisely what Sparhawk wanted them to be doing, full time.

Now the Waterfield hay barn, behind the harness shed lean-to from which Cullross had discovered the small wagon, was not the ordinary type of frontier makeshift thrown up for fodder storage. It was a bona fide barn with two floors and a spacious hayloft. Getting down to present points, there was attached to the open front of that loft a still serviceable winch for hoisting up heavy loads of baled hay or sacked feed from below.

What Linn Sparhawk calmly proposed was to windlass the little wagon up to the loft, roll it through to the rear of the barn, lower it by ropes out the loft's other open end and so on down to the ground below, outside the corral wall.

Simple? Well, they all already knew their man was not to be confused with average folks.

Sparhawk was undaunted by their head-scratching and other, more direct, expressions of doubt in his competency. With the wagon safely outside the corral, he went on, it would be no trick at all for them to let themselves and their livestock out through the rear window of the stationhouse; especially, he enlarged, since he already had Sim at work with his Bowie knife and bulging muscles revising downward this particular window casement into a full-sized and proper back door—something Sparhawk personally felt the Mesilla Station to have long been in need of.

It would take Sim, he estimated, the best part of an hour to pry the required number of adobe bricks out of place and to do so in a manner and degree of quietness which would not attract any undue interest from the guerrilla guard across the street. It would, further, take the rest of them easily that long to truss up the wagon, get it up into and through the hayloft and roped back down to the ground outside, without, in their turn, they made "more racket about it than six pickaninnies with a possum up a gum tree."

Since there was, too, no more than sixty minutes of solid darkness remaining ahead of moonrise, the Alabaman concluded, "we had better get started to scratching, if we're going to raise any dust at all."

Well, how could any sane person argue with a diseased imagination like that? The best thing to do with a madman is humor him, Lucy Henderson was the first to decide, and had the good sense to suggest as much to Frank Swango. The latter reckoned she was right and Doc Harnaday conceded that since nobody else seemed to be giving a good damn about losing his hair, he wasn't going to be miserly about hanging onto his. Jake Bergerman muttered something in agreeing German and Cipher Reno Sanchez sighed, "Ay de mí!" adding that he had no true idea it would prove so much trouble to be an americano but that inasmuch as he had said he would be one, why, "por Dios," he would. Sim still being busy on the new door and Price Cullross not eligible to vote, that was substantially that.

As with the others, Lucy Henderson had no idea the daft scheme could actually be brought off and, being a woman, never did rightly understand how it was. But this is what she did know. Shortly before nine o'clock on a certain April evening in 1861, there stood assembled on the ground outside the rear wall of the abandoned Waterfield stage station in Mesilla, New Mexico, the following mixed array: one fancy springbed wagon; one spirited roan saddle gelding; two seasoned coaching mules; two flashy bay carriage horses; four adult male Americans; one German-born Jew; one half-breed Mexican boy; one bought-free Louisiana plantation slave; one lately Union-employed, presently very willing to travel, white girl.

Then, shortly after nine o'clock, there was nothing and nobody standing behind the American Mail Company's station in Mesilla.

There was only the narrow set of iron-rimmed wagon tracks snaking off down the river to vanish among the aromatic mesquite and fragrant juniper of the New Mexico uplands. And by the time the moon came, brief minutes later, the tough, pungent grasses were already springing back into position to rub out even the wagon tracks.

Shortly, no mortal record remained that seven desperate men and a disguised white woman had set out in a single lightweight wagon to cross 300 miles of silently waiting Apacheland.

9

A mile south of Mesilla they turned northwest through the open range to cut into the Tucson road west of the sleeping town. Linn was driving, Doc riding gun for him. A hundred yards ahead, cameo-clear in the increasing moonlight, Swango led the way on his roan.

The rest of them sat hunched, knees touching, across the narrow bed of the wagon. Cipher Reno, Bergerman and Lucy Henderson were on one side; Sim and the again silent Price Cullross on the other. Balancing the load on Sim's side was a grotesque third party; a sloshing mannequin made of their lone water barrel topped by the sack of flour, side of bacon and bag of coffee beans which composed their remaining supplies. Sparhawk had built the crude figure, crowning it with his own shapeless hat. He had done so with the apparent idea of cheering up the weaker members of the expedition, namely Lucy Henderson, Jake Bergerman and the Sanchez boy. He had even gone to the trouble of introducing his creation to them as "Slim Pickens," late of El Paso and points south, a traveling man headed west for his health.

But they should have known by then that the Alabaman seldom operated entirely on passing fancies. There was nearly always a practical aspect to his little jokes. In this case he had not put the flour sack atop the keg and Sim on guard alongside it for fun. Lucy Henderson was the one who found this out when she asked the burly ex-slave for a drink.

"I'm sorry, missy," he told her. "Mr. Linn has said not to move the things off the barrel."

The thirsty girl stood corrected, and enlightened. Slim Pickens was not laughing. Clumsy-humored in conception, or otherwise, Sparhawk's crude dummy meant business. Their water was already being rationed.

As she and the others mulled over this disturbing news, Swango rode back to say the Tucson road lay just ahead. He and Linn and Doc held a subdued conversation, to which Lucy Henderson was simply too tired to listen. After a while she felt the wagon move forward again. She remembered it striking the firmer going of the stage road. After that she must have dozed, for the next thing she knew it was long past midnight and they were stopped once more.

Swango's roan was again standing alongside the wagon. A second muttered conference was in progress. This time the Union girl listened, and learned a few things well calculated to keep her and her fellow passengers awake the rest of the night.

They were forty miles west of Mesilla. The long road ahead angled north past Cooke's Peak and the lower horseshoe curve of the Sierra de las Uvas range.

Just off the road, scary and still in the glaring moonlight, lay Goodsight, the third of the abandoned Waterfield relay stations west of Mesilla. Fourteen miles beyond it was Mimbres Springs. Eighteen miles past the springs was Membrace Station nestled in the protective shadow, albeit some actual miles south, of Fort Webster, their first night's destination.

Webster, toward which Swango was now preparing to scout their advance, was one of the half dozen New Mexican posts still garrisoned to guard the last troop withdrawals from southeast Arizona. It was overdue for abandonment but at the time of their approach still activated.

Its commander, Major Robert Mobry, was an officer well known not only for his fiery Confederate sympathies but also for his considerable knowledge of the Apache. From him Sparhawk counted on getting the best possible picture of the situation obtaining currently among the mutinous *rancherías* of the red men, particularly those of Cochise's Chiricahuas and Mangas Coloradas' Mimbreños over toward Apache Pass.

He hoped, as well, but with less reason, to get an escort of troops to Tucson. Failing that and given prohibitive news about the Indians, he felt they could still get permission to accompany the troops back east, camping safely at the fort until they left; provided Major Mobry was due his order to move out soon and could feed eight civilians meanwhile.

In addition, and in any event, the listening girl now gathered from his low-voiced proposal to Swango and Doc that he meant to leave Lucy Henderson in the Major's official charge.

Miss Lucy was both a government employee and a pretty woman in the same shapely package; a package which, sex considered, would be mighty awkward to handle on any unscheduled freight run through Apache country. His exact words were: "No matter she's some gaunt and looks sort of undone in those old clothes of mine, she still won't pass inspection for anything but a woman under half a mile."

Frank Swango said that was right and that the only thing boyish about her was the haircut Sparhawk had given her. "And," he warned, "it takes more than a set of stable duds and a short clip with the sheep shears to blind a man, Indian or white, to as outstanding a set of social distinctions as hers."

The shotgun rider's flattering summation was supported, if a bit tainted, by old Doc Harnaday's agreement that "any goddamned Mescalero, Mimbres, Cherry Cow or Tonto who couldn't spot the waggle to that flossy's seat would be ninety-nine years old and not out lookin' no more."

Sparhawk said that, choice of language aside, they had got his main point: one way or another they had to get shut of *Miss Lucy at Fort Webster.* The matter being thus agreed, Frank spun the roan and faded into the night again. Linn touched up the bays, Doc cursed the mules, the lightweight Democrat wagon leaped forward. They were under way once more.

The miles and hours were rattled under in swift succession. The first gray of the four o'clock false dawn found them rolling over the last rise in the lovely floor of the Mimbres Valley, south and east of Fort Webster. They had made sixty-one miles in seven hours, a spanking average of nearly nine miles an hour. Thus they were running right on Linn Sparhawk's seemingly exaggerated schedule, and the surprise of that perked them up like the cup of hot black coffee they would soon be brewing beneath the blessed safety of Fort Webster's frowning walls.

Eight miles and sixty minutes later they were drinking in another fact. It was just as strong and twice as black as any dawn-halt coffee, but nowhere near as blessed.

Why is it that man can tell a deserted dwelling from afar? What primal instinct surviving from a distant, hunted past lets him know that the habitant is not at home, that the lair is empty, the cave abandoned, the hearth grown cold?

With the new dawn flushing up hot and clear behind them, the El Paso fugitives sat upon the low bluff six miles east of Fort Webster and knew the garrison had gone. Where, how, why or when the last Army outpost in southwestern New Mexico had been stripped of its troops did not concern them. Only the fact they had gambled heavily on finding Fort Webster still occupied—and lost—mattered now. They all knew it; they all accepted it. Each sat in the wagon looking silently at the others, all sharing the same dark thought, none daring to put words to the common fear.

Finally, it was Linn Sparhawk who found the right way to say it. "Well," he drawled, favoring them with his sad, soft smile. "I'm put in mind of what Abe Lincoln said when he stubbed his sore toe: 'It hurts too much to laugh and I'm too old to cry.'"

"Yeah," wheezed Doc, hawking to clear the morning phlegm out of his throat in the nasty way an old man will. "Put another way, there's nobody minding the store down there and we're apt to be up to our hocks in Indian customers any minute."

"Like as not," admitted Linn. Then, calmly, "We'll know shortly why business is so slow. Yonder comes Frank."

Swango, still riding out ahead, had been nosing around the silent post long before they drew up on the bluff. He was now spurring his mount their way.

"Never sprinkles but what it comes a cloudburst in this country," he said to Linn, stepping down off the roan. "Guess what?"

"My guess got us into this," replied the other, not smiling any. "I yield to the gentleman from Fort Webster."

74

"Thanks," bowed the tight-lipped shotgun rider. "I pass the gavel to Sergeant A. E. Zimmerman."

"To who?" growled Doc.

"The last man out of Fort Webster," said Swango. He handed Sparhawk a crumpled sheet of notepaper. "This was pinned on the barracks' door. It tells us where we are."

The Alabaman read the note to himself, his normally labored breathing increasing perceptibly as he did. When he had finished, he passed the note along, dropped his empty hand to his side, sat staring out across the brooding valley of the Mimbres.

"Well," rasped Doc, unwilling to wait his turn at the note, "where are we?"

Sparhawk broke his gaze from the valley. He looked at him a long moment, his strangely colored eyes hollow and dark shadowed.

"In trouble," he said quietly. "Let's get under cover."

The Mimbres River rises many miles northwest of Webster. Near its source and for several leagues thereafter, it flows bright and sparkling upon the surface of the arid land. Then, some miles north of the little fort, it plunges underground to run thus the entire remainder of its length until it empties into its nameless sink in Chihuahua.

This seemingly extraneous bit of hydrography was important to the El Pasans. In the dry bed of the Mimbres, a short distance from their present vantage point and quite a ways below the fort, a succession of work details from the post had sunk three splendid hand-dug wells. These composed the most reliable source of good sweet water in that country.

More to the present concern of the worried travelers, they contained the only water between Mimbres Springs, passed in the dead of the previous night, and Ojo de la Vaca, commonly and incorrectly called Cow Springs, the next water west of upcoming Membrace Station.

That is to say, they ordinarily did. When Linn drew up the teams on the bank above them, it was found that Webster Wells had vanished. Beyond the cluster of cottonwoods which marked their previous site, the bottom of the Mimbres ran as smoothly sanded as an ocean beach at low tide. The comparison, while inaccurate, was apt.

"Flash flood," said Frank Swango, confirming the fact. "Mark, yonder, how high she hit." He jerked a reins-calloused thumb toward the line of limb-caught debris edging the willow scrub at the base of the cottonwoods. "And look at that damned sand. That's fresh. She's shifted channels and sanded over the old course so smooth a peach-twig dowser couldn't find it in twenty stabs."

Doc Harnaday sniffed, spat and added his professional agreement on the caving-in and covering-up of Webster Wells. "Yep, that's all new stuff. She's not piled anything that far up the bank since I started on this run the fall of '57. And, like you say, that present channel's bare as a Mexican baby's backside. Yes sir, mister, that was some high water."

They were talking, partly, to give the others time to steady up and get over the shock of the wells being gone. Linn knew that and chipped in to help them do it.

"I venture she was a real gully-washer, all right," he began. "But then look at the watershed you've got up there." He gestured to the north. "Except for what the Gila takes, the Mimbres gets water from the whole of the Pinos Altos foothills, which are nothing but the south spur of the main Mogollons, practically speaking."

Neither of his fellow talkers appreciated the little Alabaman's effort.

"Thanks," said Swango, "for the drainage lecture."

"Yeah," gritted Doc acidly. "Sometimes, boy, I wonder about you. You got any bright ideas what them Pinos Altos foothills are famous for putting out besides run-off water?"

"Well . . ." started Linn pleasantly, but the old man huffed him down.

"Well!" he parroted him, "leave me show off my own goddamned eroodification." He paused, glaring at the thin Southerner. "Up in them precious watershed ridges of yours, not fifty miles from where we're standing, is something else which comes awashin' down this here channel every so often. And with no more warnin' than back-canyon floodwater. Something old Kit Carson himself wouldn't have stood here waiting for. Not even with 500 of Charley Bent's tame Cheyennes to hold his hand. I mean the Apaches, boy! That country up yonder is the main range of the Mimbres and the Gilas, you damp-eared fool!"

The oldster had to stop and spit again to lower his pressure before tapering off.

"Why, hell's infernal fire! the Mimbres fancy them pine hills so much they wanted to fight the whole United States Army for them. That was on account of the government

76

dealing with the Spaniards to get title to the Pinos Altos back in '47; instead of dickering with old Mangas, who plainly figured *he* owned them. Which he did, by God, lock, stock and mud-dobbered wickiup!"

They had none of them ever heard Doc let off such a long head of steam, but even so he wasn't done yet.

"Jesus, boy, you couldn't comb out a worse snarl of Apache burrs if you curried the whole Indian tail of New Mexico—with the mane of Arizona throwed in for good measure. Now I reckon we'd better leave off standing here weeping over a set of washed-out wells."

He put the third tobacco juice period to his speech, wiped his whiskers on his sleeve, returned his scowl to Linn.

"And I'll guarantee you," he growled, "we'd better do it before some of Mangas's boys start drifting down from your damned watershed to see what's happened to the soldier boys over to Webster. That note's near a week old. My guess is we ain't got all day to get under that cover you was just talking about. Ten gets you one they're already curious and crawling the rimrock to smell out what took Major Mobry off so suddenlike."

His mention of the note and Major Robert Mobry flashed the image of Sergeant Zimmerman's eloquent scrap of paper once more before all their eyes.

The brave noncom's farewell had been brief. Two weeks ago the little company's first lieutenant had died of dysentery. Five enlisted men had preceded him. Ten days past, orders by Indian runner had come from Colonel E. R. S. Canby, Commander of the Department of New Mexico, at Fort Craig, to abandon post as the war was considered to be but a matter of hours away.

That same afternoon the regular weekly Pinos Altos patrol had come in minus its sergeant and the company's other lieutenant. Major Mobry was the sole remaining officer and he loyal to the South.

Two hours later he was gone, resigning his commission in a letter left with Zimmerman and going back with the Zuñi runner to offer his services to the Confederate Army.

Zimmerman proved a soldier's soldier with the pressure mounting. He still had Mobry's orders from Canby and his men still had the strength to form up a column of fours to carry them out. Six days ago he had struck the regimental colors, hauled down Old Glory, and left Fort Webster to Mangas Coloradas and the winds of time. In so doing he had signed off his military adieu with a fillip of frontier irony

77

which had Frank Swango and Linn Sparhawk exchanging a look of accusation and guilt which on the one hand would have withered a rock and on the other melted a mule's heart.

The last four lines of Sergeant A. E. Zimmerman's farewell to New Mexican arms read:

We shall march for Fort Fillmore, as directed, bypassing Mesilla. We shall remain at that post until a courier may be gotten through to Fort Craig for additional orders. We shall in my opinion be fortunate to make it so far, and will be grateful indeed to cross the Rio Grande, God granting we get sight of it. The Indians have been very quiet. . . .

Such professional candor, plus the disheartening disclosure that they had driven within a hundred yards of a detachment of Union troops, and adventure's safe end, at Fort Fillmore, could do nothing but heavily increase the travelers' already burdensome sense of foreboding.

Watching Frank Swango now, as he nodded in terse agreement to Doc's terminal promise of Apache nearness, added nothing to their dwindling store of faith in the expedition's doubtful future.

The shotgun rider's lean head turned slowly, studying the northern hills. He seemed to take forever about it, checking back time and again to some detail of ridgetop or arroyo whose main geography was a strain for the others to make out, before at last breaking off his gaze and grunting simply, "All right so far. Nothing yet."

No one answered him, for there was nothing to answer about. He looked back at the far hills again, his voice sharpening. "Doc's right, all the same. We know Mobry ran a weekly patrol up there. From that, there's no doubt Mangas will miss the soldiers when they don't show up."

"Yes," said Doc grimly, "and he'll come alookin' for them like a wolf that's smelled a first-fresh heifer with a wet calf." The old man peered off up north in his squinting turn. He shook his head, hurried on. "We'd better pass up the fort, I figure. Hide out down the river at Membrace Station. She's Apache-burnt and that's fine for us. Leaves no reason for further attention from the red devils. Let's get a move on, Linn boy."

Sparhawk said nothing. Clucking to the bays, he shook up the lines. The gingery geldings swung out from under the scrubby motte of riverside cottonwoods, still having spirit enough to cut and shower back shoe sods with the driving dig of their start. Behind them the slower mules lumbered to make up to the gait and get in stride with them. Both spans were going a full gallop in fifty yards.

"Old John was a big, square-bodied man, mean and tough as a Brazos beefsteak." Doc Harnaday, talking to make the miles seem shorter and the Mimbres Apaches farther away, spoke of the head of the American Mail Company as though he were already gone on to greater rewards, a not uncommon practice when little people tell of their brief personal encounters with the flesh and blood of the famous. "He signed his first contract with the postmaster general to carry the mail to California on September 17, 1857," the old driver went on. "Now you may not realize it but that's less than four years gone!"

Sparhawk and Lucy Henderson, squeezing close since the start from Webster Wells to share the cramped pitch and sway of the Democrat's seat box with him, nodded that they did realize it, and Lucy said, "Isn't that wonderful, just four years!"

It was an inane remark, meant to encourage Doc to keep talking just for talk's sake, and conveying no real interest whatever in what he might be saying. The back-East girl was learning the game. And fast. Minutes ago, back at the vanished wells, she had not been familiar with its rules; had not realized it was being played, when Frank and Doc and Linn had dwelt, seemingly overlong, on the drainage of the Mimbres River and the recent Indian history of the Pinos Altos foothills.

Now she knew, and now she was herself joining in. Back there, they had done it for her. Here she was doing it for others. She glanced over her shoulder at the huddled figures of white-faced little Jake Bergerman and big-eyed Cipher Reno Sanchez. Both were pale and tight-lipped with fear, but the talking game was keeping them from giving way to it completely and she felt suddenly warm and good, on top of her own fear, that she was being allowed to "ride up front" and help out on the way to Membrace Station.

It was a funny kind of a game, all right—none of its players admitted to himself he was involved in it—but the main thing was, it worked, if you hit the ball back when it came your way.

"Go on, Doc," she said, fighting the little silence which had set in. "What happened after Old John got his contracts for the California run?"

"Well," said the old man, happy to be off again, "first thing was financial troubles. But you know what Old John said to them lily-livered stockholders of his? He said, 'Boys, by Christ'—uh, begging your pardon, Miss Lucy, but Old John, he was always one to cuss quite a bit. . . .'"

"Yes, not like some we know," Sparhawk wedged in drily.

"Now, God damn it!" snapped the bearded stager, "you want to hear the history of the Waterfield Line, or you want to set there making your spurrous incinerations?"

"Ease off, old-timer," Sparhawk laughed. "I reckon Miss Lucy wouldn't have asked about Mr. Waterfield, hadn't she wanted to know about him."

"That's right, Doc." The tall girl turned her green-eyed, soft-lipped smile on the offended storyteller, purposely snuggling up to him and away from Sparhawk with the warm reassurance. "You go right along now. Don't mind Mr. Sparrowhawk; he's hardly what you'd call a history student."

"Why now I reckon that's so," admitted the accused soberly. "I've always mainly had an interest in what makes us tick in our own times, so to speak. I agree with old Voltaire. He figured history was a waste of time. Allowed it was nothing more than a written-down register of the crimes, follies, misfortunes and general all-around damnfooleries of mankind. Now there's a man makes sense to me. Who wants to stomp around kicking up yesterday's dust when we got more than enough of today's to choke on?"

Lucy Henderson took a revised look at Linn Sparhawk. For all his backwoods idiom and sidelong shyness, you could not entirely dismiss a stablehand who successfully mixed vintage Voltaire with Waterfield stage-line manure. Particularly when he could pitch you a stinging forkful of one or a sharp quote of the other with equal ease and accuracy.

"Well, all right," she was grateful to hear Doc take up grudgingly. "Like I was saying, Old John he says to them chicken-hearted shareholders, he says, 'Boys, by God, a man's got to be able to mail a letter in New York and have it to get to San Francisco faster than Vanderbilt's goddamn steamships take it through the Panama Canal! We got to get a stage 2800 miles in twenty-five days. Now then, you still saying it can't be done?'

" 'Yes!' yelped everybody together. 'We're still saying it. There ain't a single damned chance that you can do it!'

"So, naturally, what does Old John up and do? Why he

just up and does it! Oh, let me tell you, them were the days, them were the days. . . ."

He drifted off, savoring those golden yesterdays in the sad, far-eyed way an old man will, and they didn't have the heart to urge him on right away, game or no game.

"Well," he finally began again, "you can believe it or not, but that first mail-stage to leave California for Missouri got from the Golden Gate to the Saint Louie office in twenty-four days, eighteen hours, twenty-six minutes. Old John was in business and by God he's been there ever since.

"Why, do you know that just before Congress passed that fool franchise-shift bill and knocked him out of Texas, he'd got our schedule pared down to twenty-one days and a few hours? Why, for the love of God, that's only three weeks!"

"Remarkable," drawled Linn Sparhawk.

"Remarkable?" barked the old man. "Hell, it's impossible!"

This time when the silence set in, it stayed. The game was run down. After their short laugh at old Doc's last remark, Linn and Lucy let the road-rattle of the wagon wheels and the muffled hoofbeats of the galloping teams take over the conversation.

Off east, the sky was rapidly turning pink, its rose-flush tokening an unseasonal warmth for the coming day. The distant, rimming hills on the lovely valley, however, were still cool and black.

Somewhere far back in them a coyote yipped lonesomely. The thin echo faded off across the wind-still valley flats. Nothing answered it. The harness jingle and hard breathing of the teams again usurped the oppressive quiet. Lucy Henderson stood it as long as she could. Then, suddenly loud, she blurted out her personal surrender to the unspoken fear which had been their constant, grim outrider since that moment above the Mimbres when the true meaning of Fort Webster's abandonment had sunk in upon all of them.

"Doc!" she pleaded, "what about the Indians?"

The old man never lost a chew on his quid of Bulldog cut-plug. He shifted it, spat to windward, waved a gnarled, veiny hand as though she had asked him what he thought of the South's chances to win the war.

"Why, pshaw, little lady, they never was nothing to worry about! Nothing at all. Oh, a little scrape here and there in past times, maybe. I'll grant you that. Some mules run off at one station, a brush *ramada* bonfired at another. You know,

81

pesky little things like that. No real trouble though. We always got the stages through."

"Doc." It was Sparhawk, soft and gentle.

"Yeah, yeah?"

"You lie like a lame mule in full gallop."

Doc Harnaday looked out across the passing sage. He spat once more safely with the wind, shook his grizzled head reflectively.

"You know, Miss Lucy," he said to his slender seatmate, "I'm coming seventy-three years old this summer. I got one arm stiff from a saber cut at San Jacinto, one leg gimped by a slug of grape at Monterrey. But I will be a suck-egg son of a bitch if I can't tie my good arm behind me, stand on my bad leg only, and still whup me the living daylights out of any skinny little Alabama bast—"

"Whoa up! Whoa up!" laughed Sparhawk. "Remember my delicate health, Doc. Also your professional dignity. You wouldn't want to take apart your best patient, would you?"

The old horse doctor consigned something unquotable to the confidences of his beard and subsided once more. He did not attempt to return Sparhawk's good humor, and it was clear he did not consider the latter's cryptic reminders of their relationship either fair or funny.

But the Alabaman was not worrying about what Doc Harnaday thought. He had his mind on Lucy Henderson and her unanswered fears.

"About those Indians, Miss Lucy," he said carefully, "it's this way. Along in '55 or '56, Major Steen, for the Army over in Arizona, arranged a good peace with Cochise—he's the one I told you was chief of the Chiricahuas, the bunch Doc calls the 'Cherry Cows.' Anyway, they're the biggest and mostly the boss tribe of the Apaches. Well, Cochise he kept his promise to Steen. He rode herd on the other tribes, keeping all of them right in line with his own Chiricahuas. The settlers, freight outfits and Waterfield stages started going through pretty smooth. Then, like always, others of the red rascals couldn't stand it so peaceful. Also they began to get eyes for our stage stock. Some of them, like Benito, Victorio, and naturally old Red Sleeves—that's Mangas Coloradas, head of the Mimbres—they just couldn't get over drooling about what high grade horse-stuff Waterfield was sending us to run the line with. So they began raiding our stations, killing our agents and stock tenders, burning our buildings and running off those choice relay-team horses.

"Well," he shrugged, smiling at her, "some unhung genius back in the home office told Mr. Waterfield he'd heard the Apaches wouldn't be caught dead riding a mule. Right quick, all the horse teams were pulled off the coast run and mules put in. Just as quick, the Apaches showed their gratitude. It got rougher than ever. You see, what the intellect back East had not told the Old Man was that horseback Indians down here would rather eat fat mule than prime buffalo. So the mules caught more hell than the horses ever had.

"Still," he grinned, "the stages did manage to keep getting through, what with the Army garrisoning the main passes and patrolling the roads in between. This went on a year and a half. Then in mid-'60, Apache fever broke out like cowpox. The rash ran from Gila Bend to Yuma.

"First off, a bunch of Tontos wiped out the stage station down to Gila. Then some Mescaleros took apart one of our stock corrals out here past Mesilla. Killed the tender and his four kids and carried off his wife, after first cutting out her tongue when she went to pleading with them to let her babies live. There were a dozen other station scrapes and stage shoots. A bunch of Red Sleeves' boys once ran the Tucson coach clean into San Simon, killing the conductor forty feet from the gate into the station yard.

"This kind of thing was pretty quick due to break the Army's hands-off-the-Indians policy. Just this past February, it did. A dumb cavalry lieutenant named George Bascom, out on his first patrol, got Cochise into a peace-talk trap over in Apache Pass and nearly killed him. Naturally Cochise jumped the nearest white settlement in retaliation. It happened to be a Waterfield station. Two of our top linemen, Culver and Welch, got killed. The Indian Agent J. F. Wallace, went out to talk with his old friend Cochise about the flare-up. He found out his old friend wasn't his old friend any more.

"Cochise grabbed Wallace and carried him off to be used in trade for his wife—that's Cochise's wife—who'd been wounded and taken prisoner by that idiot Bascom in the Apache Pass business.

"To shortcut it for you, Miss Lucy, the good old Army told Cochise to go to hell and hauled off and hung six of his bucks to make sure he would. Well, he did. He simply cut up Mr. Wallace into pieces too fine to count, and that's the war that's on out yonder right now."

He broke off to gesture vaguely to the west, as Lucy Henderson and his other listeners shook with a chill certainly

83

not born of the warm April morning. Then, shaking his shaggy head doubtfully, the Alabaman went on.

"By now the Army's pulled out all the troops, or most all of them, and Cochise has thrown in with the other chiefs who wanted war right along. Now that he's quit walking the white man's road and painted his own face black, there will simply be no stopping the murderous likes of Nachez, Nakay-do-klinny, Chatto, Loco, the young Geronimo and, most of all, Mangas himself. We've even heard that Eskim-in-zim and Ka-ya-ren-nae are out with the others, and they're the friendliest Apaches and best people you'd want to know."

Again the signficant pause and again its matching shudder from the slim girl at his side. He looked at her, and quickly around at the others in the wagon bed, including them all in the words which still went, ostensibly, to her.

"My guess now is that this will turn into the longest, bloodiest Indian war on record. And what Doc hasn't wanted to tell you and the others is that since it got started there hasn't been a white man to venture out of Mesilla, Sante Fe, Tucson or Tubac, without he was hair-cut and hung up by his thumbs for his trouble."

He intentionally lowered his voice, not to avoid the final attention of the wagon-bed listeners but to insure it, and concluded quietly to his immediate companion.

"So that's what about the Indians, Miss Lucy. It isn't my idea to add any worries to the ones you're already carrying, but there comes a time to quit storying and tell the truth. I reckon this is it."

The last pause was hardly a pause at all. "If they catch up to us there'll be no question of begging or buying our way out of it. It used to cost twelve bags of corn to get past old Mangas and his Mimbres at San Simon Creek. Now all the gold in the Federal treasury wouldn't let you dip your little toe in that water. The Apaches are charging one price now, the same as Old Nick charges to get past the seven circles of the Styx."

"You mean . . ." gulped Lucy Henderson, not having the nerve to go ahead with it.

"Yes, ma'am," Linn Sparhawk finished quietly for her. "If they catch us they'll kill us."

The station at Membrace was not actually far below Fort Webster. It was a liver-jolting ride in the lightweight Democrat but they made it in reassuringly little time. Once there, they worked swiftly. Five minutes after arrival they had the little wagon parked inside the ruins of the corral shed where it would not show beyond the walls. In another five minutes they had got themselves and their livestock hidden in the roofless remains of the stationhouse. It was not yet six A.M. when the big wait began.

It was hot. For mid-April it was very hot, and it caught them bad. They had their three horses and two mules standing either partly or entirely in the relentless brassy glare of the still early morning heat. They, themselves, could hide along the bases of the mud walls following the sundial creep of life-saving shade around the charred perimeters of their bake-oven prison.

The two priceless teams and Frank's fleet gelding could do nothing to escape the thickening choke of the furnace heat. They stood and panted like dogs. Their human tenders lay along the walls, watching them through the wrinkling mirage that ran along the mud floor distorting reason along with vision. Helpless to aid them in any way, they could do no more than fight for their own rapid, shallow breaths and pray for a rise in wind to break the deadly heat lock that was dehydrating their animals.

Sparhawk, Doc and Frank Swango crawled together in the foot-wide shade of a half-fallen roof timber at the far end of the single room. They whispered in short, conservative strings of words, saving their strength, guarding the movements of their drying lips.

Doc, who had spent most of his seventy-odd years in the Southwest, could not remember a spring day with such a sun. Frank, forty years and more a dweller in the high deserts, could recall none earlier than mid-May at these altitudes. Linn could not match their wisdom of experience and added nothing to the labored conference. However, he nodded agreement that they must not let the others know how rough things really figured to get, barring an almost impossible weather change.

Yet though he brought little enough to the brief meeting, the Southerner took more than enough away with him. They were in possibly fatal trouble here. The very fact the heat was freakish and wrong for the time of year added to its menace.

Returning to his place near Lucy Henderson along the front wall, he did his best to evade her gasping questions. The girl was not to be put off. She sensed his fear and caught

85

it from him. She did not need to know what had been said by the men now. Instinctively, she understood there was something wrong with this day beyond its pure hotness, and so she lay panting along the wall with Linn Sparhawk and the other El Pasans, sharing their unstated hopelessness and the grimly developing reasons therefor.

They had something less than twenty gallons of water left in the barrel. There was no more to be had, saving for an eighteen-mile drive one way, and sixteen the other. Yet if they let their draft animals dry out in the withering heat, all the water west of the Rio Grande would not help them. It was a bad choice.

The sun drove down. The mules were still all right but the Waterfield bays were beginning to shake. Frank's roan had dropped his head. The heaving flanks of all five animals ran with sweat. That was virtually pure water. It had to be replaced.

There was no longer any choice. At ten o'clock the men began to ration the water to the stock. Sim carried the barrel to each animal in turn, holding it lightly as a backyard well bucket while the poor brutes drank. A gallon went to each, Linn marking the levels with a piece of charcoal on the side of the oak staves. A quarter of a keg was gone with the first watering. At two P.M. they had to have another. And at four, a third.

At that time the travelers also had their second rations of the day, making an eight-pint total for them. Frank, who was bossing the dispersal, did not like to issue this much yet knew he must. They could not deny themselves water any more than they could their horses and mules. Man dehydrates too. The Mexican kid and the girl had both been heat sick, vomiting twice each. Bergerman was fish-belly gray, shivering with the cold of approaching prostration. Linn Sparhawk looked like hell. And there was no relief in sight. The sun burned on.

The barrel was now ominously easy to lift. In it were less than three gallons of water. The frightened, heat-exhausted travelers thought they were going to die and felt it would be a privilege to do so. But they were wrong, and Frank was wrong. Relief was coming and they had won their wait-out.

By five o'clock it had cooled wondrously. A moist wind blew in ahead of some swiftly rolling cloud banks up northeast. A five-minute crashing of thunder and lightning drove in a drenching April shower which soaked the dessert three

86

inches down. As quickly as it had blown up, the little storm drifted on, grumbling and complaining off into the southwest where it presumably had some more May wildflowers to awaken and some more spectacular New Mexican rainbows to build before sunset.

The skies over Membrace Station cleared off, the fresh breeze held, the revived land gave forth its fragrant, grateful breath. The Waterfield crew stood up and walked about like men and women again, thankful for the simple favor of senses and sanities retained. They were all right. And they were going to be all right.

Their stock was in good shape. Each of them was fit to travel. The Apaches, had they been watching the ruins of the burned-out relay station since six A.M., could not have seen a single movement to lead them to suspect the presence of the El Pasans. It was a remarkable feeling. They had cheated the elements and outgambled the Indians. All of them felt a little taller for having done so.

They came out of the ruins to stretch their limbs and then to lie quietly on the damp, cool ground in the long shadows of the eastern wall. The others watched Linn and Frank make a small, clear-flamed supper fire. When the aroma of boiling coffee, broiling bacon and rising trapper's bread began wafting their way, Mangas Coloradas and his Pinos Altos Apaches seemed remote indeed. And when the boys served their suppers—Lucy Henderson's actually brought to her on a salvaged shard of station crockery—the sinister foothills of the Mogollons may as well have been in Montana.

They ate their food and drank their coffee, their only conversation the eloquent one of smacking lips and smiling, silent nods.

The burned bacon and stick-twisted flour dough were breast of wild turkey and plantation spoonbread. The coffee, evil enough to creosote a fence post, was prairie ambrosia. Even Price Cullross, untied and unattended since the past midnight (would he prefer the company of Apaches to theirs?), had to speak out and congratulate the chefs—his first friendly words in nearly twenty-four hours. And so they all luxuriated there in the blessed relief of the stationhouse's sunset shadows and in the purely lucky fact that the Apaches had not picked this particular day to come down to investigate the abandonment of Fort Webster.

Presently the men, ordering Cullross out of earshot, got, low-voiced, to their next decision. It was a wise one, welcomed by all. Its original suggestion came from Sparhawk, but by that time and under those circumstances, even Frank Swango was ready to turn around and go home.

They had, the Alabaman pointed out, refreshingly little room for arguing march routes. Doc and Swango had dwelt at length upon the all too apparent danger of the Apaches to the north. Cipher Reno, who could smell Southwestern weather as well as any Pueblo or Zuñi snake dancer in the business, had predicted today's heat was but a beginning. Unless and until a real spring rain broke it up, there was going to be a hot spell to put down in the history books. Sim, whose African powers of prophecy were vouched for by Linn, had warned them that the Indians were "somewhere out there right now." Even considering the fact the big Negro had indicated his "somewhere" with an arm sweep which took in half of New Mexico, no one had laughed. No one laughed, either, as Linn soberly backed up his black shadow's "powers," and the little Southerner hurried on.

The smartest thing they could do, he thought, was to turn tail and run for Mesilla and the safety of Sergeant Zimmerman's troops at nearby Fort Fillmore. As soon as it was full dark, he recommended to Doc and Frank, they should hook up the teams and dig out. If the Confederates were still hanging around Mesilla, they could flank out around the town and hit across the river directly west of Fillmore. But the better chance was that Cullross's boys had given up and gone back to El Paso. In any event, the risk they themselves ran in heading for the Rio Grande was nothing to the Apache exposure they stood to suffer by staying on at Membrace Station or, crazier yet, trying to push on west to Dinsmore's Station at Cow Springs.

That closed the Alabaman's case. No one appeared ready to argue any of its obvious conclusions. Twelve hours under a blistering sun had brought the reality of the Apache menace home to all of them in a way the earlier verbal warnings had not begun to manage. Any last doubt in this direction was now cooked out of the last of the "loyal Northerners" by simple, sweat-caked example. When men the hard likes of Frank Swango would lie along a stifling mud wall breathing adobe dust and drinking salt sweat and not daring to get up and walk around from sunup till sundown, no one in his or her right mind was going to question the sincerity of the situation.

The teams were brought out, picketed and put to graze for the remaining hour until complete darkness. Sim wheeled the wagon out of the corral shed, repacked their food and water, laid out the harness. It was still but a few minutes past six, the beautiful Mimbres Valley lying calm and clear in the deepening pool of sunset shadows, when they saw something in the sky—cotton-boll white against the lucent green in the east. Blanket-fanned and blanket-broken, rising swiftly into the still air, hovering there far above the distant unseen rocks, a peculiar series of ballooning puffs suspended silently in twilight space—Apache smoke.

10

They watched the ascending smoke signals in wordless fear, waiting for Doc Harnaday to decipher them.

At last the old man lowered his peering squint, cursed and spat.

"Mimbres," he said.

"Figures," grunted Frank Swango. "What else?"

"What do you mean, 'what else?' You can see where they're squatting. Right square astride the stage road between us and Mesilla. Along about Goodsight, I'd say." Doc was testy with it, and Frank shook his head.

"You know what I mean, old-timer. What else in the smoke?"

"Nobody reads Apache smoke perfect, God damn it! Not if he's a white man, he don't."

"Doc, I know that." Swango was strangely patient with him. "What does it say?"

Watching them, Lucy Henedrson saw the old driver's eyes shift anxiously her way.

"Well, hang it all, Frank, maybe we'd ought not to—well —uh—I mean—well—I mean the little lady!" he finished defiantly.

Frank waved a hand at Lucy without looking at her.

"Doc," he was still riding him easy, "the 'little lady' is in this up to her elbows. It's mostly her party if you want to look at it that way. Leastways, she gave out the invitations. Now you go on with that smoke talk; she might as well know what she's in for—her and the others with her."

"Yeah, I reckon," agreed the old man unhappily.

"Well, damn it, firstly they've cut our wagon track and have got us pegged correct for conveyance, color of complexion and course of travel. Three short puffs, that's 'white man.' Four shorts and a long reads 'wagon.' One long is 'west.'"

He stopped there, shaking his head and muttering to himself, still not liking to talk Indian smoke signs in front of a woman. But Frank was crowding him at once.

"There was more. Two longs and a short."

"Yeah," grudged Doc. "That just means to sort of come on in for a closer look-see."

Frank nodded, eyeing him. "And . . . ?" he said.

"And what?" snapped the old man.

"Doc, don't put off on me. I seen that very last puff. After the two long and the short. Almost like a period or signature, it was. Just the one last quick puff, all by itself, and not another damn wisp nor stray nor spiral after it. Now you tell me how sharp I am at guessing Mimbres smoke. Wasn't that their . . ."

"Yes," interrupted the bearded driver hurriedly, "it was." Then, looking at Lucy Henderson again, "But damn it all, do we need to spell it out loud?"

"We do."

With the statement, Frank turned from him to the others.

"Folks we're in real trouble," he told them quietly. "You heard Doc name that smoke. It's Mimbres, and they ain't roasting no mule with it. What it's saying is that they mean to run us down and kill us."

He watched them to see how they were taking it and to give them time to handle it, each in his own way. When he saw no one was going to break, he gave them the rest of it.

"It's a right bad deal and I'm not going to tell any of you I like it, or that there is any bright side to it. I don't and there ain't. We're just going to have to fort up and fight."

"Where?" wondered Linn Sparhawk, voicing the question in all their minds.

"Where the hell do you think?" snorted Doc Harnaday. "I taught you better than that, boy. Nearest water of course, you damn fool!"

"Cow Springs?" echoed Linn, saying it as though he was praying he'd guessed wrong.

"Maybe," suggested Frank.

Doc came around on the shotgun rider, frowning.

"Maybe?" he challenged.

"Yeah," rasped the other, "maybe." He looked westward, pale eyes narrowed. "Maybe more smoke from over yonder, maybe not. Maybe they got us blocked off over Cow Springs way, too, and maybe they ain't. Maybe we'd best wait up a bit and see, and just plain maybe, all by itself, for the pure and simple hell of it. Comprende 'maybe'? Quizás. Tal vez. Acaso. 'Maybe,'" he finished acidly. "You got it?"

"Could be," admitted the old man.

And "Maybe" grinned Linn Sparhawk, to ease things all around and especially for the girl and young Cipher Reno.

Then they waited out Frank's "bit." It seemed like an hour and a half, yet it was not over ten minutes.

The second smoke came from the northwest, about five miles above Fort Webster and between them and Cow Springs, east and west as Frank had anticipated. It merely acknowledged the first signal from the Mesilla side, and signed off. There were no more smokes after that, north or west or east or anywhere. The Mimbres were through talking.

Doc and Swango and Sparhawk consulted briefly. The rest of them listened intently. There was no more effort to guard or censor the discussion. Even Price Cullross was included, if by no more than the virtue of not being excluded.

It seemed likely, the three leaders agreed, that what had happened was that the Pinos Altos Apaches, missing the regular Webster patrol, had indeed started down to investigate. Then, evidently figuring that if the soldiers had pulled out they would have gone eastward, the main band had split somewhere above the fort. One bunch had swung over to cut the Mesilla road, the other had loafed on down along the Mimbres toward Webster.

There was no way of knowing how many Indians they had to deal with. It took only one buck to build and fan a signal fire. They might have nothing but a handful of scouts over there on the Mesilla road, or they might have half the tribe there. The guess and the gamble belonged to the Waterfield refugees.

Doc Harnaday figured they had best turn around and race the Mesilla bunch for Mimbres Springs. Neither the Apaches nor themselves could reach the springs before dark and the former would quit and pitch camp the minute the light went. The odds were therefore certain, as Doc saw them, that they could beat the Indians to the water at Mimbres.

91

Furthermore, the old man argued, they would then be that much closer to eventual and real safety via soldier help from Fort Fillmore.

Swango agreed, repeating his dictum that there was literally nothing to do in an Indian surround save to fort up and fight. They had food for ten days on careful rations. There was water inside the walls at Mimbres. They had plenty of the right kind of firearms and, the saturnine shotgun rider added pointedly, they had the shooting-eyes to go with them.

"Yep," Doc bobbed his beard quickly, "and we got enough of them slick-loading brass cattridges to kill us off all of Cochise's cousins this side of San Simon."

For a promising moment it looked as though there would be no dissent, but Linn Sparhawk delivered his usual minority report only slightly behind schedule. He began it with an obstinate headshake.

"I don't know about that," he said. "It's dark in thirty minutes. Right? And the teams are fresh and wanting to go. Agreed? All right, now, if we make our run all the way to the Rio Grande, instead of stopping short at Mimbres Springs, we've got at the most no more than half the Apaches to get past. And we've got nighttime to help us do it. On the other hand, if we fort up at Mimbres Springs we'll have all of them on top of us come daylight, or damned shortly thereafter. Now for God's sake, Frank, where's your sense in that?"

It was as worked up as any of them had seen the little Alabaman get. Moreover, the content of his words troubled them deeply. Yet they all knew there was no substitute for experience in fighting Indians. The slender Southerner was a stablehand. He had to be wrong. Uneasily, they waited for Doc and Swango to decide it.

"My sense in that," replied the latter to Linn's challenge, "is that the stage roads of this whole plateau are littered with the bones of tinhorn sports who didn't have the brains to fort up before morning." He paused, staring at his questioner. "You want more," he said softly, "I'll give it to you. Like this. You name me just one fort-up you ever heard about, that was set up in good time, with plenty of food, water, guns and good shots, that didn't make out all right in the end. Any one will do; don't rush yourself."

Sparhawk was in over his head. He knew it and he backed off and quit.

Frank's voice gentled. "Kid, they're just like wolves. If a pack of them jumps you and you run, you're dead. If you stand fast and make a circle, you got them beat. They'll try

92

maybe two, three stabs to make sure you're not just hooking your horns, then they'll tuck their tails and go quick alooking for easier meat. Ask Doc, he'll tell you."

"Frank's right, Linn." The old driver's tones were softer too. "It ain't like we had a coach and a six-mule hitch, with me and him up on the box and eight or nine good pistol-shot passengers in the tonneau. Look around you, boy. Count noses. Tell me how your total turns out."

Sparhawk looked around. It got very quiet. If he were counting "good-shot" noses, he would have to stop when he got past himself, Doc and Swango. The rest of them, possibly excepting Cullross as an unknown quantity and Sim at Bowie knife range, were about as useful in a Mimbres Valley Indian fight as a fifth ace in a Fort Worth poker game.

It was at this point that the big Texan finally cut himself in on the deal. He did it by breaking his stubborn silence for the second time in forty-eight hours.

"Sparhawk is right," said Price Cullross flatly. "But you two old fools will have your way regardless."

"What?" grated Frank, swinging around.

"Schiller said it," shrugged the Texan calmly. "You might recall it, Sparhawk, 'Against stupidity the very gods themselves contend in vain.'"

"Schiller was a surgeon," answered the Alabaman soberly. "He always cut too much. Matthew said it better in the New Testament."

"What the hell you insulting sons of bitches talking about?" demanded Doc edgily.

"Guidances from the Bible on the general subject of bull-headedness," said Linn.

"Such as?" asked Swango with warning softness.

"'They be blind leaders of the blind,'" quoted the Southern youth just as softly. "'And if the blind lead the blind, both shall fall into the ditch.'"

"Say it in English!" blustered Doc.

"All right," agreed Sparhawk gently, "it goes like this: 'none of us knows what we're doing or where we're going.'"

"Speak for yourself, kid." Swango caught him up, still low-voiced. "I know what we're doing and I know where we're going."

"Naturally," sneered Price Cullross. "We're hooking up the teams and heading back to Mimbres Springs for a good old-fashioned fort-up."

"Naturally," said Frank Swango.

And that was the way it was.

93

11

They had to wait out the sunset's lingering retreat, Frank insisting on it. The western bunch, he said, had been too close when they answered the eastern smoke. Should they take the notion to push their ponies, they could come down on them before full nightfall.

It was almost certain, he added, that they would not do this. They would far more likely ride to cut them off from Cow Springs. Or at least to swing out that way to make sure they had not yet got that far. But with most Indians you seldom knew and with Apaches you never did.

So they waited. And worried. In that upland country, daylight hung on like a lover saying good night. Lucy Henderson, for one, thought it never would get done kissing the distant hills and go on home to bed. Yet it was only thirty minutes before it did. And another brief twenty before Frank said, "All right, she's deep enough. Let's get out of here."

The worried girl knew that last expression from her hills country childhood. It was a mining term meaning "I quit." When a coal digger said, "She's deep enough," his implication was that the management had allowed the timbering in the stope to get too skimpy, the bore of the shaft too shaky, or the air in the drift too stale. Which meant there was just too much danger to life and limb building up in the situation for a man to stay in it a minute longer than it took him to pick up his tools and clear out.

Apparently Frank's colloquialism made sense to the others too, for Lucy Henderson was not the first into the wagon by several. In fact, had not the handsome Price Cullross paused gallantly to hand her up, she would have been last. But the florid Texan's unhurried bow and Stetson-swept "After you, madame," restored a little needed perspective, while his following critical comment that it was a fine night for "culling a herd of black cats," settled the nervous girl down just right.

There was something definitely salutary in the aromatic

Western idiom, Lucy Henderson decided. She was finding much comfort in its lean reassurances, and further aid from the tough cut of the men who gave them out—say Price Cullross for present example. Yet she had no more than relaxed to one Westerner's drawl than she was straightening up to another's.

"I think I'll take Sim and ride ahead," said Frank Swango, addressing Sparhawk. "I might go past some sign he'd spot, happen he sees as well in the dark as you let on. What you say, kid?"

"I say you're right. Sim, will you please go with Mr. Frank and watch out for any signs of the Apaches?"

"Yes, Mr. Linn, I will gladly go."

"Will he want a horse?" asked Swango.

"No," Sparhawk shook his head, "he'll run by your stirrup. It's only eighteen miles."

To Lucy Henderson's surprise no one questioned the laconic deprecation of such a formidable distance. Later she learned that it was nothing for an Indian to trot eighteen miles or, if need be, 118 miles. She found out that a man on foot could run down the swiftest desert stallion or wear out any other four-footed brute which drew the breath of life. But this macabre knowledge was not hers that long-ago night at Membrace Station, and so she wondered at Sim's accepted ability to pace Frank's saddle mount all the way to the next water, and went on listening.

"All right," nodded the silver-haired shotgun rider, "you ready, Sim?"

"Ready, Mr. Frank." The big Negro's perfect teeth gleamed quickly. "You tell me, please, if the horse gets tired."

"I believe the black beggar means it," muttered Price Cullross. "He gives me the creeps."

"Yeah," grunted Doc. "And ain't you glad he's doing his creeping on our side?"

Cullross didn't answer, nor did he need to.

Frank turned the blue gelding and was gone. Sim, floating like a dark feather off his near flank, went with him. Doc Harnaday spoke to his wheelers, shook a line at his bays. He did not curse. Linn Sparhawk cocked his Springfield. They moved out. Membrace Station and the dry bed of the Mimbres River fell behind and were lost in the first half-mile.

Four hours later, with the moon shining brightly as a newly minted dollar, their teams were shouldering into their collars to pull through the deep sand of the dry wash just west of Mimbres Springs. One quarter of a mile north, up the wash, lay the actual springs themselves. One quarter of a mile east, across rising ground, lay the station.

It was a few minutes past midnight when Doc pulled the teams to a halt in the middle of the old Waterfield corral and let his passengers sit there soaking up the silence and the lonesomeness.

No one said a word. Not even Frank Swango had the nerve to try and fool any of them about that place. Back at Membrace Station it had seemed like a dearly distant goal, a desirable place to gain, an objective that was important, that really meant something. Looking at it in the cold moonlight of successful achievement, it was terrifying.

The weathered adobe and stone corral appeared to be some fifteen paces wide by twenty-five long. Its walls must have been all of nine feet high. Across the rear of the compound was a sod-roofed shed. It seemed originally designed to serve the dual purpose of stock shelter and fortress catwalk, as an armed man upon its roof could clearly command the surrounding terrain and still be protected by the continuing rampart of the masonry wall.

In the near, southwest corner of the corral was the stationhouse itself. It looked to be 15 x 20 feet in size and had had its beamed roof burned through and its interior gutted by Apache fire, the same as its mate at Membrace Station.

The entrance in the front or south wall of the corral was just wide enough to pass an Abbott & Downing coach, and not a wheel-hub wider. Its heavy gates of cedar-plank construction had long ago been torn off to feed the nomad cookfires of the Apache.

The whole place reeked of dried pony droppings, moldering stage-mule manure, charcoaled timbers and the noisome stinking dust of human desertion. All around it, crouched in a circle like patient, watchful wolves, the ancient mesas of high New Mexico looked down upon the little station at Mimbres Springs—and waited.

Somewhere off in the eastern hills a coyote yammered with the crazed wildness which never fails to startle the oldest listener. Westward, disturbed in his night stalk of sleeping birds down among the rushes of the spring marsh, a dog fox scolded back in his breed's sharply querulous manner. To the north, plaintively long drawn, compellingly lonely, the cry of a buffalo lobo came from high up on the granite shoulder of Cooke's Peak. From the south came only the murmuring stir of the night wind sneaking up out of the wash to rustle the soft gray curl of the grama grass.

The lonely travelers shivered and knew the nightmare was real and that its name was Mimbres Springs. Even Frank Swango's calm voice, complete with its usual arid strength, failed to warm the deepening chill.

"Come on," said the shotgun rider, swinging down off his restive roan, "we're going to have to rustle our backsides, folks. We got four, maybe five hours till seeing daylight. My hunch is we'll need every minute of them and then some. Let's go."

"You ain't just whistling 'The Yeller Rose of Texas,'" growled Doc uneasily, reaching with his ancient boot for the front-wheel hub. "This place is a far piece from being forted up proper. We'll need to dig some before we can rightly say we're ready for company. Everybody down and start shoveling, by God! Come on, you bastards! Get a move on!"

"Well," Sparhawk muttered tiredly to himself, as he eased down out of the Democrat to join the cursing Doc, "I reckon we might as well. 'The foxes have holes, and the birds of the air have nests; but the Son of man hath not where to lay his head.'"

"What's that?" barked the old man belligerently.

The little Alabaman paused, his pale face lined with fatigue, his oddly blue eyes dark with the pain of the wasting sickness that was in him.

"Matthew," he said quietly. "Eight, twenty."

While the others fell to their various tasks, Linn assigned himself to Lucy Henderson.

Taking from the wagon some blankets and, to the sleepy girl's surprise, her old yellow straw suitcase, which for some reason of misguided Southern chivalry he had again smuggled into their baggage at Mesilla, he guided her solicitously toward the stationhouse.

It had been voted, he claimed, to see that she got some rest. There was nothing she could do to help, anyway, and the best thing for all of them was for her to get out of the way and stay there. Besides, he added, her nerves would be greatly benefited by a few hours' sleep, which same she could handily get between then and sunrise. Left unsaid was the grim fact that those few hours of sleep might well be the last she would get between that or any other sunrise. However, Lucy needed no reminder along those lines. No one could look at Mimbres Springs in the still light of a midnight moon and be guilty of making any extensive plans for the future.

She followed the Alabaman without complaint, or comment, as ready to quit as a new puppy which is suddenly all played out and only looking for a quiet corner to collapse into. She was already half asleep when Linn led her through the low doorway into the charred ruin. Yet the place had about it an aura of past tragedy which would not be denied. It rose up and met Lucy Henderson the moment she crossed its rotting threshold. It was there to greet her like a clammy hand; and she shivered and was all at once no longer sleepy.

The single room was, as it had appeared to be from the outside, about 15 x 20 feet. It had one small door in the east wall, a single shoulder-high slit of a window in the corral-side, or north wall. There were no openings of any kind in the outer walls which were, in effect, the south and west walls of the corral itself.

About the one inside window hung some pathetic shreds of scorched calico; the woman's pitiful small touch in a man's brutal world. Lucy's lips twisted bitterly. What a travesty! She found herself suddenly very angry, and the anger brought with it a flash of strength. Then, turning away from the burned curtains, she saw something else, and the fight went out of her with sickening speed. Protruding from beneath a fallen roof timber was the crushed, out-flung arm and sun-faded, curly hair of a faceless baby doll.

Ordinarily she would have been equal to such a little thing, but she was not. Caught and held as the broken creature was in the glaring well of moonlight which fell through the hole in the roof timbers, it completely unnerved her. Sparhawk, who was arranging her blankets, heard her low cry and leaped back to her side. He saw the doll, but did not let the staring girl know that he did. Instead, he gently took her by the shoulders and turned her away. "Count to ten and look back," he advised her. Then, as she obeyed, he smiled. "All right. Now what do you see?"

She shook her head slowly. The doll was gone and she knew he had done something with it, yet she just answered, "Nothing," as though his little kindness had worked its intended mercy.

"Moonlight's like that," he told her soberly. "It'll fool you blind. Always got to look twice to be sure."

It was a good reach but it didn't stretch quite far enough.

98

Sparhawk saw that it didn't. He seemed, somehow, in his diffident way, to be always able to see how things were with Lucy Henderson. In the present moment he not only knew that sleep had vanished for her with the hidden doll; he read and answered as well the wordless question about the broken toy in the white-faced look she now gave him.

"Yes, ma'am," he said, being deliberately impersonal. "This is the place it happened. You'd have guessed it sooner or later, anyway, what with the curtains and all."

He was right again; she had, indeed, guessed it. She could even remember his exact words describing the family tragedy. She saw them as clearly before her as though he had written them down for her that past morning on the swaying seat box of the Democrat, south of Webster Wells.

. . . then some Mescaleros took apart a stock corral out here past Mesilla. Killed the tender and his four kids and carried off his wife, after first cutting out her tongue when she went to pleading with them to let her babies live. . . .

"Yes," she admitted to the Alabaman, "I think I knew this was the place the minute I saw the curtains. Guess I was fighting it down all right, though, until I saw the doll."

"Let's go back outside, Miss Lucy." He took her arm and she did not resist. "You can help Sim and me fetch the water from down at the springs if you want."

"The water?" she said uncertainly. "I thought somebody said there was water inside the walls at this station? They did too! It was Frank," she remembered defiantly, as though the fact it had been the shotgun rider made disagreement impossible.

"I know," her companion murmured, apparently as reluctant as she to question Swango's infallibility. "But nobody guesses the hole card right all the time."

"What are you getting at, Linn?" Lucy was in no mood for parables of the poker table. "Come right on out with it, whatever it is!"

He shook his head, mumbling some excuse for not answering, and she took a new set at him. If irritation wouldn't work, perhaps some of his own type of out-West talk would do the trick. Forcing the smile, she lit into him again.

"Now, see here, I'm tired of being treated like the old-maid aunt down to spend the summer, you understand? You boys are stuck with me and I wish you'd admit it and quit carrying on so damned noble about it!"

"I read your smoke, ma'am." He acknowledged the clumsy try grinningly. "What else?"

"This else," she said, still feeling for the Western way to say it. "You'd better start waving your blanket back at me. I want to know what's going on around here."

"Miss Lucy," he nodded, the smile gone and the little charade over, "it's the inside-water, like you guessed."

He pointed to the far corner of the room. "There's a camouflaged cistern eight feet deep yonder by the fireplace. The station crew used to keep it full of hauled water for emergency use in case of Indian trouble. Frank figured the Apaches hadn't found it and that it would still be holding whatever water was in it at the time the Mescaleros burned the place."

She nodded back to him, realizing he hadn't said all he had in mind to say about that cistern. "Linn," she asked him, "what did you figure about there being water still in it?"

The Alabaman was humble but not deceitful. His answering shrug was as quick as it was candid. "Reckon I didn't figure," he said. "Reckon I knew. You can't fool an Apache about water. He can smell it the same as a wild horse. Otherwise he couldn't live in this country. I allow you'd have to say I guessed they'd have sniffed it out and either used it up or ruined it long ago."

"And?" she prompted uneasily.

"It was a good guess, Miss Lucy. Sim and you and me will have to haul every barrel we can before daylight. There's nothing down that cistern hole but adobe dust and dry-rot spiders."

When Swango learned of the water situation, his jaw went tight. But by his voice one would have thought he and Sparhawk were discussing the best place to put down the hamper for a Sunday School picnic. Nevertheless, he agreed quickly enough to Linn's proposal that the latter and Sim take the barrel and start for the springs. The powerful black man would carry the water while Linn sat shotgun on the waterhole. The only question came on Sparhawk's inclusion of Lucy Henderson in the assignment. And it came blunt and quick.

"I don't see the call for the little lady to tag along, kid." Frank was as close as he ever came to a scowl. "You got some special reasons, or you just lonesome and wanting to be sociable? Seems to me she can be more real help to us up here at the station. We got plenty to do, I'll promise you,

100

before we're ready to argue with them Apaches, come daylight."

"Sure, Frank, sure you have. Hell, I know that. But this place is giving her the creeps," explained Sparhawk. "It's getting to her and she needs to get away from it for a spell. Sort of get her mind on other things. You know what I mean, Frank."

Lucy had previously observed that Frank Swango never smiled. He didn't do so now. Yet somehow she felt that down inside he was pleased about something. Something he could see about her that she couldn't see about herself.

"Sure, kid," he said in soft reply to Linn's urgent explanation, "I reckon I know what you mean. You two run along. Me and Doc will have this rock barnyard forted up tighter than the bung in a green-oak barrel before ever Sim gets back with that first keg of Mimbres gin."

"Thanks, Frank. Thanks a whole lot," was all the homely little Southerner said, as he took Lucy's hand and called out to Sim to get the keg and come along. But the watchful girl knew that with their parting exchange of looks, Linn Sparhawk and Frank Swango had shaken hands over a man-to-man understanding they would never share with her or any other woman.

Mimbres Springs had been a favorite white travelers' watering place since its modern discovery in the fall of '46 by Colonel Phillip St. George Cooke and his famed Mormon battalion on their memorable march from Santa Fe to the sea. Before that, and untold centuries before that, it had been one of the main camping points on the great east-west Indian trail, the so-called "Apache Road" of the Southwest. In more recent times, specifically since September of '58, it had served as the sole water supply for Mimbres Springs Station on the American Mail Line to California. In addition, it was one of the ten historically never failing wells on the long dry run of the Waterfield route from Horsehead Crossing on the Rio Pecos to Yuma Station on the sedge-grown banks of the Big Colorado.

Lucy Henderson now listened to Linn Sparhawk recount this olden history as she sat with him upon a dune above the spring trail watching the moonlit skyline while Sim filled and toted back to the station the first barrel of water.

As she listened to the story, she looked at the beauty of Mimbres Springs, disturbingly weighted down by the vague sense of endless time which hung about the place.

The main pool was some fifty feet across, a glittering jewel of clear water. Swango had not been wrong to call it Mimbres gin; it was indeed that transparent and silvery.

Around its sanded edges stretched a marshland of graceful reeds and cattail rushes. Beyond, standing like sentinels posted to keep watch over this treasure of the wastelands, were the ancient cottonwoods and their flanking mesquites. The seed of the latter doubtless had been brought to this desolate oasis in the droppings of the Spaniards' Arabian horses.

Crossing the marshy ground, and going out to deep water, was a rock-filled causeway which passed immediately below their sand-dune lookout. This construction, Linn told the now relaxing girl, was built in modern times by American Mail's advance work crews, as a part of the immense engineering and surveying labors which had gone forward for a full year before the first Celerity splashed across the Pecos and the stage route to California became a scheduled fact instead of a stock promotion dream. It was down this same smooth path, only moments later, that Sim came padding to fill the second barrel, interrupting Sparhawk's story and changing his subject with alerting suddenness.

As for Sim, he only glanced up in passing, checking to make sure they were still on the qui vive, then just grinning and trotting on.

But Sparhawk continued to stare off after him, a warning look of innocence on his pale features. Lucy Henderson lost some of her drowsiness and took heed. She could not be sure in his case, but in others before him that look had reliably presaged some morally questionable move.

Presently Sparhawk looked over at her.

"Excuse me, ma'am," he said, and slid down the dune and disappeared.

She saw him reappear on the causeway below, to trot out and join Sim at its end. The two talked quickly. Then Sim nodded his massive head, picked up the filled barrel, and started back up the grade toward the station. The Alabaman was back at the dune shortly, innocent as ever.

His companion was of a mind not to like the studied blamelessness of his averted face. It seemed to her that she had seen that exact look on that same face previously. In fact, she suddenly remembered when and where she had seen it. Then she was sure she didn't like it. It was the same bland disclaimer of all evil intent which had preceded her visit to Lucia Sanchez's resort back in El Paso.

102

"Sparhawk," she said, "what were you and Sim talking about?"

"You," he admitted at once.

"All right," she proceeded carefully. "What about me?"

"Nothing much I guess."

"Well, guess again. How much?"

"Well, I just told Sim that since it was such a grand warm night and since you hadn't had a good dip since your plunge into Luz's irrigation ditch, I thought you might want to take a swim while we were down here. I mean to say as long as we are down here."

"Just what do you mean to say?" demanded the girl at his side.

Up to then she'd had no idea he knew about her swim at Lucia Sanchez's. It somehow upset her that he had found out about it. "Well," she repeated, jumping the question again at her gentle-voiced companion, "what do you mean?"

"Well," he countered easily, "I mean that seeing there's no sign of the Indians yet and you being the lone girl with a bunch of stubbly-bearded menfolks and this being likely your last chance this side of Fort Fillmore to freshen up, I thought you might cotton to the idea of taking a spring-water bath."

The idea was not without merit, actually. Its supporting logic even seemed reasonably sound. But by this time Lucy Henderson knew Linn Sparhawk.

"And was that all you thought?" she inquired caustically.

"Well, nigh," he hedged.

"I see," she nodded, trying to keep calm. "What else?"

"Well," he took off evasively again, "as you know, I'm a great hand to go along with President Lincoln on domestic-policy matters. I side with him especially strong on the subject of being helpful. Now he said in his Cincinnati speech just this past February that he held that so long as man existed it was his duty to improve not only his own condition but to assist in ameliorating mankind's as well. It's a cinch he meant womankind's too, but just didn't want to say so for fear of offending somebody's mother."

"Sparhawk," said Lucy Henderson desperately, "what in God's name are you talking about now?"

"Still about taking baths, far as I know, ma'am."

"Well, what about taking baths?" she blurted out before thinking it through.

"Nothing much—only that I reckoned I might take one with you, Miss Lucy."

She gasped and drew away from him so quickly that he jumped to his feet and left her sitting alone on the saltgrass of the dune, his own attitude one of readiness to run should she come for him.

As for Lucy, she had gone as far as she intended to go with his Southern shenanigans. She wouldn't pretend for a minute that she was insulted, for obviously he had not meant her to be, but neither was she going to let him charge any more of his cow-country jokes to her account. She looked back at him, deliberately borrowing one of the local sagebrush sayings to let him know as much.

"All right, fine," she said. "And who's going to mind the store while we're gone?"

She waited on him, completely confident she had him cornered.

"Nobody," he slipped away nonchalantly. "Sim says the Apaches haven't arrived on the scene yet. That's the same as a money-back guarantee. Let's go."

She shook her head, half amused, half genuinely concerned. "Sparhawk," she asked him tolerantly, "do you think I'm crazy?"

"A little bit, Miss Lucy," he said softly and without awkwardness. "Aren't you?"

Lucy Henderson looked at him. Down the hill in the moonlight she could see Sim coming again from the station. The stillness was so complete she could plainly hear the muffled fall of his bare feet in the dust of the trail, and the light, swift urgency of their cadence drummed its way into her mind, returning her to the moment's reality. Of a sudden she could feel time running through her clutching fingers like loose sand. How many hours away was the sun? How many miles behind it, the paint-smeared ponies of Mangas Coloradas and his savage Mimbreño Apaches?

She stood up quickly, coming to face Linn Sparhawk in the moonlight.

"I guess I must be, Linn," she told him low-voiced. "Let's go . . ."

As Sparhawk lay there thinking, many things were made clear to him. Many questions were answered, many vexations quieted, many mysteries made transparent. But the greatest mystery of all was to remain forever unsolved in the mind of the little Waterfield stock handler.

Price Cullross was an adventurer no less than Lucy Henderson. He was a rapacious rascal who, like the girl, made

104

social capital of his natural good looks and inherent lack of social compunction. He had no more morals than a stud mustang but, God knew, he was a man. And a very handsome, eager, entirely courageous man who, Sparhawk was satisfied, had never left the auburn-haired Henderson girl in one moment's doubt that he was hers for the first asking. . . . Frank Swango stood six feet, three inches tall. If there was a solitary molecule of his lean body that wasn't all male, it must have curled up and died for lack of company long before Lucy Henderson met him. There was nothing about Frank Swango that a knowing woman would want to change. He fascinated the Yankee girl, as any other man would be blind not to see. Nor was the attraction purely physical. Frank's character was as hard and compelling, and little doubt as deadly, as the polished barrel of his Army Colt. Withal, he was a dangerous, saturnine, exciting man who read women as though he had written the original book about them. And to his dying day he, Sparhawk, would remain convinced Lucy Henderson could have had Swango too, as Cullross before him, for no more than the least beckoning of bold eye. . . . Why then, in the name of a supposedly just and reasonable God, a bewildered Alabama boy would be asking himself till the end of time, did she choose to wind up at that Mimbres Springs swimming hole with a bedraggled, drowthed-out specimen like Linn McClellan Sparhawk . . .?

Worse yet, coming back to the immediate moment from that far land of just thinking about it, what in the further name of the good Lord above was she doing still lying there with him alongside that desert Shalimar?

Why was she stretched out there beside him on the warm sand of that tiny bar on the north bank of the springs, letting the moonlight continue to bathe her beautiful body and invade her close-cropped, shapely head?

Why was it that the lingering touch of his grateful hand in hers was allowed to remain, and even encouraged to stay; no, even refused permission to go?

Why had she lain thus with him this hour and more past, listening to him repeat his clumsy litany of her endless charms? Why was that dreamlike look of utter content still relaxing her soft lips? Why were the New Mexican stars reflected as brightly in her jade-green eyes as in the sparkling pool of the spring? Why had she come here with him, why had she stayed, why had she let it happen . . .

And then that last, greatest mystery of all. Why, oh everlasting why, had she picked an expatriate failure of a small-town Southern weakling like Linn Sparhawk with whom to fall suddenly and forever in love?

12

Linn and Lucy Henderson came back to the station with Sim and the last barrel of water about half past three. Neither the Alabaman nor his companion had heard a sound or seen a shadow at the spring. But Sim had.

The latter had suddenly thrown up his head and frozen dead-still. He had sniffed the freshening dawn wind as warily as any big jungle cat detecting the first sign of the two-legged hunter. He had even rumbled deep in his cavernous chest like an angry lion, before turning to Linn and muttering, "They are out there now, Mr. Linn. You and Missy had better hurry."

Not needing to inquire who "they" were, Linn and Lucy had started on the run up the hill toward the station. They had arrived out of breath and well ahead of Sim, but with plenty of wind remaining to warn the others that the Apaches were drawing near.

Now, unable to sleep after half an hour's futile effort, the restless girl got up and climbed to the roof of the station-house where Doc Harnaday was on guard.

She wanted to talk to somebody who knew Linn Sparhawk, and her other choice (Swango was standing the watch atop the horse shed) was apt to be touchy on the subject. She now realized that Frank had knowingly let her go to the springs with the young Southerner, well aware the latter wasn't after water. But she didn't care to press her luck with the quiet-eyed shotgun rider.

Besides, Doc knew Linn better than any of the rest of them. The old driver knew too, to judge from the two or three terse references she remembered being made, what it was that physically ailed the Alabaman.

Doc seemed glad enough to have company. Also, perhaps by premonition, he acted strangely gentle and contrite.

"Well, Miss Lucy," he said in answer to the anxious girl's question about Sparhawk's sickness, "I ain't no medical doc-

106

tor, as you can plainly see. But I reckon I can tell you what's the matter with the boy. And I don't believe it makes any difference to him now, so I will tell you. Ordinarily, you know, he wouldn't stand for it. He long ago put me on my bounden word not to say anything about it. Not to anybody. He said he didn't want folks bothering him on account of him being down. Which was really to say, providing you know Linn Sparhawk, that he didn't want to be bothering folks on account of him being down."

"Yes, that would be like him, I think."

"You think right," said the old man.

"When the Lord poured Linn, it was the last of a pretty thin and watery mix. But when he broke open the mold, something pretty special had set up inside."

"I'm beginning to believe it," murmured Lucy Henderson.

"Well you'd better," growled Doc. "That boy's got something in him that shines out like a ranch-window lamp on a stormy night."

"Yes," she said. "And whatever it is, it shines to the disadvantage of the rest of us. What is it, Doc? What is there about Linn that makes the rest of us look second-rate? Yet that makes us resent him at the same time it makes us appreciate him—maybe even love him."

"Part of it," replied Doc feelingly, "is his being so sick. It's just like a poor damn dog that's four weeks gone into distemper. He's breathing fast, coughing pus, passing blood and fixing to die by daybreak. Folks just naturally take to anything that's mortal sick or bad hurt, like that. Yet they can't help being upset by looking at it, either. It's the feeling we get when we see a hunchback dwarf or a cripple-born kid. We're sorry as hell for them but we don't really and honestly want them around where we have to look at them."

"Doc, I don't think that's it with Linn."

"Well, no, not the whole of it, maybe. He's got that inside light like I said."

She let it go, thinking back to his dragging in of the sick dog analogy, knowing it had been done deliberately.

"Doc," she said levelly, "have you been trying to tell me Linn is going to die?"

"I have," said the old man simply, "and he is. He's got the lung fever, girl, got it bad. Had it ever since he come out here and likely long before that. It's why he come to Texas to begin with."

"But he doesn't cough!" she protested hopefully. "I've

107

never heard him cough even once. It can't be consumption without coughing, can it?"

"It ain't the coughing kind. It's the quiet kind. Kills a man like a knife in the belly. Not much of a mark outside but his guts all broken and bleeding inside. Yes, I'm telling you he's going to die, Miss Lucy, and I'll tell you something else."

He paused, peering east and west along the gray ribbon of the Waterfield stage road before finishing softly. "He ain't going to die alone."

His confused listener recoiled without understanding the exact meaning of the old man's last words. "Now what are you trying to tell me, Doc?" she muttered. "I thought you and Frank were sure . . ." She started to say she had thought they believed the fort-up to be entirely safe, but the bearded driver interrupted her abruptly.

"Me and Frank was wrong—dead wrong. The boy was right. He was right all along. I know that now. It's like something you can't explain; like the ache in an old man's bones when the weather's fixing to change." He looked at her, dropping his voice for emphasis. "I'm an old man, miss, a mighty old one. And my bones are aching something fierce."

"Doc, you mean we should have kept going?"

"Yes," he said quietly. "We should have made the full run for Mesilla and the Rio Grande last night, win, lose, or come a dead heat, just the selfsame dead-right way Linn said we should."

Lucy Henderson could not argue that belated admission. She could only agree with it. It had been her own conviction the little Southerner had been right back at Membrace Station, and she had lacked the courage to stand by him. Now it was too late; there was no use crying over it, past admitting it. She and Doc understood that and they understood one another. There was no more to be said.

It got very quiet. They sat there; Doc crouched along the front wall, continuing to stare east and west through the thinning night; the lonely girl huddled in her blanket against the west wall, staring at nothing and thinking about Linn Sparhawk.

Behind her, down the hill, the bobolinks and redwings were beginning to stir among the misty rushes of Mimbres Springs. Somewhere in a mesquite tree out on the *llano* a mourning dove started her sad lament. Down by the spring again, feeding toward the water up the wash from the south, a pair of desert quail began their bright chuckling talk. Up the wash, working down toward the spring from the north, a topknotted bachelor cock answered them cheerily. Lucy Henderson smiled, thinking back to the time a million years ago when, atop the Celerity between Coyote Wells and Mesilla, Linn Sparhawk had shown her how to imitate and answer back those same clear sweet quail calls.

It was a very pleasant memory, Lucy Henderson thought. Doc Harnaday definitely disagreed. He was at her wall in one scrambling slide across the roof, his old eyes squinting downward toward the mist-hidden marsh, his gnarled hand cupped to his ear. Poised there, he held his head cocked like an early morning robin listening for the faint scratching of the invisible earthworm beneath him.

He did not listen long. The next moment he was at the edge of the burned-through hole in the stationhouse roof calling down to the exhausted sleepers below, "Everybody up down there! On the double! We got company!"

He was back at Lucy's side in an instant, cocking his heavy Sharps bullgun and peering once more into the curling mists of the springs.

"Doc," she whispered fearfully, "what is it?"

"Well," said the old Waterfield driver, carefully punctuating the opinion by shifting his quid of cut-plug and spitting springward, "I'll tell you three things it ain't." He laid the bullgun's octagon barrel across the adobe parapet, nestling its worn butt stock lovingly to his cheek. "It ain't no three damned desert quail working north and south up and down no damned dry wash toward no damned drink at Mimbres Springs, New Mexico!"

It was still some minutes of five, the new day yet a dingy sort of an all-cats gray and just showing the least pink flush over toward Mesilla, when the Apaches came over the east wall at Frank Swango's station on the horse-shed roof.

The other defenders never found out by what side-gully route they got up beneath Frank's wall, or why they had kept moving through the night to make an attack before full daylight. All they ever knew was that one minute they weren't there and the next they were.

Frank was calling across the corral to Doc, checking on the earlier quail calls down by the spring. His back was turned, for fifteen seconds, to the east wall. He did not see the first Indian appear behind him. All he saw was the leap of old Doc's Sharps coming to shoulder and the roar and flash of it going off, followed by the whistle of the bullgun's big slug ripping across the corral toward him. Then he whirled and saw the painted devil who had slithered over the wall behind him.

The Apache was armed with a settler's wood ax. He had this weapon raised for a slash at Frank's head when Doc's bullet put a period above his left eyebrow. He threw his hands to his face, spun like a spiked top crazily over the edge of the roof to strike and lie still upon the ground below.

At the wall, the scaling ladder by which he had come up at Frank, was moving again. The shotgun rider leapt away from it as he would the buzzing tail of a Texas rattler. He flashed his Colt, throwing the shot into the face of the second red man as he topped the parapet. The latter pitched forward onto the horse-shed roof, dead before he hit its weathered sods. But after him came three others, too fast to count. Frank's Colt went off twice more, each shot centering its target. The fourth shot went wild and the fifth was never fired. The last Apache over the wall, screened by the still upright bodies of his dying companions, hurled his war ax at Frank from a distance scarcely greater than his sinewy arm's length. The murderous blade turned only once in its flight before burying itself to its helve in the shotgun rider's chest, high up near the base of the throat.

Frank's gun fell from his spasming fingers in the same instant Doc's second shot, fatally delayed by the Sharps' slow-loading action, spun his assailant off the horse-shed roof with a ball through his lower abdomen.

Frank, still on his feet, took two lurching steps to the wall, pulled the scaling ladder up onto the roof, turned back, stumbled to his knees, slid sideways of the shed, fell soddenly atop the Indian who had axed him. Bounding limply off the latter, his slack body sprawled motionlessly in the puddled dust of the corral.

There was absolute silence on the mesas beyond the walls of the Waterfield station at Mimbres Springs. The outer stillness was echoed by that within the tiny quadrangle of sunbaked earth which they enclosed.

Linn and Price Cullross, on guard at the front gate, where the wagon had been overturned and entrenched to close the narrow entrance portal, had seen nothing. They still saw the same.

Puzzled, Sparhawk shook his head. Evidently the five bucks who had tried for the horse-shed roof had acted on their own and independently of the main bunch. Well, thank God for that. It was a well-known Indian habit, this trying to steal a little premature glory. And it was a trait of red

110

insubordination which had saved more white lives than all the regiments of cavalry ever stationed on the frontier. For which, again, thank God.

Of course, had the eager ones won their gamble to strike the big coup before their slower fellows might come up, a man wouldn't be standing there thanking God or anyone else. The five bucks would have been the live heroes and the remaining members of his own party the dead fools. As it was, the Apaches were dead and he and his friends were still alive—or at least they might stay that way if they got a move on.

With the last thought, the Alabaman yelled up to Lucy Henderson to come down off the stationhouse roof and look to Frank, while he sprinted for the unmanned horse shed, leaving Price Cullross to hold the front gate.

The white-faced girl ran down the inside adobe stairs and out across the corral. She was at Frank's side as quickly as she could possibly get there, and it was not quick enough.

When she dropped to her knees at his side, taking his lean gray head into her lap and crying like a child for God to please not let him die, Frank Swango was already dead. His pale eyes were calmly closed, his sun-bronzed features untortured, his grim lips peacefully curved. Perhaps it was a smile, perhaps not. Lucy Henderson always thought it was. And beneath it, she was sure, his handsome face held the satisfied look of a man who had known what he was dying for; a man who had realized at the last that he had found a company of fellow humans upon whom he need not fear to turn his back and in whose separate or collective presence he need not be afraid to unbuckle his gunbelt.

Some such inadequate sentiments were still struggling to be put into words which might relieve her pent-up feelings when Linn Sparhawk came back down from the horse-shed roof to stand at her side and say it, with big Sim's deep-voiced help, far better than she could ever have done.

When she saw the Southerner's slight shadow and glanced up, she could see he already knew their friend was past hers, or his, or any human help. As he stood there, Sim drifted noiselessly up. The Negro giant stared down at Frank a moment, made a curious sign over him, stepped back, looked up at the sky, muttered something in his native tongue, turned and growled something equally unclear to Linn.

"What did he say?" she asked Sparhawk dully.

The latter hesitated, thinking.

111

"I'm not too perfect on his African talk," he said at last. "The best translation I could give you would be in Shakespeare, not Swahili. It was in *Hamlet*."

Lucy Henderson waited, knowing he would go on.

" 'He was a man,' " the slender youth quoted softly, " 'take him for all in all, I shall not look upon his like again.' "

After Frank's death the unbroken quiet outside the walls continued. It was not a natural quiet. The least experienced among the fear-bound watchers in the corral could tell that. Or thought they could. It just did not seem possible to them that one single Indian could keep that still, let alone the several dozen which Doc Harnaday felt certain would compose the Apache band for which they were waiting. But the old man was insistent. They were out there, all right. He could feel them.

But Doc Harnaday was wrong. The Apaches were not out there. It was noon—a terrible, torturing nerve-wrack of nearly seven hours—before they saw the first Mimbreño.

Then they saw him in a way that would make a strong man weep tears of weakling salt. He came on a gallop, not from the east where they had been mainly watching since the attack on the horse shed, and from which direction Doc still thought the main bunch must appear, but from the west.

Behind him rose a column of dust, such as would be put up by a good many more than a few dozen mounted men. The dust was moving along the Waterfield road, toward the springs, from Membrace Station and Fort Webster, and the same glad question leaped into the minds of all the watchers on the rooftop. *My God! Could it be that some westernmost column of retreating troops had come upon the deserted fort and was force-marching to come up with its erstwhile and departed garrison?*

But it was not so and the glad question had quite another and very different answer. The tower of dust came steadily on, moving at last out of sight behind the cottonwoods of the spring. There it stopped, settled, died away. Five minutes crawled by.

The advance Indian came out of the cottonwood grove riding his pony down the wash to the south. They could not see him clearly because he was below the lip of the wash, and they followed his course by the thin spurts of dust put up by his trotting mount. When he reappeared after a second interminable five minutes, it was to stand posed atop a

112

rocky outcrop commanding the station from a safe 600 yards away.

The Apache sat up there against the raw blue sky for a long time looking across at them. The only movement in either man or mount came with the noon breeze, which rustled first the pony's shaggy mane, then its master's equally harsh black locks. The air was so clear and the Indian so still, his white watchers could plainly make out the typical abrupt cut of the Apache bangs shadowing his fierce eyes.

While the warrior sat thus, Linn Sparhawk studied him silently through his field glasses. After a time Doc Harnaday said to him, "All right, boy, call him off for me slow and careful. Tell me, most particular, what kind of a coat he's wearing."

Linn nodded without taking the glasses down. "Tall for an Apache, real tall. And big. Thick-bodied as a bull. Got a head the size of a nail keg. Tough and craggy-faced but not mean-looking. Appears level-tempered, maybe even friendly. He's showing some age, hard to tell how much, and he sure is wearing an odd outfit, all right. Regular sort of a suit or uniform rig of some kind. Sure like nothing I ever saw on an Indian before. Looks to be of blue broadcloth. Mexican pantaloons, a full frock coat and, so help me, a double row of big brass buttons all down the front of it. The pants are slashed from the knee down, Mex-style, with real bright red flashings inside. The coat is . . ."

Doc had heard enough.

"The coat," he broke in on Linn raspingly, "is lined with the same red silk as the gussets on the pants. The sleeves of it have been knife-slit clean up to the elbows and he's wearing them turned inside out and rolled up like a damned shirt so's the inside red will show."

Linn took down the glasses, his smile tight around the edges. "Might as well throw these away," he gestured with the glasses. "You're seeing him better than I am."

The old driver did not hear him. His eyes were far away, and they were seeing considerably more distance than lay between his listeners and the oddly attired Apache on the outcrop.

"He was give that coat," he said, "by a sheep-brained idiot of a U.S. Indian Bureau commissioner named John Bartlett. That was God knows how many years ago at a peace talk over at the Santa Rita Copper Mines. He ain't wore nothing else, rain or shine, since. Saving for one thing. That's a dirty-

113

white dress shirt with stud buttons and no collar, which I'll guarantee you he's wearing this minute with the shirttails aflapping loose outside his blue Spanish pants!"

He paused, grimaced bitterly, spat over the wall. "He's better than middling agey and calm-faced like you say. Ugly, you might call him, but not vicious nor shifty-eyed. And he sits his pony proper and poker-backed as a preacher on Palm Sunday. He looks old and grandpa-gentle enough to trust your wife with while you're out of town, or to take your kids on a picnic to Big Bend. But he's a paid-up-for-life member and Grand Swami of Mimbreño Lodge Number One, goes by the proper Apache monicker of Mangas Coloradas and will kill you quicker than Comancho cholera or Rocky Mountain spotted fever."

"Red Sleeves!" gasped Lucy Henderson gratuitously.

"As ever was," agreed the old man.

The following stillness was excruciating. Then Doc nodded. "Happen any of you got a spare prayer stashed away, you'd best dig it out and start sending up them spiritual smoke signals. Barring help from up yonder, we've come about as far as we're going to go. If God don't lead somebody to stumble on us by accident, or if He don't make it so's one of us can get through to Mesilla and Fort Fillmore to fetch help, we're done for. Them's the main pack of Mimbres Apaches yonder, and you can set your clock by that."

They heard him say it. They saw his reference nod go toward the springs and the cottonwood grove behind which the big column of horse dust had disappeared. And as they did, each of them got pale and tense and pinch-mouthed with the same terrible bit of thinking back.

The old man's words had just confirmed one more of Linn Sparhawk's soft-voiced advices. And done it brutally. The main Apache group had not been over toward Mesilla and Goodsight Station as Doc and Frank had guessed. It had been camped at Cow Springs exactly as Linn had wanted to gamble it would be. Between them and the safety of Sergeant Zimmerman's forces at Fillmore last night had stood only the five-man scout party which had made the original smoke signals on the Mesilla side and followed them in for the dawn attack which had killed Frank Swango.

Still more maddeningly tantalizing was the opportunity obtaining through the long morning's stillness just past. At the time of Frank's death Mangas Coloradas had been thirty miles west of Mimbres Springs Station. Had they set out for Mesilla any time within a full three hours after the shot-

114

gun rider died, they could have beaten the Apache band to the Rio Grande by an easy sixty minutes and never pushed their strong, fresh teams out of a rolling rangeland lope to do it!

They all of them just stood there, deathly sick with the pure heartbreak of it.

13

With Frank gone they knew the odds had changed. There was no one who could take his place and no one who rightly thought he could. But Price Cullross, as the frontier saying went, was a man who would have a go at a circular saw. The Texan simply refused to let rough luck deal him a hand he would not pick up and have a try at playing out. In this case he had his try the minute Doc Harnaday finished advising the tight-lipped company to start talking to its various gods about sending somebody to lead it out of the Mimbres Springs bulrushes.

"I am not what is known as a praying man," apologized the Confederate guerrilla leader, "but if the price is right I have been known to speculate a bit now and again."

"Well," growled Doc, "suppose you get to speculating on some way to outsmart Mangas."

"You won't outsmart him," said Cullross, "but you might outsimple him."

Doc scowled him down. The veteran stager did not care for the new crop of Texans coming along. They all had too much to offer of advice and not enough of action. Since the days of Captain Jack Hays and Ben McCulloch of the Rangers, real men had got scarce as Lincoln Republicans in the Lone Star State. The Johnny-come-lately likes of this Cullross boy were no more true Texicans than, say, Jake Bergerman or Ceferino Sanchez.

"What the hell kind of Sesesh talk is that?" he finally demanded of the San Antonian.

Cullross laughed, holding up his hands in mock surrender.

"Old Man," he said—he never called him anything but that—"what would you think would be the last thing a half

115

dozen poor white devils might try, providing you were Mangas Coloradas and had them cornered twenty-to-one?"

"I ain't in the mood for guessing games."

"Get in the mood," advised the big Texan, his face hardening.

"You go to hell!"

"No," said Cullross, "you go to thinking."

Doc went through the motions of a ferocious scowl but he was beat. "Thinking what?" he huffed.

"What it was you and Swango said was the last thing a white man should do when jumped by Indians. You remember. What you told Sparhawk when he wanted to make an all-out break for Mesilla yesterday evening."

Doc's scowl dissolved guiltily. "Run," he admitted, so softly the others had trouble hearing him.

Cullross nodded. "I'll grant you it's a little late in the day," he smiled, "but sometime after dark tonight I'm meaning to climb aboard Swango's roan and make that little run you were talking up a spell back—you know, the one to fetch the Yankee cavalry from Fort Fillmore."

"You're crazy," said the old man.

"So was Sam Houston, but he made a state out of a quarter million square miles of sagebrush."

"I still say you're cracked!"

"No, just cheerful. Like a bee-stung bear. Or a fly-bit bull."

Even Doc had to grin at that. This Price had more brass than Grandma's bedstead. But no sooner did the old stager start to twist his lips a little than Linn straightened them out for him.

"If anybody's to ride for the river, it should be me," he said quietly. "I know the best crossings and back trails and can get there by the surest and fastest riding at night as will have to be done."

"Mr. Linn"—Sim's voice was completely unexpected— "let me go for you. I can run afoot, saving you the roan horse. He is a good horse and you will need him later."

"Thanks, Sim," said the little Southerner, "but it's got to be me on Mr. Frank's horse. The roan's a racer, as you well know, and if I can get him through the Indian lines, there isn't a Mimbreño mustang in New Mexico will ever head him this side of Messilla."

"Let me go for you," pleaded Sim. "Please let me go for you, little boss."

"No, and that's final." Linn reached up to put his thin

116

hand on the great broad shoulder. "You're needed here, Sim. You're our watchdog; our nighttime eyes and ears."

"No Apache can catch me, Mr. Linn; and the one who does will never tell his friends about it."

"Sim," said Sparhawk gently, "it's not that simple. I know you're not afraid of them. Or a hundred more like them. But even you can't outrun an Indian pony in the first burst of speed. Should they see you before you got well away, you wouldn't have a speared lion's chance in short grass. They would ride you down like a crippled game-beast, surely you see that."

Sim shook his head, muttering his disagreement in guttural African, but he stepped back and said no more.

Cullross at once took up where he had been interrupted.

"All right, friend Sparhawk," he nodded good-naturedly, "what makes you think you can give the roan a better ride than I can? Beyond knowing the country better, that is."

"Two other things: knowing the horse better and being more cut to size for proving it. Blue Bolt is like a baby with me. I hackamore-broke and neck-reined him for Frank, and he will go with me quiet as a meadow mouse. That's vital. Quiet is something you couldn't get six feet from the front gate without. Those Indians have ears delicate as dandelion fluff. The least jar will bring them down all over you. The nub of the other thing is that it's fifty-two miles to the river and you outweigh me sixteen ounces to the mile."

Cullross grinned.

"A reasonable argument, that last," he conceded. "But there's just one trouble with it—I've got a better one."

"What's that?" asked Sparhawk.

"Me," said the Texan.

It was Linn's turn to grin. And to back off.

"Well, now it's true, Mr. Cullross, I'm in no condition to wrestle you for it, but you strike me as a man who will bet on the color of the next card, blindfolded."

"Yes, and turned three times around in his chair to boot," said Price Cullross.

"Very well then, sir. . . ." Linn fished in his pocket, bringing out a verdigrised twenty-five-cent piece. "How about tossing a coin for it? Heads or tails. You call it on the spin." He didn't wait for the other's agreement but threw the quarter at once. "Heads!" barked Cullross belatedly.

The worn coin hit the dirt, not bouncing in the deep dust. Linn leaned over quickly to look at it. He smiled happily, picked it up, put it back in his pocket, shrugged, turned away. "Tails, you lose, Mr. Cullross," he said. Then before Price or anyone else could challenge the questionable ruling, he swung his glance off south, threw up a warning hand and added suddenly, "Everybody back to stations. Keep your eyes peeled sharp. Our red rooster's disappeared down off his dungheap yonder."

They all turned, seeing that Mangas Coloradas had indeed gone from his rocky lookout while they had been discussing the ride-out for Fort Fillmore.

Old Doc jutted his beard. "Now, by God," he calculated dourly, "we'll see whether the red son means just to flap his wings and crow to show off how fancy he is, or whether he really aims to fly up in our faces. We'll know soon enough."

"How so?" said Cullross, no student of Indians but under the circumstances eager to learn.

"By the bite of his spurs sunk shank-deep in our backsides," growled the old man.

Linn Sparhawk laughed softly. "That's a pretty good trick, isn't it, Doc? Flying up in our faces at the same time he's putting the petmakers to us from behind? That's sort of both ways against the middle with a kick in the pants thrown in for confusing good measure, I'd say."

"You'd say right, too, boy." Doc's answer came quick and without the laugh. "It's the way they operate. Raise all hell out in front of you with fifty bucks, while five sneak in behind you and slip a goddamn butcher knife between your shoulder blades."

"I know," Linn quieted him, "but my guess is they'll not hit us, front or rear, today. I reckoned all along old Mangas was waiting for something and now I reckon I know what it was." As he talked, the Alabaman had raised the field glasses once more, this time peering through them toward Fort Webster and the Pinos Altos foothills.

"What is it?" asked Doc Harnaday, squinting and shading his eyes to follow the point of the glasses.

"An audience," answered Sparhawk softly, and handed him the glasses.

The old man took them, bringing up quickly. They all saw the tilt of his ragged beard steepen sharply.

"What the devil is it?" demanded Price Cullross.

"Company!" groaned Doc, gritting his stumpy teeth. "Oh God A'mighty—kids, squaws, dogs, old people, pack mules, cookpots—Jesus—the whole pirooting kit and kaboodle of them come down to set up camp and see the fun!" He put

118

down the glasses, saying under breath and to himself, bitter as lye water, "Well, that does it. If we wasn't in over our hocks before, we sure as skunk juice stinks are up to our bellies now."

His listeners did not hear his concluding remark. The mere mention of women and children approaching brought a misbeat of hopeful excitement to their anxious hearts. Now, surely, things would be different. With their families here, with their patient squaws and butter-fat little babies to soften their fierceness and with their sage old elders to counsel moderation and restraint, now surely the Apache men would decide to go slow, would, quickly enough and as Frank Swango had predicted, raise the siege and wander off to look for other, easier game.

Doc Harnaday knew better. He saw the mistaken gladness leap up in his friends' eyes and he knew what they were thinking and what he had to tell them.

He held up a big-knuckled hand. "I'm afraid this ain't exactly good news, folks," he said. "Was I you, I wouldn't let the idea of them Apache women and their button-eyed young ones get mixed up in my mind with normal human beings."

"What are you saying, Old Man?" asked Price Cullross.

"Just what I did a minute ago. If our fat wasn't already well done, it's fell in the fire and burnt to a chitling crisp now."

"How's that, Doc?" It was Lucy Henderson's turn and she took it, still satisfied that the appearance of their blanketed mates could not help but exert some "civilizing" influence on the murderous aims of the Apache males. How could it be otherwise? They were women, weren't they?

Again Doc sensed the unspoken, wrong thinking; stepped on it before it could spread. As was his fashion, he spat and bobbed his whiskers to warn them this was a considered opinion.

"Folks, if I had my druthers," he said, twisting his mouth to the bad taste of the thought, "I'd sooner get caught alive by a hundred Apache bucks than dead by six of their squaws."

He stopped, shook his head, went on again. "Apache women are so ugly they wouldn't stand no chance in a beauty contest with a blue-nosed baboon. But they've got the faces of little pink-nubbined cherubs compared to the hell that's inside of them.

"Happen they hadn't come down to sit in on the show,

119

we would have had a fair chance. Old Mangas might well have got bored and wandered off after a spell. Injuns will do that, you know. They're like kids that way. They bore pretty fast if there's nobody around to show off in front of. But that's all changed now, all changed. With the squaws here, everything's different. There's no need of our guessing what they'll do now."

His voice trailed off into another headshake, and they all sat there thinking it over.

"Señor Doc," Cipher Reno's question wavered bravely out of the stillness, the voice small but steady trying to be a man among men, "que hubo? Que pasa con los Indios ahora? What weel they do now, Doc?"

The old man looked at the boy. He handed the field glasses back to Linn Sparhawk, picked up his rifle, checked its breech to see that it was loaded. Putting his bony hand absently on the half-breed youth's dark head, he patted him quickly and awkwardly.

"They'll stay now, kid," he said, and walked off and left it just that bobtailed, four-word way.

There wasn't a shot fired the rest of that day. The Indians didn't even bother to keep a lookout up on top of "Mount Mangas," as Linn was calling Red Sleeves' elevated outcrop.

They seemed to act as though they didn't quite know what to do about their cornered prey. A few of them rode up and down the west side of the wash, appearing to study the lay of the land around the station. Half a dozen crossed over north of the corral and climbed a mesa to the east, evidently for the same purpose. The trapped El Pasans could tell from the obvious motions and handsigns of the Apaches that the latter were discussing them and what to do about them, yet they went about it so calmly and unhurriedly that the group began to wonder hopefully if the red men were not beginning to consider letting them go.

This possibility was not entirely the deduction of the inexperienced members of the party. Even old Doc was puzzled.

"Well, by God, I frankly don't know," he frowned in answer to Jake Bergerman's gentle-voiced query on the subject. "It could be they've gone soft since last I fought them. That was in '58, when we first started running west of El Paso. Matter of fact, it was this same Mangas Red Sleeves rascal that time, too. But like I say, Jake, I just don't rightly know what to think." He wandered off, shaking his head, and Linn took up the question where he had abandoned it.

"There may be a chance they'll pull out, at that," he suggested, thinking out loud. "The main thing is not to get nervous and shoot before they do. Like Doc says, you just can't tell, but the way they're acting, it does begin to look a little hopeful now."

"Well, Señor Leen," objected Cipher Reno who, deserting the Alabaman somewhat, had taken to being much with Jake Bergerman of late, drawn to the little Jew by the latter's fatherly comfort and good counsel and by the common loneliness of strangers in an alien land, "that isn't true. The Apache *jefe* has seen our two fat mules and our three good horses. He has seen, as well, how few we are. What then of these things? *Entiende Ud., señor?*"

"I see, *amigo*," admitted Linn, "and you are right. An Apache will cut out his mother's kidneys for a good piece of mulemeat."

"Or," amplified Doc, "his father's *cojones* for a brace of blood horses like them Waterfield bays."

"Ach!" sighed Jake, palming his small hands. "It just doesn't make good business that they should let us go. If it is white blood they want, where will they get it any cheaper? And with a little brown and black mixed in for nothing extra charged? Ah no, my friends?" He put his arms around Cipher Reno proudly. "We have talked of this thing, the boy and me. We know what is the truth here. It is hard to fool an old man and a boy. Very hard, my friends. You don't have to hide this thing from us. The boy and me, we are not as afraid as you think."

"Maybe we never thought you were afraid, Jake," smiled Linn Sparhawk.

"Thanks," said the little bookkeeper with great dignity. "It is good to hear that."

"*Si, señor*," added Cipher Reno gravely. "*Es muy bueno.*"

"All right! All right!" snorted Doc, embarrassed. "That's enough medals passed around. Let's get back down to cases."

"Sure," said Linn. "What'll the first one be?"

"The first one is I got a bad notion everything over there to the spring ain't so all-fired rosy that we can start waving good-bye to them red sons just yet."

"I'll buy that, Old Man," said Price Cullross, coming to life. "You got any special idea what they might be up to?"

"Yes and no."

"Never mind the no."

"Good enough. Now then, supposing I'm right and Mangas wants mainly to show off for the women—I mean as long as they're down here and camped and all?

"Well, sir, there ain't no better way in the Apache world to do that than to take off the rest of the day to talk it up, which I will bet you last summer's sweat they're doing this very minute."

"Go on," said Cullross, no longer easy about it.

"All right, it goes this way. From the talk comes the rest of it. And quick. Along about sunset—and I mean *this* sunset—they get all painted up, break out the drums, take on a bowlegged load of *mescal*, *pulque*, *tiswin* or whatever corn or cactus-mash poison the squaws brung along from home, light a fifteen-foot bonfire and proceed to put on one hell of an all-night scalp dance before saddling up and swarming us under come sunup tomorrow morning!"

Cullross stood back, his curiosity quenched. Past Doc's dismal opinion there wasn't much point in probing the brighter side of their prospects. The old man had been there before; he ought to know all about it. Nonetheless, the big Texan made an honest try or two. It was charity wasted. Doc remained adamant. The Mimbres were building up to a big dance.

"Come sundown, you'll see I'm right," he argued. "The drums will start up and they'll do an Injun buck-and-wing till broad day."

"Then what, Doc?" Lucy Henderson had to know.

"Then us," said the old man. "Pared apart and parboiled for breakfast."

"Well," observed Price Cullross, still trying, "It's a social spirit not unknown to the white brother. Who wants to eat when there's still redeye around? Many's the time I've said myself, 'What the hell, Daddy? Putting on the steaks already and there's still some white mule in the old brown jug?'"

"Yeah," grinned Sparhawk. "Or, 'Good Lord, Mama? Supper on the table and the gin's not gone?'"

The grizzled driver was not amused. "Laugh and smirk all you're a mind to, boys. We're sitting here like a rack of hump ribs over a roasting pit. They know we're done to a turn and that we ain't going to sprout any wings and fly away. Meanwhile they're just letting us set and sizzle to keep warm till they're ready to pick us apart."

"Doc," Linn told him compassionately, "you missed your calling."

"Yes, sir," agreed Price Cullross. "You've got all the endearing young charms and overwhelming good humors of a hung-over undertaker."

The old man glared at them. He puckered up and spat over the wall savagely. "It's a natural pleasure," he grated, "to have along two such unmiscerated comedians." He split the glare down the middle to accommodate both of them. "I just don't know what we'd do for laughs at tomorrow morning's show if it wasn't for you boys."

"Coming to that," offered the big Texan, unabashed, "if these Mimbres put on as good a night show as a corn dance I once saw some Mescaleros stumble through, they won't be in any shape to go on stage tomorrow morning."

"I hope not," grunted Doc, cooling down but still on the dismal side. "I've heard tell, though, that Mangas himself don't touch the stuff. However, you never know. Apaches and hard liquor are like soldier boys and syphilis—kind of hard to keep apart."

"Services," announced Cullross in sepulchral tones, "at the funeral parlors of J. T. Harnaday at ten A.M. tomorrow morning. Interment: the beautiful Mimbres Springs Memorial Park. No flowers, please; the kinfolk won't be there to appreciate them."

Doc didn't answer him. These two youngsters weren't fooling anybody but themselves. Doc Harnaday knew where they were. And who they were all looking at. Men, especially rash young men, will joke about Death when he is known to be in the neighborhood. Old men never laugh about dying. That is because Death is closer for them. He isn't only in the neighborhood for the old ones but coming right up their street, turning in their front walks and standing on their front stoops, just outside the door. Doc knew the look of him well. He had seen him through the door before.

In that following long moment on the rooftop of the Mimbres Springs stationhouse, he took another good look at Death. Then, because the others couldn't see who was waiting there just beyond the corral wall, and because they were young and had a right to be brave and to laugh, he forgave them both and only nodded quietly to Linn Sparhawk, "Well, boy, I think you'd ought to go down below and get yourself some sleep. It's most five o'clock and you'll want to ride by eight."

123

"That's so, Doc," murmured the Alabaman, the guilt of his having helped Cullross rawhide the old man showing in the way he dropped his eyes. "Price, you get me up, will you?"

It was the first time any of them had heard him call the Texan by his first name, and the hard-faced adventurer seemed to like the sound of it.

"Sparrowhawk," he answered warmly, borrowing the affectionate corruption of Sparhawk, "you can trust me like a brother. I'll be down to tap you gently at ten minutes before the hour. Blue Bolt will be under saddle and set to go. Rest easy, Old Son. Henry Price Cullross III is on the job."

Linn smiled gratefully, touched his fingers to his forehead in an awkward little wave and started for the station-house stairs.

The big man stepped after him, calling softly.

"Kid . . ."

Linn turned around.

Cullross held out his hand. "Just for luck," he said. "Like the Old Man says, you never know."

"You never do," answered Linn Sparhawk soberly, and took Price Cullross's hand with quiet pride.

14

At six o'clock sunset the Apaches began getting ready for their dance. The El Pasans could see them with unpleasant clearness. It was no more than just out of long rifleshot to the big campsite in the cottonwoods beyong the spring. The trees were placed well apart, there was no underbrush. The early twilight was calm, the air clear as distilled water.

The *tiswin* went around in colorful dried-gourd drinking vessels. The antelope horn, wolf-skull and horse-tail headdresses were unpacked and put on. The startling black and white and yellow ochre war paint was mixed and daubed on, the tall narrow cowhide drums unslung from their carrying covers and started into their primal rhythms. The cookfires were ignited by the prehistoric spinning stick method, and fed carefully into proper beds of roasting coals. Beyond their growing light, hung head-down from a handy cotton-wood limb and looking strangely like a giant, naked jack-rabbit, was the gutted carcass of the fat pack mule slaughtered for the coming feast. On the near side of the fire the drummers squatted on their hams picking up the beat of their own deep-grunted chant. Faster and faster moved their calloused palms; still deeper and more excited grew their barking cries. Their hunched bodies swayed and bent grotesquely low to the increasing cadence of their wild music, and shortly, in response to the savage call, the headdressed dancers began to move out and around the fire in a sinuous, stomping, body-whipping snake line of growling, drink-crazed warriors whose weird cries and whirling gyrations the white watchers found morbidly hypnotic.

It was like watching the gallows makers erecting outside the window of their prison cell the scaffold upon which, in the drear gray of the coming dawn, they would be hanged by the neck until they were dead.

They could see the carpenters. They could hear their busy hammers. They knew what they were building and for whom they were building it. Yet they could no more rid their imaginations of the grisly picture by taking their eyes from it than could the condemned man shut out the ticking of the prison clock by putting his fingers in his panic-stricken ears. So they watched it and they suffered it and they kept their fearful silence like their fellows around them—frightened halfway out of their remaining wits but not man nor woman enough, any of them, to admit it to each other and so be done with it.

Meanwhile the sun went down. Night came on. The dance built drunkenly to its climax. Sim and Cipher Reno saddled Blue Bolt and brought him from the horse shed to the stationhouse. The powerful black man dug away the dirt and moved the overturned wagon in the gate just enough to pass a horse and rider by it. With that, it was time for Price Cullross to go down and awaken Linn Sparhawk—their Fort Fillmore courier and their last best chance to be alive tomorrow night.

"I'll go down with you," whispered Lucy Henderson to the Texan. "I want to say good-bye to Linn."

Sim and Jake and Cipher Reno moved forward out of the dark muttering their own desires to bid farewell to the popular little Alabaman.

Price Cullross demurred.

"Let me talk to him first, Miss Lucy," he suggested. "The

rest of you too. Then I'll send him up to see you all before he rides out. He'll likely want a minute to come awake and get ahold of himself down below."

"All right," the tall girl agreed. "But call me down there before he comes up here to see the others. I want a minute alone with him."

"His luck," said the handsome Texan, in tones meant for her hearing and not the others. "I wish it had been mine."

"It might have been, Price!" she whispered impulsively, drawn to him in that minute by his quiet, rock-strong way. "It truly might."

"Yes," he answered, reading her charitable intent and accepting it like the Southern gentleman he was. "A man draws all kinds of hands in a lifetime." Then sweeping off his wide black hat and bowing in that sardonic, good-humored way of his, "The shame of the House of Cullross salutes you, ma'am. Old Henry's poorest son regrets he has but one life to offer in the service of his Union lady."

With that Price Cullross was gone. They heard him feeling his way down the adobe stairway; then some muffled sounds of talking in the room below. This was followed by the soft thud of Blue Bolt's shoeless feet—the gelding had been unshod by Cullross while Linn slept, so that no iron might strike a rock spark or ring out a warning noise in the dark—moving quickly toward and through the corral gateway, and then, suddenly, nothing.

The stillness stretched warningly long. Lucy Henderson sprang up in premonitory alarm, her heart pounding with a fierce, nameless anxiety. But old Doc's taloned hand shot out of the darkness, slamming her rudely back down upon the roof decking.

"Get down and keep down, damn you!" he hissed at her. "You want to give him dead away before he's forty feet gone?"

"But, Doc, he didn't come up to say good-bye!"

"Hell, I know that. Course he didn't. Good-byes are for people who ain't coming back. Now hush up your noise and leave me pick him up in the glasses."

She subsided and presently the old man had centered horse and rider moving east on a fast walk.

"I can make them out fine," he muttered happily. "He's got the roan nose-wrapped proper and is hand-leading him off to one side of the road, careful and quiet through good heavy brush. Good, good. Right where he ought to be. Now he mounts up. Still holding him in a fast walk though. That's

126

right, boy, that's right. Easy, easy. No sign of trouble anywhere. Picking up a little speed now—and, there—he's gone
over yonder rise safe and sound. Thank God. Not a peep nor
a pry out of the murdering Mimbres the whole way. Jesus,
I am glad."

He dropped the glasses, wiping his eyes to get the "straining" sweat out of them, or so he claimed.

"Well, the boy's made it," he muttered weakly, after a minute. "I'd have died with him, happen those red apes had
jumped him just now."

"I reckon two of us would, Doc," breathed Lucy Henderson thankfully.

"Three, missy," muttered Sim at her elbow.

"Cuatro," corrected Cipher Reno Sanchez.

"Fünf," concluded Jake Bergerman happily.

The full company having voted its heartfelt favor of the
soft-voiced Southern boy, they all fell silent awaiting Cullross's return and his report on Linn's departing words for the
various ones.

Shortly, they heard his step on the stationhouse stairs,
then saw his shadow rise out of the stairwell's greater blackness. He took a step forward, mumbled something inco-
herent, staggered and fell face down on the rooftop.

Lucy was the first to reach him.

As she did, the climbing moon broke its thin rim clear of
the far-off Florida Mountains, lighting up the night like a
cabin lamp. The starting girl gasped and felt her heart stop.
The man on the roof was not Price Cullross. It was Linn
Sparhawk.

When they turned the Alabaman over they found a
crumpled note tucked into his shirt pocket. Lucy Henderson
unfolded it and read it aloud to the rest of them:

Sparrowhawk—
Herewith in grateful return of the 2 x 4 love-tap you loaned me
back in the old El Paso courtyard. I'll try to bring Miss Lucy
and you a suitable wedding present from Fort Fillmore. If not,
three cheers for the Stars and Bars, and God bless us one and all
until we're better paid. Yr. Obt. Svt.,

                                            H. P. Cullross III

There being scarcely any postscript any of them could add
to that, none of them tried. Back of Linn's ear they discovered the goose egg-sized lump which figured from the

opening line of Price's note. By that they deduced the Texan had hit him from behind. But they could not decipher the "grateful" part of the note's reference to the blow until Linn regained consciousness and told them Cullross had confided to him down below that he had really meant to shoot Lucy Henderson that night in the El Paso courtyard and that he was eternally grateful, as things turned out, that Linn had hit him and kept him from doing it.

Old Doc growled that the "sneaking Johnny Reb" no doubt meant to rejoin his guerrilla friends in Mesilla and had no more honorable intention of trying to reach the Union troops at Fort Fillmore than he had of continuing on up North and enlisting in the U.S. Army at Fort Craig.

But Linn shook his head in rebuttal and said no, he reckoned they still none of them rightly understood Southerners. For money-back certain, Price aimed to do the right thing. It was just that, like so many down South, he couldn't keep his regional ego in line. When there was a chance to play the lead, he wasn't going to settle for any spear-carrying parts.

With Price it was just like it was going to be with the whole Confederate Army when the war really got under way—ten commissioned officers for every fighting private in the line—and six of the ten full generals with no military training past riding a horse and handling firearms since they shed their milk teeth. There was, the Alabaman nodded softly, only the one remaining thing a person had to say for the rough-riding Texan. Price Cullross was, like Frank Swango before him, and taken for all and all, a man.

After Sparhawk's simple tribute things got very quiet again on the stationhouse roof. Sporadically, the prayerful group catnapped and whispered the night away. There was no chance for decent sleep. Not with the way the Apache dance was going. It must have been pushing three o'clock in the morning before the Mimbres decided to wind things up with some sort of an initiation or trial-by-fire for one of the bucks.

The watchers on the roof saw his fellow warriors dragging this unlucky candidate up to the main fire, but by the time they got the glasses on them the Indian audience had swarmed so thick around the initiate they couldn't make out what they were doing to him.

But they could hear it. The poor devil's inhuman scream would have lifted the hackles of fear in a deaf-mute. It was

128

literally hair-raising. Old Doc came rearing up off his blanket fumbling groggily for his Sharps and yelling, "Give 'em both barrels, boys! They're over the walls!"

Linn grabbed him and tried to quiet him down by explaining it was just one of Mangas's braves getting branded in one of their regular war-lodge ceremonies—most likely a young buck out on his first war party—but the old man wouldn't quiet. He kept worrying about that yell and wanting to talk about it. Linn still wouldn't listen to him. The Alabaman believed what he had told him, and beyond that didn't want Lucy Henderson to have to hear any more Apache talk than was minimumly necessary. There was Cipher Reno too, and poor gentle old Jake. No use working them up past what was needful, either. He stood fast in front of Doc's instinctive concern over the yell and finally the old man gave it up and said, "Well, hell, whatever it was it's got me and sleep as come apart as a poor-tied pack and a pitching mule. Might as well set up and chat cheerful, I allow."

He did just that too, regaling Sparhawk and Lucy Henderson until five o'clock daylight with tales of the old '49 and '50 days of staging through the California Sierras. He carried on about Three-Fingered Jack, Dick Fellows, Manuel Montez, Black Bart, Joaquin Murietta and all the other Mother Lode badmen, large and small, as though he had been raised with them on the same bottle or at least slept with all their sisters or witnessed their wills or rendered them some other such bosom-friendly service as would make him forever their dear pal and trusted partner.

The plain truth was, his listeners knew perfectly well, he had left California's gold camps well before any of the rascals had got famous and, in fact, well before most of them had even taken up hoisting Concords on a professional basis. Still they let him ramble on, and actually were more than glad to do so as his improving mood fitted in nicely with their own burgeoning hopes.

For they were both thinking of Price Cullross riding for the Rio Grande. They were praying hard for him and for themselves. And they were beginning to believe firmly there was a real chance he would save them.

And why not? The Texan, with his very fast horse and unseen getaway, could actually do it. He *could* get through to Fillmore and back with the Federal troops in time. That was the simple truth. It really was.

He had left at eight o'clock. That meant he could easily

pull the fort by midnight on a racer like Blue Bolt. Then give the Fort Webster boys that were resting there another six hours to mount up and make the return ride to Mimbres Springs. That was giving fair time. That wasn't stretching the facts or being blindly wishful. And the result had to be, for certain, that come six o'clock sunrise they could all expect to look out over the front wall and see Price Cullross riding back at the head of that blessed blue cavalry patrol of Sergeant A. E. Zimmerman.

In one respect they were right. When they looked over the front wall that morning they did see Price Cullross. Only it was not six o'clock, it was barely five o'clock. And the big Texan had not ridden back, he'd been carried back.

They stood staring down over the gateway wall at the contorted figure lying on the ground ten feet from the overturned wagon blocking the entrance to the Mimbres Spring corral. None of them in the first minute of realization were able to move or speak. Then Linn Sparhawk said, "All right, Sim, go out and get him," and the big Negro dropped over the nine-foot-high wall like a puma easing down off a mountain ledge. He scooped up the limp form of the guerrilla leader and sprang to the top of the overturned wagon in the gate and on into the corral with his burden. The movement required no more time nor effort than it might take a jungle man-eater to leap a native kraal, seize his victim and bound back over the encircling thorn boma. But Price Cullross was not asleep; at least he would never awaken again.

When Sim brought him into the stationhouse Linn and Doc were already down below to receive him. There did not appear to be a mark of any kind upon him, but Lucy Henderson, peering down unseen from the burn-through in the roof, saw Doc immediately turn the Texan's body over and then let it fall quickly back to lie face up again. As the terrible grimace was still twisting the old driver's face and just before Linn looked up to catch her spying at the rooftop hole, the horrified girl heard Doc say, "God help him, boy, that screech we heard this morning was his."

"Oh, Lord, no! That wasn't Price," groaned Linn. "It couldn't have been, Doc! No white man could make a noise like that. God, he just couldn't . . . !

The old man shook his head the way a dog will with a dirty piece of meat in his mouth; one he wants to get the sand and grit and bitter-leaf and bits of stick off of.

He got up and went to stand in the doorway, the faint

130

pink of the coming sun touching the gray marble of his face. Lucy Henderson had never seen such a look of sick fury on the features of any human being.

"He could," he answered Linn, thick-voiced, "with the fire-heated barrel of a broken rifle shoved up his bowels to the breechlock."

15

They never found out how the Apaches caught Price Cullross, or when, or where. The best guess was probably Doc's. The old man allowed they had let the Texan get over the rise on purpose, having him under watch and stalk the whole way. Then, once out of sight of the station, they had jumped him. They were like that, Doc said. The Mimbres most of all and Mangas most of the Mimbres.

Even his own people recognized his special talent for torture. They didn't call him Red Sleeves up in the Pinos Altos. That was his own vain choice of titles, taken from his pride in his famous red-lined coat. They called him "El Gato," after his Mexican name meaning "The Cat." And like a cat he was, Doc averred.

First trap the game. Then let it think it was going to get away. Even let it actually escape. Let it get a good start toward precious freedom. Let it begin believing it was safe, start thinking joyous thoughts of life's regained sweetness. Then *whoompff!* land on it with all fours. Seize it skillfully in your teeth so as not to harm a hair of its terrified head. Bear it back to your denning spot for your mate and the cubs to play with. Then, when the time came, when all had had their fill of hurting it short of death, kill it with the utmost pain and cruelty possible.

"And," muttered the old man in morbid conclusion, "the way poor Cullross went under wasn't bad news only for him. The quick quietus they gave him shows they mean not to fool with us no more. They'll come for our hair, now; there's no middleways maybes about that."

He paused to spit dispiritedly.

"It's why they took the trouble to sneak the boy's body

up here in the dark of this morning. Injuns are funny in ways like that; they're weird funny. They'll near always tell you just what they aim to do to you, providing a man knows how to read the signs they leave. And God knows, I know how to read 'em."

Doc trailed off, wagging his stained beard and muttering to himself. He had run out of hope and of ways to hide the fact from his friends.

The latter nodded and said nothing. They were back on the stationhouse roof once more, just the three of them— Linn, Doc, Lucy Henderson. Of the others, Sim had gone to carry Price's body to the horse shed to lay it out with those of Frank and the five Apaches. Cipher Reno had trotted ahead of him to take up the watch atop the horse shed, and Jake Bergerman was in the stationhouse room below trying to prepare breakfast for the full company.

As to eating just then, not a one of them wanted to. But Sparhawk had insisted they must do so. Strangely enough, no one had questioned him when he gave the order. At a time when, on a basis of past experience, it would seem that Doc should have succeeded Frank Swango in command, the El Pasans, including the old man himself, were looking to the consumptive Alabaman.

Now the latter was studying the grizzled driver, then saying, "Doc, you sure about the meaning of them leaving Price out front just now?"

"As sure as I am that spit travels smoothest downwind. Why?"

"Well," said Linn, "I always figured that if a man let me know he was going to hit me, it gave me the choice of ducking or hitting him first."

"I'll set still for that option. What next?"

"Well, there's clearly no place to duck hereabouts."

"So?"

"We swing first."

"And?"

"We've been holding our fire, figuring not to stir them up. Right?"

"As spring rain in sprouting time. So what?"

"So they're doubtless doing plenty of wondering about us right now. 'What's the matter with those white fools?' they're asking themselves. 'They've had plenty of good chances to shoot at us, why haven't they done so? Are they low on ammunition? Do they have only two or three old guns which are not much good? Are they all new to this country? Do

132

they not know there is an Indian war going on?' and all such questions as that. Do you follow me, Doc?"

"Not very far, boy. Back up and take another short run at it."

"All right, you said Mangas was like a cat, Correct?"

"He's licking poor Cullross off his whiskers right now, ain't he?"

"Yes, he is."

"Well then?"

"Well then, it was curiosity killed the original feline, wasn't it?"

"The original what?"

"Cat."

Slowly the light of Linn's idea dawned on Doc Harnaday.

"Curiosity, by Christ!" he burst out. "Say, boy, I do believe you've hit on it. Why, God damn it! If we can lay low enough to lure a big part of them real close in, we can really clobber them!"

"We can," smiled the pale-faced Alabaman, picking up his field glasses once again. "Run over and call in Sim and Cipher Reno for breakfast, while I give a look-see to the 'matoo-shunal alblooshuns' of the Pinos Altos Apaches."

"Watch your language!" snapped the old man, the spirit of the game flickering up in him momentarily. "There's a lady present."

"On your way, Sir Walter," grinned Sparhawk, trying to play it out. "And while you're about it, keep your bony old backside down off the skyline."

It was a perfect opening either for a return line of their little play, or for one of Doc's run-of-the-mill profanities. The latter, significantly, said nothing, his unwonted silence suddenly reminding his other listeners that but for the past moment's quick-fading flare-up of excitement over Linn's Apache-luring proposal, they had not heard the doughty old driver utter a really heartfelt curse since Price Cullross had called him down for overruling the Alabaman back at Membrace Station.

It was a curious and not a reassuring omission on the old man's part, but his companions were given little time to explore its likely causes. Doc scuttled across the roof to the stairwell, taking obedient care to stay below the lip of the wall, as ordered. He backed crabwise down the stairs, not even a mumble of protest marking his retreat. Once out of the stationhouse below, he loped swiftly across the corral to the horse shed. He was back shortly with the sphinxlike Sim

133

and the very worried Sanchez boy. Behind them came faithful, smoke-grinned Jake Bergerman bearing his gallant effort at breakfast for six al fresco.

No one let on the fare was atrociously bad. All accepted their shares of the half-raw bacon and fried flour-paste pancakes, complimenting Jake on their goodness, forcing down both the food and the falsehoods with grimacing gulps of the truly fierce cistern-water coffee. As they did, Sparhawk kept field-glass watch on the enemy.

The Apache camp was by this time alive with activity, the general purpose of which required no glasses to make clear. The Alabaman was only seeing it bigger than the rest of them, not any better. He was the detailed translator, nonetheless.

The Indians were, he reported tersely, clearly getting ready to attack them. The ponies were being run in from the grazing herd. Rifles were being removed from their leather covers and checked for function of action before loading. Face paint was being freshened, war charms fastened on, headdresses shaken out and donned.

Across the morning fires, mesquite-spitted slabs of mulemeat were roasting in great abundance. And across the smoking slabs of mulemeat, battle instructions were being issued by Mangas Coloradas himself, strutting and posturing and striking himself in the chest repeatedly, the while leaving no doubt in the minds of any of his viewers, white, red, brown or black, that he fancied himself tremendously in a new wide black hat of Texas cut and Confederate cavalry brimcurl which he had not worn the day before.

It was this throat-tightening scene ending with the Mimbres chief stalking arrogantly about in Price Cullross's familiar black Stetson which Linn Sparhawk described in field-glass detail while his companions watched with him and listened without an interrupting word.

When he had finished, he began quietly giving out his orders for their own counterattack.

"Now then," he advised, waving toward the Apache preparations, "don't strain yourselves in that direction. Pay attention to me, not Mangas. It will take him some time to get them steamed up to make their big move. Meanwhile, here's ours and I honestly believe it is a good one."

As he went along expanding on his idea to draw the Indians in close for a surprise broadside, he talked quite seriously. Yet now and again, as he could see one of them beginning to weaken, he would throw in a quick smile or one of his

134

salty phrases to buck up his frightened companions. Before long he had them listening with more than their ears. Shortly, they were beginning to think a little. Even to believe.

He freely admitted the success of the gamble depended on his questionable guess that the Apaches would do what the lay of the land around the station suggested to him that they would. Which was that they would make their real play from the west wash, the closest-in good cover to the corral walls.

His words, unsupported, would not have done it. But old Doc, who had fought the Mimbres and the Comanches before them for thirty years, said that he rightly felt the Alabama boy was ninety-eight percent correct in his Apache guess, and the others took heart from that and perked up by the minute.

As Sparhawk outlined it, their position was this: In picking the site of the Waterfield station at Mimbres Springs, the American Mail Company's route surveyors had picked exceedingly well. The thin Southerner, as he talked, sketched a deft map on the stationhouse wall to demonstrate for his friends why this was so, and why his resulting idea of a west-wash assault by the Indians was a sound one.

Yet he did not try to delude them. Beyond its supposition that the Apaches *would* rush them from the direction of the dry wash, there lay the remainder of the defensive gamble in his guess: the risky placement of all their firepower behind the west wall of the stationhouse roof, leaving all other points around the corral unguarded for that whole dangerous time of waiting which now lay between them and the first wild yell of the Indian charge—wherever it might come from.

Still, if he was right, the damage they could do to the Apaches in the space of five seconds at a range where the powder blast would burn their shaggy bangs, would be appalling—even by Mimbreño standards. If he was wrong, it would be the last mistake he ever made or any of the rest of them ever remembered him making.

He concluded by reviewing their own ability to hurt the Apache. The review was, in all, hopeful.

Linn himself, like so many plantation-reared Southern youths, was a swift and certain shot. He had passed on a degree of this skill, via random instructions behind the Waterfield horse barn, to Cipher Reno Sanchez. Sim, although not handy with either rifle or revolver, was a master of the shotgun. He had picked up the art of smooth-bore wing-shooting while teaching his former owner's young son to shoot upland birds. He would be no threat to the enemy beyond forty yards, but what he could do with Frank Swango's cylinder-bored double twelve under thirty yards would be something you wouldn't want to watch. Doc Harnaday and his old Sharps could, by the crusty oldster's own indelicate admission, "hit a yearling bull in the bung at 900 yards," provided, of course, that the critter "had his tail up, just so." Jake Bergerman had never fired a gun in his life, nor had his hands on one, by his own plainly scared statement. But he could be taught to load, point and pull the trigger by dry instruction inside of half an hour, granted the Mimbres held off that long. Coming to Lucy Henderson, she was a Southern girl raised in the Virginia hill country. While certainly no Indian fighter, she knew which end of a maplestock muzzle loader the wad and patch went in.

So then, that was it.

The Alabaman finished his listing of their military assets, held up his hand to quiet their still doubtful and immediate questions. Obediently they fell silent, awaiting his final words for whatever they might prove to be worth.

Lucy Henderson never forgot those words. She was equally sure the others didn't forget them either; and that they found in them the same strength and spirit with which to go on as did she.

He regarded them a moment with his soft, quizzically shy smile, the steadying light of complete assurance showing in his blue-green eyes. Then, spreading his pale hands in that simple, all-warming gesture of his, which somehow or other seemed always to make things look better than they really were, he said it to them very quietly.

"I just want to remind you all of something the Lord gave us to fight with that beats guns and bullets all hollow. It's from Romans 5:3. Likely you'll remember it. In it we're told to rejoice in our sufferings, knowing that suffering produces endurance, and endurance produces character, and character produces hope, and hope does not disappoint us."

He looked at them another little time, and added gently, "It's that hope I'm talking about and counting on. The Lord's hope, folks. He won't let it fail or disappoint us, if we ourselves don't fail it or disappoint Him. I reckon you know that and believe it as sure as I do."

"Amen," said old Doc softly; and he didn't say it to be smart or sharp or wise in any way, but only to let Linn Sparhawk know that they did believe with him and that they were, each one, grateful to him for the Word.

After that there was no more talk. Their lines were drawn, their lives committed, their weapons primed, their prayers said. Only the waiting remained.

About seven o'clock the Indians began to move.

The survivors in the Waterfield corral could see them mounting up and slipping away from their camp among the spring-swale cottonwoods.

Some rode north out of the grove, some south. They left in small groups of three or four warriors, making no fuss. It looked as though they were up to anything but massing for an attack on the adobe-walled stage-line fortress. None of them went near Linn Sparhawk's much discussed western dry wash. In twenty minutes the last of them was out of sight and the camp was quiet save for the movement of the squaws coming and going about their open-air housework, and the incongruous laughter and happy splashing of the copper-bodied little boys and girls swimming in the spring.

"Looks to me," worried Doc to Linn, "like they're swinging wide to go clear around and come at us from the east, same as their five friends did Frank yesterday. I'm beginning to wonder a mite about that west wash idea of yours, boy."

"Well don't," advised the Alabaman, about as short with it as any of them had heard him be with anything. "It's exactly what I expected. Them going around to the east that way is pure bunkum. They want us to think that's where they're going."

"Sometimes," said Doc, "it don't pay to be too smart. Not with Apaches. They wrote the book on being foxy."

"Precisely so," nodded Linn Sparhawk, and went right on watching his empty dry wash.

An hour passed. Two. Three. Between the station and the spring not a lizard stirred. Ten o'clock came.

Across the wash now the Apache women sat against the boles of the ancient cottonwoods smoking their short stone pipes and puffing on the evil black Sonora *cigarillos* which were their preferred addiction. The children still played in and about the spring as oblivious as children everywhere to the wickedness in the hearts and minds of their elders.

Suddenly old Doc straightened. He had just turned for the hundredth uneasy time to check his conviction that the west wash was now out of consideration as an assault base and that the Mimbres meant to attack from the east, or high ground, side of the station.

None of his companions saw his pouchy eyes widen but they all heard the strangled yell which accompanied the stricken look. It was a wordless yell but its warning was more compelling than many a prepared speech. They—all of them, save Sparhawk who never took his eyes off the western approaches—spun around to see what it was that had so choked up the old man he couldn't do better than a bug-eyed sputter.

When they saw it, they knew exactly how Doc Harnaday felt. Their own heartbeats came up in their throats so thick and heavy they smothered their breathing and made their stomachs sick.

Over along the crown of the eastern mesa a line of mounted Apaches bristled against the morning sun black and menacing as the guard hairs of an angry wolf's back. Even as they discovered them, the Mimbres threw up their rifles and fired them, one-handed, into the air. They reared and spun their painted ponies, screamed insults and unspeakable threats at their cornered victims. They galloped wildly back and forth along the mesa's rim, shaking their guns and their gaudy war lances, giving out their yammering, crazy war cries and in general starting the sort of hackles-raising ruckus that horseback Indians always do before any kind of a final charge.

But in this case there was something patently spurious about that demonstration on the mesa. Its mounted line was too thin, for all the milling effort to make it appear otherwise. Look out. *Tenga cuidado.* They were up to something. Watch the devils.

Doc and Linn had counted the Apaches out of the cottonwood grove earlier that morning. Their figure, give or take a dozen they might have missed, was near a hundred head. Yet those ugly beauties doing all that yelling over on the east mesa would not total half that number.

Question: Where were the other fifty? Companion question: What were they up to?

The breath-held white party got both answers in the next instant, when the heavy crash of Linn Sparhawk's Springfield behind them brought them whirling back around to face west again.

Where the missing fifty Apaches had been was exactly where Linn had said they would be, *in the dry wash.*

And what they were up to was racing on foot and bent

138

double, swift and silent as so many wind-driven cloud shadows across the open prairie between Sparhawk's wash and the west wall of the Waterfield stage-line station at Mimbres Springs, New Mexico.

The Apaches, like all desert Indians, were trained to run from weaning age. Only the Mojaves and perhaps the Pimas in their Pueblo days produced greater runners. The brush-lipped rim of the dry wash lay not over 150 yards from the stationhouse wall. The first of Mangas Coloradas' straining braves had gained a third of that distance when Linn shot him through the hips, sending him thrashing to the ground.

Indians are unpredictable. A man learns that fast in the Southwest, and the Alabaman knew it well. Sometimes they act like stampeding buffalo. If you drop a front runner those behind him will pile up against his body or split around it to veer off, and the danger of being overrun is past. Sometimes they are like wolves with hydrophobia. If there are fifty of them and you shoot forty-nine, the last one will still be coming at you if he has to climb a pile of his own dead ten feet high to die with his teeth in your throat. Mangas Coloradas' Mimbreños were not running like buffalo that day.

Doc got the second one at seventy-five yards. Cipher Reno excitedly centered his first one at fifty yards, where Linn's second shot dropped the fourth Apache. At twenty-five yards Doc got his second and Linn his third for a full count of six. Five yards from the foot of the wall Cipher Reno fired again and got the seventh buck squarely through his evil, upturned face.

That ended the first carnage. But it did not stop the Apaches. Doc and Linn had not yet reloaded and for some reason Sim had not yet fired at all. The girl, Lucy Henderson, had frozen at the first sight of the screaming warriors and had not even raised her Springfield. The fatal seconds whipped by, faster than fired bullets. They had not stemmed the red charge and the Apaches were now under the wall.

With Doc and Linn coming to their feet to stand and fire straight down, the first clot of them, swarming directly below the white riflemen, began to pyramid upward against the weathered stone and adobe of the corral wall.

They came up its vertical surface with the inhuman agility of chacma baboons. They were over its top, onto the stationhouse roof, before the dazed minds of the defenders could record the fact. They carried no ladders, flung no ropes, used no scaling equipment whatever. They simply swarmed the

139

wall like prehensile-handed apes. There was no stopping them, and Linn's and Doc's shots disappeared into their climbing mass with no visible effect.

It was then that Sim calmly came into action with Frank Swango's chopped-off shotgun. There were eight or nine Indians in that first topping wave over the wall. As they foamed onto the stationhouse roof the giant Negro, who had been standing quietly at the inner edge of the roofdeck, fired from the veteran field gunner's "ready" position, the gun halfway between hip and shoulder, shoved up and forward.

The range was perfect, just distance enough beyond point-blank to open up the pattern of the cylinder-bored gun. It was beautiful in a terrifying way.

His white companions could hear the heavy #2 shot slithering into the close-packed Apaches like a blowing rain driving into an overripe and heavily headed field of wheat. It was even more like the whacking feathery smack of #7½'s swung dead into a straightaway breaking covey of bobwhites. There was the same split-second pause between the acrid blast of the black powder and the pocking spatter of the shot getting home fifteen yards out—that endless moment when it is certain birds have been hit and are going to start dropping all over the place but when, as yet, not one has faltered in its bombarding flight.

The kindred moment before the Apaches began to drop before Sim's gooseloads was just long enough for the awed El Pasans to read the strange look on the face of each of the stricken savages; that look so familiar to every man who has ever advanced in the face of galling fire; the staring, unbelieving, bewildered look with which the comrade at his side grabs his bowels, or his side, or his chest, or his throat, and cries aloud without uttering a sound, "Oh no, not me, it cannot be me, it must not be me . . . !" And yet it is him and must always be him.

So it was with the dying Apaches. The first to spin and fall backward over the wall took two companions with him. All three were dead before they hit the ground, as were the other two who pitched forward and fell onto the roof rather than over the wall. In the same instant two more were clawing blindly to find their way with eyes no longer seeing from faces not recognizable as those of humans. Doc smashed the skull of one with his steel-shod Sharps' butt, and Linn split the head of the other with the swung barrel of his carbine. Both Indians fell twistingly downward upon the now hesitating swarm of their living fellows below.

The last survivor of the topping wave had fallen inward and was crawling around on the rooftop with his intestines trailing out, to be caught and crushed by his own tortured knees. In a display of brute strength and callousness not to be exceeded by the red enemy, Sim seized the dying warrior by one ankle and whirled him bodily outward and around his waist like a hammer thrower before popping his brains out against the rough mud of the wall and heaving him downward after his more fortunate, less slowly dead fellows.

It was too much even for the Apache stomach. The Mimbres broke and fled back for the wash. They had taken in the three minutes of their wild rush and wall-scaling assault against the Waterfield rooftop an incredible fifteen casualties.

Not even the merciless children of Mangas Coloradas cared for that kind of arithmetic. There was bound to be a long quiet spell while they sat back down around their cookfires and more carefully refigured their tactical problem. And there was. Yet the grateful El Pasans had barely turned to one another to start enjoying the respite than they discovered it was not so easy to subtract fifteen from one side and nothing from the other and still come out even.

It was Doc Harnaday. He was trying to grin and cover it up by pressing his gnarled hands hard against it, but the blood was coming out between his clutching fingers, and his face had the gray, far-off look of a man who has seen his last sunrise and is peering ahead into scenes the unstricken cannot behold with him.

He had been hit, apparently, when he stood up with Linn to fire down into the Apache pyramid just before it spilled over the top of the wall. The wound was a gaping three-inch hole high in the chest, right over the great artery of the heart. It had not been caused by a bullet but by a rusted piece of carriage bolt fired out of an unrifled Mexican army musket of muzzle-loading vintage. It was the kind of weapon and charge a man could laugh at past fifty feet. But the Apache who has used it on Doc had fired from five feet, and the old man's life was pumping out through a hole that would have killed a grizzly bear or bull elk.

His stunned friends didn't know whether the old man knew he was done for or not. And they never found out. When Linn Sparhawk spoke to him, he was gone.

141

16

When Sim came back from the horse shed there were only five of them left upon the rooftop of the Waterfield station-house. It was fifteen minutes after ten in the morning of the second day. The weather was without wind, very clear, well on its way to turning off hot again.

Across the wash there was no sign of Indian life. The children had left the spring, the squaws deserted their camp-work, the bucks returned to the grove and disappeared into its central, thickest stand.

Somewhere up the wash a quail chuckled half-heartedly. Down in the rushes of the marsh a redwing cleared his rusty throat in disinterested cross-complaint. Then nothing.

It got so quiet the rooftop watchers could hear in the powdered dust of the room below them the tiny-footed scut-tlings of the fingerling house lizards which infested every abandoned or little-used dwelling in the Southwest. The air was like crystal. They could see well over a quarter of a mile away the swarming, sun-green glint of the bottle flies blow-ing the carcass of the dead mule in the Apache camp. The stillness was a tangible thing, its import as ominous as its appearance was innocent.

It was at the moment of its deepest hush that the Mimbres women began their death song. The sound put the fear of God into all of them. The keening of the human female over the body of a lost loved one is one of the most disturbing sounds in the human world. It was bad enough in its civilized form, as most of them had heard it coming faintly from the single black-clad widow in the wings of the village chapel. As it now burst tearingly from the breasts of two dozen pagan Apache squaws in the first agony of their mass bereavement, it was completely demoralizing.

It was against this nerve-wracking background that Linn Sparhawk told them the next sixty minutes could bring the crisis of their ill-fated adventure. The degree of the women's grieving would decide it, he said. The entirely unexpected death of so many of their warriors might be blow enough to impress even the Apache imagination. Or it might prove just irritant enough to goad the Mimbres into a third suicidal rush. This rush, should it come, the little Southerner believed, would be disastrous to the defenders. Their remaining forces were simply too few to withstand another determined assault.

There was nothing to do, he concluded, save to wait and to pray—meanwhile keeping a sharp watch. While Sim and Cipher Reno mounted that watch he, Linn, would work some more with Lucy Henderson and Jake Bergerman in teaching them to load and handle the Springfield carbine, a job he had begun the previous day. Should the Indians' actions indicate a decision to starve them out rather than rush them, he added, Sim and the half-breed boy would have to man the horse-shed roof. Pending proof of such intent, however, they were to stay with the others on the stationhouse roof.

Even as the Alabaman completed his brief instructions for their conditional deployment, the Apache women stopped singing. It was immediately apparent that some other decision had been made. The bucks reappeared and began slipping out of the grove to go north and south around the station elevation. All were mounted, all rode in full view. There was no hurry, yet no indecision. Here and there in their circling ride, as a condition of local rock or brush or drainage gully suggested a good firing point, they would drop off a small detachment of two to five bucks. In half an hour they had invested the terrain around the Waterfield corral, and the helpless group within its walls was for the first time literally surrounded. It was to be a siege.

During their thirty-minute dispersal Linn Sparhawk had counted 124 of the enemy. With their women, children and old people there had to be nearly 300 Apaches camped in the cottonwood grove. The Alabaman knew the meaning of such numbers. He did not keep the fact from his friends.

Mangas's camp, he told them frankly, comprised an uncommonly, and ominously, big band for a breed of desert Indians who ordinarily hunted or traveled in small wolf packs of ten or fifteen braves and their families. Any time more than that number gathered together in one bunch it meant bad news for everybody but other Apaches. The Mimbres had shown up in force to begin with, but now it was clear that still more braves had come in during the past night. This would indicate they had been sent for. Which in turn indicated that Mangas had no intention whatever of moving on. They had to face it, Linn said quietly: the odds building against them out there in that sunlit stillness, barring a pure miracle of unsolicited military rescue, were insurmountable.

Three men—one sick with consumption, one foreign-bred and unfamiliar with firearms, one of an enslaved dark race with every reason to hate a white skin as passionately as any Apache—did not in themselves make a very good hand. Add to them only one half-breed Mexican boy and one Virginia settlement girl, and the pot only looked farther away than ever. Taken with all the gambler's gall in the history of showdown poker, their five cards would never stand up in a nightcap game with the Mimbreño Apaches. Particularly when it was remembered that the latter were the fiercest family division of an Indian people infamous from Hueco Tanks to Dragon Wells for its irrational actions and inhuman cruelties.

No, if Mangas meant to make this the last game, there was no doubt he could clean the table.

Yet, having made his compulsively honest survey of their chances following Mangas Coloradas' move to put a siege line around their high-walled adobe prison, Sparhawk now dispatched Sim and Cipher Reno to the horse shed as outwardly unperturbed as though he were Ulysses Simpson Grant ordering up more artillery on the last day outside Appomattox courthouse.

While the Alabaman would not lie to his followers, neither would he permit them to despair. He was one of those rare men who will always admit the true facts of an adversity, then set out to make a liar of logic, regardless. And such men do not surrender.

"Our main worry right now," he reassured his dispirited listeners, "is to make sure we don't let them sneak a good shot in close to where he can snipe us crazy. Now, believe me, friends, if we can do that one thing—just keep them back where they are, being quick and accurate with our shots at any who try to move up—we may still have this little war headed for a stand-off."

He waited a moment, giving them time to see any hope they might in that, then went on. "They have no way of knowing how bad hurt we are and providing we fire fast and true at every attempt they make to improve their positions, they're not going to find out. Beyond that, they don't seem to me nearly so ambitious as they were this time yesterday. I know one thing that's no guess. We've killed more Mimbres bucks in two days than the Waterfield outfit has put under in four years of running fights with all five main Apache tribes. You can't discount that kind of statistics. Not even if you're an Indian.

"Still, we've got to be extremely careful about this thing of letting them find out we're in such bad shape. The only way they can do that is to work a man up to where he can see inside the corral. There's one place, on all four sides, where they can do that. I reckon you can see it without me pointing it out for you."

They could, and that was a fact. Sparhawk waited deliberately, while they all studied the low sandstone ridge which commanded the station's south wall, midway between the front gates and Mangas's original lookout.

Its menace was clear even to Jake and Lucy. The ragged brush of its crown and the bouldered rise of its low flanks would hide a dozen braves. Its maximum elevation was the height of a man above the tops of the corral walls. A sharpshooter gaining its crest could command all but the very front wall shelter of the stationhouse roof, and entirely all of the horse-shed roof. From this advantage, and given time to evaluate and average up the emptiness and inactivity of the Waterfield corral's defenses, the Apaches would quickly arrive at the realization Sparhawk would deny them at all costs—the knowledge that the trapped party was reduced to five members, of which two were a gray-haired old man in settlement clothes and a Mexican half-breed boy no bigger than the pony-soldier gun he was trying to hold up and point across the horse-shed wall.

That sandstone ridge, Linn knew, had been the one really bothersome topographical feature to plague the route surveyors at the time of the selection of the Mimbres Springs site. They had even tried to drill and blast off its crown to get it below wall-level of the station, but the stubborn rock had defied them and they had accepted its strategic significance and gone uneasily west to stake and chain the Membrace Station site.

But whatever twinges of conscience may have accompanied the survey crews westward those four years ago, they were as nothing compared to the painful appraisals now being made of the same engineering mistake by Linn Sparhawk's nervous listeners.

When the shaggy-haired Southerner was satisfied the latter had absorbed the full tactical menace of the sandstone ridge, he made his final conclusion regarding it.

"Just remember," he told them softly. "If the Apaches get

145

to that outcrop and see they've got us hurt bad, they'll be over the walls from all four sides in less time than it will take us to let out the breath we're holding right now."

It was getting on toward four P.M. The others had long ago gone to their stations, leaving Linn and Lucy alone on the stationhouse roof. Yet in the entire dragging time they had been there, the Alabaman hadn't said one further word about the Indians, leading the frightened girl to assume he was still trying to think of some way he might mercifully tell her what he *really* thought of their situation.

He was, in fact, even now continuing his apparent effort to avoid the subject by making his seventh or eighth unnecessary check of his changed dispositions: *Sim at the wagon blocked front gate; Cipher Reno on the horse-shed roof by himself; Jake Bergerman limping around in the middle of the corral proper, leading the lazy-footed mules in an eccentric circle designed to stumble up just enough dust to intrigue and concern the Apache curiosity over what their victims were up to that might bode possible ill for themselves.*

Watching the deliberately preoccupied Southerner, Lucy Henderson decided she would assume no more, and so caught his averted eye and put it to him in a calm way he could not deny.

"Linn," she said, "I don't believe what you've been telling us about our chances. We're not going to get out of here and you know it. Now I tell you I am not afraid and I want to know the truth. I think I deserve that, don't you?"

He looked at her a minute and said quietly, "Yes, I think you do. But I rightly and firmly believe we've taken some of the flap out of Mangas's shirttails and can turn this thing into a Mexican stand-off, given any luck at all."

She studied his reply. Considering the hours and events which had passed since that morning's attack and the little Alabaman's moral lecture at noon, there did indeed seem to be some small evidence to support his stubborn optimism.

Three individual Indians had made sneaks to get in closer to the corral. Two of these had come in against Cipher Reno at the rear wall, the other one at their own station on the front wall.

The Mexican boy had driven his pair back with a brace of very good shots, getting major flesh wounds in both cases. Linn felt he had only creased his Indian, a big ugly buck who appeared to be directing immediate operations along the south wall; Mangas, being in over-all charge, issued his orders from the safe remove of the far south elevation where they had seen him the previous day.

This third Indian, Linn thought, might be Lobo, a sub-chief of treacherous reputation and high tribal rank, white report placing him second in command among the Mimbres to Mangas himself. If such a thing were possible, he was rumored to possess an even more violent hatred of Americans than his vicious chief. Closer to their own case, he was a renowned rifleman, said to be the finest Indian marksman save perhaps one, a little-known Arizona youth just beginning to make a name for himself—Geronimo.

The fact he had downed such a notable Mimbreño with a very long-range skull crimp was no doubt contributing measurably to the present state of Sparhawk's confidence. Added to the importance of dropping a famous warrior was the further fact that the particular cover for which Lobo had been racing was the vital sandstone ridge. Had he made it, all bets would have been off. From such a redoubt and range even a poor shot could turn a man's hair gray using a Mexican musket and Sonora-made powder. What a sharpshooter like Lobo might have done (not even considering what he would have seen) had he been allowed to dig himself in with his fine rifle and modern brass-cased shells, would be better left unthought about.

Coming thus again to the strategic importance of the ridge, none of the corral defenders could imagine why the Apaches had not invested it during the dark of the past night, and in the end had to accept Sparhawk's tenuous explanation of the failure.

The latter claimed it to be a simple situation where Mangas Coloradas had lived up to his Mexican name of The Cat. The Mimbreño chief, he argued, had merely not wanted to kill them that fast. Good work—true art—should take more time. Mangas had palpably made previous conscious effort to have his deployed circle look loose and careless, hoping thus to lure his victims into the sort of dangerous delusion which had led to the death of Price Cullross. In the same spirit of Apache generosity, he had deliberately left the sandstone ridge unoccupied.

These ranging thoughts of the Southerner's various hopeful arguments crowded Lucy Henderson's mind during the long moment she looked back at Linn Sparhawk before replying to his gallant calculation that a little bit of ordinary luck was all they stood in lack of to win a bloodless or "Mexican" stalemate from the Apaches as of this late afternoon hour.

"Well," she answered him at last, smiling in a wan try to match his own unvarying grin, "maybe for a change you are telling the truth. I suppose injuring that ugly Lobo and the other two could possibly be changing their minds. They've been mighty quiet."

"They have and it could," said Sparhawk. Then, softly, seeing the droop of fatigue pulling at his slender companion's shoulders, "Why don't you try to get a little rest, Miss Lucy, before the sun goes down? You clearly need it."

She smiled, not thinking about the sense of what he had said but only about that "Miss Lucy" part of it. What a strange little man he was, that he would still call her that after all they had come to know of, and mean to, one another in these brief few days. Surely, as old Doc Harnaday had said, when the Lord made Linn Sparhawk he had broken the mold and poured no more like him.

Simply to have something to say in answer to his question about rest, she pointed over toward the horse shed and Cipher Reno Sanchez and offered aimlessly, "Speaking of siestas, young Mr. Sanchez seems to agree with you. What would you say?"

Linn spun around as though she had said a dirty word, his vividly blue eyes going dark as he saw Cipher Reno asleep in the shadow of the horse-shed wall.

"I'd say grab up your gun!" he rasped to the startled girl. "And watch that damned sandstone ridge out front!" He was scuttling across the roof to the stairwell. "Whatever you do, don't take your eyes off that outcrop for a single second, you hear me? I'll be right back."

Before she could protest her inadequacy to carry out the order, he was gone, leaping down the stationhouse stairs and out across the open corral toward the horse shed. As he went, she cheated enough on his instructions to keep, or try to keep, one eye on him and the other on the dangerous elevation beyond the south wall. The divided attention was sufficient for seeing that the Alabaman reached the horse-shed roof and got Cipher Reno awakened and properly reprimanded for his dereliction of guard duty.

But you don't watch an Apache with one eye. As the weary girl crouched there smiling tightly at the half-breed boy's poignantly exaggerated despair at having failed a trust "weeth Señor Leen," she caught the flash of something white

148

in the corner of her momentarily averted south-wall eye. She snapped her head around only in time to confirm that the eye-corner impression had been correct. She had seen the flash of something white. Something white and red.

It was a piece of bloodstained cotton shirting wrapped around the coarse-haired head of a Mimbreño Apache sub-chief named Lobo. And it had flashed because its wearer had been dodging bushes and jumping rocks on his second bent-double dash for the forward sniper post on the sandstone ridge.

Lucy Henderson gasped and felt sick and wheeled to cry out her warning to Linn Sparhawk all in the same terrible minute. She was too late. Even as the Alabaman heard her and spun around to face the stationhouse, the flat crack of Lobo's rifle spat past her and across the corral toward the horse shed.

17

Lobo's bullet struck Linn high in the right chest. He told Lucy he did not think it had hit the lung but he was bleeding at the mouth when he said it and the sound of his breathing was hingey and rough, like the grating swing of an old pasture gate.

She had Sim carry him to the stationhouse against his insistence that he felt fine and was "fit to run a foot race." On the way she heard Cipher Reno firing desperately and ran ahead of Sim to dash up the stationhouse stairs. When she had reached the roof the Mexican boy atop the horse shed was reloading frantically and the brush beyond his north wall was alive with darting, dodging Apaches running in toward the corral.

She grabbed up her own Springfield and began firing across the corral past him to stem the rush for him while he got his carbine once more into action. But the next moment a whistling near-miss from Lobo, behind her, made her remember she had Indians of her own to worry about. She wheeled to face south just as Cipher Reno pumped a fresh cartridge into his Springfield and fired again at the north-side attackers.

In her haste and gunshyness of the military carbine's heavy recoil the desperate girl made no hits, but did succeed in bluffing the runners against her south wall into diving for cover and holding up where they were. Behind her, at the same time, she heard another silence from Cipher Reno and was afraid the Mexican lad had either been struck or was again out of ammunition. Or, still more seriously, had jammed a shell casing on ejection, a wicked habit the present carbiness shared with the later Springfields.

Risking a quick glance, however, she was relieved to see that he, like herself, had ceased firing only because his Indians, too, had gone back to earth. Proudly she waved to him and hesitantly he returned the salute.

They had earned the exchange of well-dones. For even though the entire Indian circle, north and south, had shrunk inward a hundred yards as a result of the probe in force, the hill country girl and the silent half-breed boy had stopped dead what could have been the last charge.

In the same pleased moment the former now heard Sim upon the stairs behind her. Turning to greet him, she lost her momentary smile. His black hands were covered with Linn Sparhawk's bright blood and his small eyes were snapping and rolling with savage hatred as he glared over the south wall toward Lobo and the brush-clad sandstone ridge.

"How is Mr. Linn?" she asked him when he stopped his animal growling long enough to swing around and face her. Having put the question, she began deliberately reloading her carbine, seeking by the methodical action to quiet and calm the fierce Massai.

But Sim was controlling himself again.

"He is very bad, missy. The little man, Bergerman, he is with him now down there. But Mr. Linn does not want to stay down there. He wants to be brought up here where he can be with you."

"Did he say that, Sim?"

"That is what he said, missy."

"Well that won't do; it won't do at all."

"That is what I told him, missy."

She caught his eye and said softly, "Sim, is he going to die?"

"We all die in our time."

"That's not what I mean. Is he going to die now?"

"No, he will not die now, missy," replied the towering black man, "he will die tonight."

The shock of his unexpected abruptness left the slender

girl stunned, but below she could hear Bergerman soothing Linn and her senses returned under the quieting effect of the "little man's" gentle voice.

"What will we do, Sim?" she asked fearfully.

"We, too, will die, missy, the same as Mr. Linn. The same as all things."

He said it without apparent emotion. There was no tremor in his voice, no evident compassion for Linn's terrible wound. There was no hint of any feeling at all, either in his choice of words or in the way he spoke them. His indifference made his white companion suddenly, seethingly angry. She wanted to cry out and curse him for his heathen callousness toward the pain and suffering of the shy-mannered youth to whom he owed his freedom from a bondage inferior to death. She did not do this, but the effort to refrain from it was obvious. Sim read her anger in the embittered look she gave him, and shook his savage, small-eared head in strangely gentle understanding.

"A woman cries like the rain, missy," he rumbled softly. "All on the outside. The fall is hard and is over quickly. A man cries inside like a deep spring. It seems dry on top of the earth but deep underground the water never goes away." He put his huge hand below his left breast, bowing his fierce gaze as he concluded humbly. "Sim cries in here, missy —inside."

She was instantly ashamed and told him so. "Oh, I'm so sorry, Sim. I should have known, anyone should!"

"No, missy," he reassured her, "nobody knows but the Lord God. If He says you are to know, you will know. What He does not say, you will never know."

It was a touching demonstration of an acquired faith in the white man's God, and the Southern girl said very subduedly, "Well, Sim, has the Lord God said anything to you yet about what is going to happen to us?"

It could have been a flippant question, but the giant Negro knew it was not. "No, missy," he replied carefully. "We can only wait now. He will show us how to die when the time comes."

The way he said it brought a strangely cynical thought to his companion. Sim seemed to be showing an odd lack of concern over losing his life. Could it be that with Linn Sparhawk dying, his faithful black shadow had decided to desert and make good his own escape? A thing he could do as easily as dropping over the wall and disappearing into the darkness of the coming night?

The white girl suddenly felt compelled to know the answer to her suspicion, for the fear of being left alone with the little Alabaman was mounting swiftly in her.

"Sim," she said cautiously, "it will be dark in a little while. You love the dark and the Apaches hate it. You know you can escape them easily, don't you?"

"Yes, missy, I know that."

"Yet you will stay, of course."

"I must stay, missy."

"Why must you? Why not go and save your own life when it is so easy?"

"I have to wait for Mr. Linn. It is an understanding we have. A thing of honer between us."

The tall girl shook her head wearily at his devious pagan cunning. He was not being honest with her, she was positive. But she also knew that it made very little difference whether he was or not.

As the late afternoon sun dropped swiftly toward Apache Pass and the Peloncillo Mountains, a depressing sense of final realization was growing within her. Compensating for it, a feeling of great independence and personal detachment from her surroundings, as though all this were happening to someone other than Lucy Henderson, was beginning to well up within her, steeling her for the end.

She looked at Sim, and shook her head idly. "Why do you say you must wait for Mr. Linn?" she asked half-interestedly, half-petulantly.

"I will not leave until he leaves, missy. We will go away together when it is time. It is an understanding, as I have told you."

The bemused girl shrugged, turned away. This last double-edged answer could mean anything, from the big ex-slave staying loyally to die with the rest of them, to back-packing the grievously injured Alabaman out through the Apache lines that night. Whichever or whatever it meant, Lucy Henderson did not care. Her tired body was beyond care, her weary mind past concern. She just sat and stared.

In that moment of defeat, she heard Linn's voice calling weakly from the room below. It was Sim he wanted, and the cat-footed Massai at once padded down to see what it was he wished. Shortly, Lucy saw the big Negro trot across the corral.

Beckoning Cipher Reno down off the horse-shed roof, he returned with him to Linn in the stationhouse. She heard urgent voices for a few minutes, then the Mexican boy came up to sit with her, bringing the information that Señor Linn had ordered everybody to stay together in the front building. It would make things more convenient for all of them, he had said.

The exhausted girl went back to her staring out across the motionless desert. The point was perfectly clear. Why argue its ugly implications? With Linn out of action they could not possibly defend both walls. They would have to surrender the horse shed and fall back to the little adobe structure in the southwest corner of the corral. There was no other logical move. The stationhouse was simply, according to the Alabaman's relayed words, the best single position remaining.

Lucy kept her face turned carefully to the southern desert. She did not want Cipher Reno or Jake, who had just come up from below, to see the hopelessness in it. Sparhawk had deliberately stopped short of the entire truth: the stationhouse was not simply the best position remaining, it was the only one.

Within its earthen walls or upon its sun-baked roof, before another day had spent its final light, the Union government's gamble to get the Waterfield office records safely out of Confederate territory would have been made and lost. Lost with that gamble would be the bold, the brief, the unimportant career of Lucy L. Henderson, from Hayden's Gap, Virginia. As the impassive Sim might say, there was no more to it than that.

They all sat there a while talking quietly. Nothing was said of their situation, Jake and Cipher Reno being as careful to avoid the subject as was Lucy. Before long the supply of small things to say became exhausted. Both the old man and the half-breed boy went back downstairs to sit with Sparhawk. On the roof Lucy was left alone with the black and crouching shadow of big Sim, and with the equally black and crouching shadows of her thoughts.

Suddenly there arose a subdued scuffle and quick, sharp cry from the room below. Then, before even Sim could move, there was the sound of Jake's feet pounding up the stairs. The next moment the little Jew was confronting them with an unbelievable report: Cipher Reno Sanchez had just gone out to hunt down the Apache who had shot Linn Sparhawk.

Shamed and grief-stricken by his assumed responsibility for the wounding of his beloved friend, the half-breed boy had just told Bergerman and the Alabaman that though he had failed to live like an *americano*, he would now do his best

153

to die like one. He had made his announcement with the monumental dignity only the Spanish attain in moments of great emotion, and before either of his adult listeners could imagine he meant it literally, he was gone.

"*Lieber Gott!*" cried out the little bookkeeper, the tears streaming openly down his face. "It is I, Bergerman, who have killed him! I should have watched him more close. It is my fault, *ach Gott!* If I had done it, what Frank said. If I had only sent the boy to his home like he told it to me. *Belieben Gott!* Help him, help him . . ."

Jake broke off, the voice-choke of unbearable grief building in his rising cry, and Sim reached forth a great black hand to comfort him.

"Be quiet, little man," the Massai rumbled in his lion's bass. "You are not to blame and there is nothing to be done. The Lord God gives and the Lord God takes away. He will help the boy."

Lucy Henderson, still under the shock of Bergerman's initial announcement, said nothing. Crouched and shivering, she remained peering over the south wall at the spot of brush between the front gates and Lobo's boulder-strewn ridge, where Cipher Reno had disappeared dragging his heavy carbine behind him.

There was a certain brutal mercy in the swiftness with which it happened. Lucia Sanchez's small brother was very brave. He was as well, and at first, cleverly able to conceal his movements by virtue of a childhood spent crawling the river brush of the Rio Grande playing at *Indios y Tejanos*. He was also a capable and careful shot, as Linn Sparhawk had taught him to be. But in the end he was trying to match stalking crafts with a Mimbreño Apache.

His slim brown hand, in moving for a better purchase with which to propel himself forward on his stomach, touched the root of the artemisia bush behind which he lay. The insignificant vibration spread upward, barely stirring one of the plant's sprays of outer foliage. It was the same stirring as would have been occasioned by a vagrant breeze. But there was no vagrant breeze just then. The Apache, Lobo, shot Cipher Reno through the head at a distance of less than sixty feet.

Lucy and Jake Bergerman sank down and sat for a long time with their backs to the front wall. Above them, Sim took over the watch unbidden. Presently, the gentle-voiced bookkeeper announced that he was going down and convey the news of Cipher Reno's tragic death to Linn Sparhawk. His heavy-lidded companion only nodded without answering. She was tired, completely, utterly tired. She did not even lift her eyes to watch Bergerman depart.

It followed that she did not see him pick up the shotgun which Sim had leaned against the wall but moments before. The big Negro, missing the weapon shortly, turned to ask the white girl what had become of it. She replied, thinking little of it, that she supposed Bergerman had taken it, for what absent-minded purpose she couldn't imagine.

The Massai's never sleeping sixth sense was not similarly deceived. He leaped at once back toward the front wall. The sight below narrowed his small eyes. With a low animal grunt he beckoned Lucy Henderson to join him. As she did so, her breath caught involuntarily.

Walking with his gray head high, his gaze never leaving the brushy crest of the sandstone ridge, Frank Swango's old twelve-gauge Ethan Allen hanging slack from his right hand, Jake Bergerman moved ploddingly toward Cipher Reno's huddled body and the rock-guarded lair of the murderous Lobo.

There was absolutely no sound from the watching Indians. And none from the solitary subchief. It was as though he and all the other Mimbres were held spellbound by an exhibition of the raw kind of courage only red men were supposed to understand and show the enemy. Or as though in their covers of brush and gully and desert boulder the Mimbreño Apaches were paying a final respect of silence to an adversary who had earned the primitive tribute.

Be the reason what it may, not a shot was fired until the stoop-shouldered little clerk was ten feet from the top of the scrubby sandhill and Lobo, thinking tribute enough had been put forward by his fellows, rose up from his juniper screen and drove a rifle bullet point-blank through Jake's chest.

The watchers on the rooftop saw the puff of dust fly from his coatfront where the slug went in, and saw the dark ring of the spreading stain between his shoulder blades where it came out. But Jake did not stop. He only faltered in his stride, one step, then came on mechanically. Before the surprised Lobo could react he had walked to within five feet of him.

As the Apache started his weapon belatedly upward for a second firing, Jake pointed the shotgun. His dying fingers closed spasmodically upon both triggers, and the double charge of heavy pellets tore the gaping-mouthed Mimbreño in half.

It was sunset. The Apaches had made no further attempt to advance since the death of Lobo. On the rooftop of the stationhouse Linn Sparhawk, Sim and Lucy Henderson waited for the end.

The Alabaman had asked Sim to carry him up to the roof when he heard what had happened out at Lobo's sandhill. He had gritted his teeth and directed the powerful black man in rebandaging his chest, making the new bonds flesh-cuttingly tight so that they might contain the fearful wound when he sat up at the wall to shoulder his Springfield for the last accounting.

His stated purpose in this sacrifice of final strength was the sentimental one of keeping the Apaches back and away from the bodies of Jake and Cipher Reno until nightfall, when Sim could go out to bring them in. Fortunately he did not have to fire the Springfield in this useless cause. The Apaches held their peace and, for some unknown reason, still continued to hold it while the sunset flamed and died.

Linn was inspired by this hiatus of silence to suggest that the back-to-back bravery of the old Jew and the little half-breed Mexican boy had purchased them, their surviving friends, some possibly very precious time.

He could very well imagine, he said, what would be running through the Apache mind right about then:

Now what the devil is going on over there in that cursed mud and rock corral? the worried bucks would be asking one another. How many of those crazy white people are left in there that they could waste such brave ones as the old man in the black coat and the little boy in the straw sombrero. Wagh! Something wrong here. Better go slow, better show a lot of that famous Apache patience. Be not curious like the cat but cunning like the wolf. No, wait, that wasn't such a good idea, either. Lobo had been a wolf and he was dead. Dead with him, too, were fifteen other brothers, and five more missing since they had made the eastern signal smoke two sunsets gone. Aii-eee! Where were Noches, Doklinny, Eskanazay, Big Mule and Noka-da-chuz?

There was something very bad going on. All the signs had said these miserable americanos were as few as seven or eight. Yet from that treacherous corral their guns had spoken as though El Gato had pounced on that missing troop of

156

Major Mobry's pony soldiers. By the sacred thunderbird, could that be possible?

Ah-hah! Look out! Who was being the real cat here? Mangas Coloradas? It did not seem so. Some hard thinking must be done soon. What should they do now? Try one more great charge on that coming third dawn, or give quietly up and go home to the Pinos Altos when the Sun God came stealing across the grass from Goodsight Station? Aye, that was truly the question—to go or to stay with that next daylight. . . .

When the Alabaman trailed off, Lucy put her arm tenderly around his thin shoulders and shook her head smilingly.

"It won't hold water, Sparrowhawk," she chided him softly. "Those Indians have no decision to make except on the safest way to finish the job."

"Now, Miss Lucy," he began, but she did not let him finish.

"It's just no use, Linn," she told him. "They're not going to give up and go home. We both know that. Now lie back and tell me that you love me. I'll listen to that."

He nodded gratefully, sighing and leaning back to rest his ragged brown curls against her cupping shoulder. She held him there beneath the lingering sun-warmth of the wall while out over the desert the crimson daylight faded, the dusk came, faded in brief turn, gave way to the blazing unbelievable whiteness of the New Mexican stars. He pressed her hand and kissed her cheek. She laughed and kissed him back, soft and quick as the touch of a melting snowflake, and they were happy for that little hour.

Linn slept after a bit and Lucy must have nodded with him, for when she awoke with a start Sim was gone and they were alone on the rooftop. Far to the southeast the moon was just spilling its first silver along the rugged spine of the Floridas. Westward, beyond the spring, the nighthawks had quit their moth-hunting to call sleepily back and forth, and from the east, up on the higher mesaland, a tiny cactus owl arose and floated down with the new moonlight to inspect the strange pair of lovers on the roof of the Waterfield stationhouse.

Lucy's first thought was for the missing Negro. Had the African-born Massai deserted them to save his own skin? Or had he gone faithfully out on Linn's last order to bring in the bodies of Cipher Reno Sanchez and gallant old Jake Bergerman?

She disengaged herself from Linn's uneasy weight, lowering him gently to their blanket. Stepping swiftly across the rooftop she came to its corralside wall in time to see Sim's great dark shadow float effortlessly over the wagon barrier at the gate and come trotting on toward the stationhouse. He carried no bodies but only a slender stick with a bulky object of some kind attached to its free end. He came noiselessly up the stairs to stand facing the white girl's accusing figure, his own huge form still partially hidden in the blackness of the stairwell.

"You didn't bring them in!" she challenged angrily. "I thought as much."

She saw his small-eared head move in dissent against the sky's lighter backing.

"You thought wrong, missy. I brought them in. They are in the horse shed with the others, as Mr. Linn ordered." He gestured derecatingly across the corral. "I went out a second time just now. On business of my own, missy."

"Business of your own?" she echoed sharply, for some vague reason suddenly afraid. "What business?"

"Only a farewell gift for the little boss, missy. You will please tell him Sim has gone free. Tell him, please, that the time of which we spoke has come. He will know from that where I have gone. You say to him, please, missy, that Sim bid him good-bye in his heart and wished that the Lord God would bless him and bring him safely home."

With the deep-voiced words he brought his right arm up out of the stairwell shadow. In his hand was a short-hafted Apache war lance. He gave the weapon a downward jab and shake. The lumpish object impaled upon it fell free. It bounced to a staring, empty-eyed halt in the day-bright light of the moon at Lucy Henderson's feet. It was the severed head of the Apache subchief Askan-do-klanny, the one called Lobo.

18

After Sim had gone Lucy cried a little from sheer loneliness and letdown. Her stifled sobbing awakened Linn who, surprisingly, seemed definitely stronger and more alert. He seemed, as well, to be under the pressing need for hurrying about something.

When his tear-stained companion told him about Sim's savage farewell gift, cryptic good-bye message and subsequent abrupt disappearance over the stationhouse wall, he at once asked her to go down and get him the dispatch pouch in which were the Waterfield records, together with some oddments of pencil and paper cleaned wholesale out of the El Paso office desk.

He refused to discuss Sim's apparent desertion, saying the girl would understand it in time and that it had to do with freedom in a sense that only a primitive would conceive of and that eventually she would understand that too.

When she accepted his dismissal of the subject and brought him the requested pouch, he took pencil and paper from it and began to write laboredly.

The first note was short. It was also singularly obscure. It consisted of a bare statement of the hopelessness of their situation, together with the identification of himself as leader and planner of the unhappy course of the misadventure beyond Mesilla, and the acceptance, by him, of all blame for the disastrous failure. He further identified Mangas Coloradas as their attacker, gave the number of Apache casualties (twenty-one with Lobo) and listed the names of the original seven Waterfield employees who had left El Paso (including Barton and O'Hanlon) with no mention of Sim, Price Cullross or Lucy Henderson. He dated the note as of the coming day and signed his name to it, consigning himself and his "brave companions" to the mercy of God. Nowhere in the note was there a solitary word of self-justification or attempt to attach any blame or claim any credit.

Folding the paper, Linn Sparhawk gave it to Lucy Henderson and told her to take it down and put it, with the Waterfield pouch and records, beneath a certain rock she would find just inside the latch-post side of the gate. She did as he bade, returning as quickly as she could. He was already busy on the second note.

He took a long time with that one, putting it down a line or two at a time, taking long pauses to study Lucy's anxious face as though that might help him find just the right phrase to describe how heartbreaking it was to die in these circumstances.

Finally, he had found all the words. He folded the last paper at least four times before he gave it to the silently wait-

159

ing Lucy Henderson. Then he said, quite ill at ease about it, that it was his will. He asked her to please take it and keep it in her possession, since it concerned her in some small degree, but not to read it until he was gone.

She nodded and put the note away as quickly as she might without seeming too abrupt about it. Her feeling was that whatever Linn Sparhawk and she had to say of good-byes, they could do a better job of them with their hands and eyes and lips than they could with the reading of any last wills or testaments.

But the Alabaman was not yet through setting his worldly house in order. When she had tucked away the note he told her to go back downstairs and bring up from below her old straw suitcase. He smiled at her surprise and said that pretty soon now she would understand why he had brought her things along from El Paso.

"I bet you still don't have any rightful idea why I did it, do you?" he asked her.

She admitted that she did not and his smile saddened the way it had the time he'd reminded them all of Lincoln's story about stubbing his sore toe.

"I knew," he murmured apologetically, "that when the time came, as I feared all along it might, I simply couldn't do for you what any real man would do for his, or any other man's girl."

"What are you talking about, Linn?" she asked, thinking he was beginning to wander. Which, as a matter of fact, she had thought he was ever since that peculiarly inaccurate note he had had her put under the rock by the gate.

"Never mind now," he said absently. "Soon enough, soon enough," he groaned desperately. "I only hope to God it works."

"What works, Linn?"

"The dress and your other pretty things in the suitcase."

She still did not understand him and was still thinking of that first note.

"Linn," she said, "why didn't you explain things straight in that first letter you wrote? I mean about the Preacher and Red Mike deserting. And then about Sim and Price Cullross and the whole change-around of people after leaving El Paso."

"I don't rightly know," he said, and clearly didn't.

"I guess I somehow just felt better about including Red Mike and the Preacher. You see, nobody knows about Sim and Price and nobody will miss them. The others—Mike and

Mr. Barton, that is—well, they were on record, you might say. They had blood and kin somewhere—people who would want to know what became of them—people who would wonder and think all sorts of possible things if we didn't list them along with the rest of us that were known about.

"Maybe it was sort of an idea to let them die a little bit better than they had managed to live. Something like that possibly. But I reckon I'll still have to say I don't rightly know why I did it that way."

His listener reckoned in humble turn that he knew very well why he had done it that way, but that he simply did not care to talk about it. It was exactly like he never cared to talk about any of the clean, decent things he did as naturally as most other men perspired, spat, chewed tobacco or fouled the air with vile language.

"Well, then," she smiled in a wry attempt to keep it light for his sake, "what about me? How come I got left out? It seems to me I should get major credit for the crime."

"It's the dress and fancy settlement things again," he said with quick seriousness.

"Go on," she nodded, sobering with him.

"I like things to come out even, you see," he explained. "The note said seven of us Waterfield men left El Paso, and if God is good and my plan for you works out, seven of us Waterfield men is all they're going to find here at Mimbres Springs Station. I guess that doesn't make too much sense to you just yet, does it?"

Lucy Henderson told him that it did not.

He smiled, patted her hand and said to her in a wistful way that was plainly half-faith and half-hope glued together with a good dollop of pure charity, that it soon enough would.

"Linn!" she pleaded with him gently. "What is it you're trying to say? What is it you mean to say?"

"Well, just this, Miss Lucy," he answered her softly and with the sad smile just touching his lips again but this time in a way that was strangely happy, "you're not going to be found here at the station. You're going to live and get away."

When Linn Sparhawk told Lucy Henderson she was not going to die, she knew he was at last and truly wandering. She took him in her arms and he did not resist or want to talk any more. His slender return of strength was spent. He was tired, he said, real tired. She kissed his damp curls and he slept quickly.

When his ragged breathing had slowed, she laid him back upon the blanket and went a little way off in the moonlight to read his will. She did not want to look at it against his wishes, like that, but she scarcely dared wait, either.

In many ways, perhaps in most, the Southerner's last testament was pathetic. Yet the pure idea of it struck the girl from Virginia as awkwardly right and beautiful. It was addressed simply to "whom it may concern" and was penned in the correct narrative style of the holographic will, starting with the standard "I, so-and-so, being of sound mind" and ending with the legal signature of Linn McClellan Sparhawk. In between reposed the brief quixotic statement which was Sparhawk's farewell to life, to love, and to Lucy Henderson.

Sirs—
I shall remain eternally grateful for the opportunity of commending to you the bearer.

Had life been less gallant I could not be in this enviable position of leaving behind such a priceless heritage as the privilege of having known Miss Lucy Lu Henderson.

In this rare woman I have found pride with its proper leaven of humility, compassion without sentimentality, sympathy without mawkishness, strength without contempt.

She has shown me how to lease my heart without signatures. How to harvest the random passage of time in its ripest hour. How to smile without knowing it. To laugh aloud soundlessly. To weep without tears.

She has anointed my life with the balm of her tenderness. She has led me to lie down in the green pastures of her dear arms. She has been of me and I of her and the being was good. She has presented to me passion without carnality, realism without bitterness, devotion without demand.

Lives there a man with need for such a woman and if to him should come this one seeking solace, let him open his heart and his arms and the stronghouse of his soul and let him admit thereto the greatest treasure he shall ever know.

I surrender it to him unwillingly . . .

Linn awakened some minutes after four A.M. When he

162

saw how late it was he struggled up and cried, "Lucy Lu, go put on your party dress! It will soon be broad day and the company coming!"

Lucy Henderson did not deny him his fantasy. She thought she knew what he wanted—to see her as a woman once more—and she got her things out of the suitcase and went below to haul water from the cistern to freshen her face and to brush and set her shortened hair as best she might. When she came again to him she was dishevelledly resplendent in her tawdry El Paso arrival outfit, and the far first gray of the five o'clock light was staining the sky behind Goodsight Station and Mesilla. He looked at the bedraggled dress, orange shoes and purple bird-of-paradise hat as though their drawn-faced wearer had just stepped, full fashion blown, from the pages of *Godey's Lady's Book*.

Lucy Henderson was satisfied then and forever after that for the one enchanted moment there in the New Mexico dawn Linn Sparhawk saw the impossibly wonderful woman he had described in his lonely will. It was not Lucille Louise Henderson, and could never be. But whoever it was, the dimming picture of her in that cheap and frowsy dance-hall dress gladdened the deep blue eyes and gentle shy heart of Linn Sparhawk, and that was all that ever counted to the girl who wore it for him that morning on the rooftop of the Waterfield station at Mimbres Springs.

She took him in her arms again. He nestled his shaggy head down upon her breast and asked her to promise that she would try to love him a little spell after he was gone. When she smiled and brushed his ear with her lips and told him that his "little spell" would be only for all the days of her life and not one second longer, he smiled back, squeezed her hand, drifted off to sleep again.

For her poor, tired Linn, it was the last sleep. When the sun came he did not answer her frightened call and, beneath the lowered sweep of his thick lashes, the flushed cheeks lay still and calm and forever more unfevered. Upon his sadly curving lips was the same wistful smile with which, the hour before, he had laid his weary head to its last rest within Lucy Henderson's sheltering arms.

She knew then that whatever of travail he had suffered in his time on earth Linn Sparhawk, the quixotic Union boy from Lowndes County, Alabama, had died at one with a world perhaps too small to understand and accept his soft-voiced kind in life. Somehow, to Lucy Henderson, the words of Robert Louis Stevenson seemed best to tell the short

163

simple story of the Southern youth she had known but five days and loved but forty-eight hours: "When I met him I was looking down; when I left him I was looking up."

The actual end came with the uncomplicated swiftness of death itself—that mercifully lucid time when all the real pain is past and only the moment of spiritual truth remains.

Linn had passed away at five o'clock. At six Sim, the black giant who had in life followed him so faithfully from Louisiana to Texas to far New Mexico, arose to continue following his "little boss" on into the "valley of the shadow" itself.

He did it in a way only a Massai could have conceived and an Apache appreciated. For some peculiar reason of their pagan psyche—possibly the finding of Lobo's headless corpse by a scout—the Mimbres had again failed to occupy the dead subchief's strategic ridge during the darkness. They made immediate shift to rectify the oversight, however, with the first of the new daylight.

It was but a minute or so after six when a foot party of ten braves broke from a gully between Lobo's lifeless post and Mangas's distant hill, to race forward and retake the brushy sandstone rise. They were already swarming up its bouldered slopes when Sim sprang into view above them.

The huge Massai came down on the stunned Apaches like a great black-maned lion, roaring up in full charge from the long grasses of the ridge's crest where he had lain the full night through in patient wait for his prey. He had stripped himself of clothes, was armed only with Lobo's war lance, yet the terrible cry with which he burst among the Mimbreño patrol would have paralyzed the heart of an African buffalo.

The horrified white girl could not see, and would never know, how many of the Indians died beneath the Massai spearman's wicked charge—if, indeed, any of them actually did die there. She only knew that in the brief moment it took the onlooking Apache riflemen to cut him down from their safely-distant cover, squat red warriors were falling around the feet of the raging ex-slave like stingless bees dropping and dying with their insides torn futilely loose around the feet of an infuriated, upreared grizzly bear. Sim's life, whatever its price, ended mercifully out of her sickened sight, behind the sandstone ridge.

Lucy Henderson thanked God for that. She stood up and smoothed her dress, adjusted her purple hat, walked across the roof and down the stairs and out of the little house below.

In her heart was a certain peace. Some things, if not all, had been made right among her ill-fated seven men at Mimbres Springs. Frank Swango had found something in death he had never known in life—friends he could trust. Doc Harnaday had gone under as any old Indian fighter would have wished—forted up and making the red devils come three-for-one. Price Cullross had won every hand of his life but the last one, and to a gambling man that was the way to play it—backing a low pair against two queens showing and betting your life the bluff will steal the pot. Dark-eyed Ceferino Sanchez and kindly old Jake Bergerman had both died for impossible ideals—and both had achieved them in the dying. Black Simon Peter had gone forth in lonely search of —and found beyond the bloodied sandhill of Askan-do-klanny, the Mimbreño wolf—the only true freedom man knows —and in the end Lucy Henderson had understood the nature and meaning of that freedom exactly as Linn Sparhawk had foretold she would.

Coming to the shy, hesitant Alabaman himself, with his vibrant voice, poet's tongue, soft drawl and unquenchable optimism, he had simply gone smilingly to sleep in the arms of the woman he had waited his lifetime to love—and how would heaven improve on that for a last memory on earth?

Lucy Henderson held her head a little higher with these thoughts and went armed with them across the corral to the overturned wagon in the gateway. Beyond it now she could see the Apaches approaching. They were mounted again, riding slowly in past Lobo's silent ridge, Mangas in the lead astride Frank Swango's quick-stepping roan. Behind the Mimbres chief she could see a pack pony bearing Sim's slack form. She nodded to herself at that, and was content.

They were bringing the Negro giant to put him to rest with the six other brave Waterfield men in the corral horse shed. With them he would no doubt suffer the disfigurements and the blackening by fire practiced by the Mimbres upon their victims. With them too, he would remain after the Indians had gone, his great body brutalized with theirs. But when, after an unknown time beneath the desert sun, some white party ventured here to find her seven wonderful men, they would not know which had been Simon Peter, the freed Louisiana slave. For what man is to say which skin was once white and which black, when all are the same charred color after the Apache has gone?

The Mimbreños did not hurry. Like Sim they could smell death. They did not need the lowering circle of the buzzards, which swept in over the corral as Lucy Henderson left it, to tell them that no living thing remained behind the tall handsome white woman in the Waterfield station at Mimbres Springs, New Mexico.

The proud girl did not look back after she had clambered over the wagon and started toward them. She was still walking chin-high and unafraid when Frank's wheeling roan blocked her way and the cold-eyed empty face of Mangas Coloradas loomed at last above her.

And so the puzzling diary of old Apache Annie, painstakingly handwritten in a good, if at times colloquial, schoolgirl English, ended as it began on a note of inconclusion.

The reservation doctor, from whose memory of that diary this account has been prepared, was definitely given to a rigorous regimen of sourmash Kentucky bond taken internally for pain as self-directed. He was, as well, addicted to the manufacture and distribution of towering narratives when under the influence of his favorite prescription, a fact admittedly not in the best interests of authenticity.

Still, he did produce certain physical properties to bolster his bizarre story of the seven men at Mimbres Springs; properties which, if not admissable as prima facie evidence, were at least provocative of circumstancial speculation.

Item: an atrociously yellow straw suitcase. Item: a frumpishly fancy street dress. Item: a pair of vilely orange highbutton shoes. Item: an impossibly purple bird-of-paradise hat.

Such articles, even though of undoubted Civil War vintage and actually found in possession of the withered reservation crone, do not in themselves constitute a convincing brief for ruling in favor of an alcoholic's historical accuracy. Yet when viewed in context with the story which old Annie's oddly blue-eyed, aquiline-featured son had supposedly allowed the doctor to read from his dead mother's diary, and which the former had been kind enough, and drunk enough, to repeat for the writer's benefit, they do pose an unsettled end-question.

Was Waska-na-chay really Lucille Louise Henderson? Or was she simply a very old Apache Indian woman with a cheap settlement suitcase stolen in some long ago New Mexican stage-station raid or cattle ranch massacre carried out, when she was a twenty-year-old tribal belle, by the far-ranging Mimbreño warriors of Askan-do-klanny and Mangas Coloradas, the elder?

Somehow it still seems the old man had the last best answer to such latter-day curiosity when he quietly took the diary from the reservation doctor and put it into the wickiup fire.

Truly, as he said in the beginning, such things belong to another time.

Henry Wilson Allen wrote under both the **Clay Fisher** and **Will Henry** bylines and was a five-time winner of the Golden Spur Award from the Western Writers of America. Under both bylines he is well known for the historical aspects of his Western fiction. He was born in Kansas City, Missouri. His early work was in short subject departments with various Hollywood studios and he was working at MGM when his first Western novel, *No Survivors* (1950), was published. While numerous Western authors before Allen provided sympathetic and intelligent portraits of Indian characters, Allen from the start set out to characterize Indians in such a way as to make their viewpoints an integral part of his stories. *Red Blizzard* (1951) was his first Western novel under the Clay Fisher byline and remains one of his best. Some of Allen's images of Indians are of the romantic variety, to be sure, but his theme often is the failure of the American frontier experience and the romance is used to treat his tragic themes with sympathy and humanity. On the whole, the Will Henry novels tend to be based more deeply in actual historical events, whereas in the Clay Fisher titles he was more intent on a story filled with action that moves rapidly. However, this dichotomy can be misleading, since *MacKenna's Gold* (1963), a Will Henry Western about gold seekers, reads much as one of the finest Clay Fisher titles, *The Tall Men* (1954). Both of these novels also served as the basis for memorable Western motion pictures. Allen was always experimental and *The Day Fort Larking Fell* (1968) is an excellent example of a comedic Western, a tradition as old as Mark Twain and as recent as some of the novels by P.A. Bechko. At his best, he was a gripping teller of stories peopled with interesting characters true to the time and to the land.